FRUM GOD

THE MOSTLY TRUE ADVENTURES OF A MODERN DAY MESSIAH

DAVID L. LITVIN

FROM GOD: THE MOSTLY TRUE ADVENTURES OF A MODERN DAY MESSIAH

2nd Edition

Published in the United States of America by:

David L. Latvin

www.davidlitvin.com

QUOTES

"Any sufficiently advanced technology is indistinguishable from magic." Arthur C. Clarke

"For those who believe . . . or want to." John Frum

PROLOGUE

This much, at least, is true. I am John Frum. Well, not exactly. I am really Joe Fray. You might remember me from a fairly popular sitcom called *Friends Without Benefits*. Not a bad show. Ran for six seasons. Made some good money, but one minor scandal and a cancellation later, and I am looking for work.

Oh yeah, I am not really Joe Fray either. That was a stage name. My real name is . . . Well, who cares? It doesn't matter. What does matter is there wasn't a lot of work coming my way. I am not kidding, nothing.

It's not like I ever really wanted to be an actor in the first place, but you would think there would still be some opportunity. After all, I was on one of the most popular shows on TV, but nope. Nothing. But that's not important just yet. This is.

Volavo is a small island in the southern part of an archipelago in the South Pacific, very, very remote and mostly untouched and unspoiled except during World War II. Then it became a fairly important way station for medium weight military vessels of the U.S and British navies.

The islanders were in awe of the men and the ships and the

uniforms. The natives there, the Bohlin, were at heart a very peaceful people, but at first they were hesitant and didn't want these trespassers there, but the white men were friendly and persistent and probably at least somewhat threatening. The Bohlin were so trusting, they probably wouldn't realize they were being threatened even if they were.

Before they knew it, the islanders, who up to this point had never seen a white man or white uniforms or even white bread, accepted them. And as I said, they were in awe of the men with their huge metal ships.

These men had tons of food. They talked into little boxes, and disembodied voices answered them. They had medicines that were miracle cures for the infections that had plagued the islanders for centuries. Even the particularly nasty version of Volavo clap was cured with just a few, small, white powdery discs from these strange and magical men. And then, only a couple of years later, they were gone. The war was over. The island was again only for the islanders, adrift and alone in a vast sea.

Almost twenty-five years later, Westerners again set foot on the island. This group, however, was a small contingent of well-meaning and almost unbearably cheerful missionaries, and what they found surprised them. The islanders were just as friendly and peaceful as ever, and they were not at all surprised by the missionaries' arrival. On the contrary, their reaction was more of a collective "Where the hell have you been? We were worried sick." What's more, the island's elders seemed disappointed in the newcomers who came in modest vessels and dressed in civilian garb with no sign of vast stocks of food, medicine, and electronic wizardry.

The missionaries were welcomed but grew more confused with each day. The elders showed them wooden ships, small and definitely not seaworthy, placed upon what looked like an altar of sorts. The ships were in the shape of the Navy vessels that had visited years earlier. The natives showed them wood boxes in the shape of the radios used by the Navy men. They would talk excitedly into them as if expecting a response.

The missionaries would ask through their translator what the purpose was for all this. Even the translator was confused. The islanders kept saying, "From. From. All for the honor of From. For the good fortune of From." They said that "From" would someday return with all of the riches of food, medicine, and gadgets. That day, of course, was February 15th, and it was rapidly approaching.

The missionaries were intrigued and arranged to stay for the big day. They watched from a distance as the normally sedate islanders made their preparations. Long story short, the day was a grand festival devoted to the memory of the arrival of the magical men in their great ships and a plea for their return, for on that day would come the promised bounty of health, wealth, and happiness.

The missionaries now realized that their hosts would not easily find the Jesus they had sought to bring them. They soon learned that the islanders had their own version of Jesus, and they believed not in "From" but in "Frum," namely John Frum, leader of the magical white men, and John Frum was coming back someday, almost certainly some February 15th. And the Bohlin were perfectly prepared to wait forever, if necessary. John Frum was their Jesus. John Frum was their god. John Frum was their redeemer.

As I said before, I am John Frum. And I returned. And they didn't need to wait as long as they might have thought.

1

PRESENT DAY

"Where the fuck is it?" asked Thomas Bush Geur III even though he already knew exactly where the fuck it actually was. "It's a remote island, practically in the middle of nowhere. And we never would have known anything about it, except a plane full of Exxon geologists had to make an emergency landing when their pilot got drunk and accidentally dumped their fuel in the Pacific. While they were there, they took a look around, and there it was—the only known deposit of corbomite in the world, the only one bigger than a shovelful, anyway. Exxon know anything about it?" asked Geur, again already knowing the answer. "No. They know it's rare, but they don't know what it can do."

Geur was talking to his friend and employee Rom Cheiro. Both were technically at the vice-president level at chemical giant Womansanto, but there were literally hundreds of vice-presidents, and there was a distinct pecking order. Geur was about mid-level while Cheiro was near the bottom and lucky to be there at all.

Both owed their positions to pedigrees of a sort. Geur, as a second cousin to George W. Bush, always seemed a little embarrassed by the more sordid parts of the family's notoriety but was certainly more than willing to walk through the doors opened by the name. He was a middling student of average intellect who was almost aggressively unremarkable. He had been graced with none of the "Aw shucks" charm of George W. and all of the good looks of Barbara. He did, at least, succeed on his own at Princeton even though he could never have qualified without the name Bush as part of his. He ended up with a hard-fought master's degree in chemical engineering with a minor in marketing that all but assured the professional level he had reached so far.

At this point, he was in his mid-forties with a wife and two kids he could mostly stand in small doses. He had been faithful to his wife of twenty years but only from a lack of energy and interest. What he was talking about with Cheiro could finally give him a name for himself. Maybe he could be some guy with political connections and a famous name, and that did interest him. The idea of real fame and real fortune was attractive to him, but it was not the burning desire of his comfortable, always secure existence.

Cheiro, on the other hand, could only think of fame and fortune, and he was also, as his friends and associates alike would tell you, an asshole, the kind of asshole who would ask you if you gained some weight when he knew you had spent months dieting and working out; the kind who would walk up to the only other people in an otherwise empty movie theatre and squinting at his ticket stub, inform them that they are occupying his seat. He wasn't really a bad guy, more funny than mean.

He owed his vice-presidency to being smarter than many, more motivated than most, and it didn't hurt that his brother-in-law was a senior vice-president, one of the real heavyweights in a truly heavyweight Fortune 100 company that was Womansanto. He was part of the team that had introduced

RoundOut, literally a billion dollar seller for Womansanto. It was a revolutionary product. It killed weeds. It killed pests. It killed child molesters. It didn't kill child molesters, but it did kill practically everything else. Who wouldn't want some?

But funny thing . . . it kept killing for a long time. In fact, if you wanted it to stop killing, you needed to buy Womansanto's follow-up product, RoundOutback. Turns out farmers, especially in the third world, would pay just about any price to reverse the effects of Roundout, what with their families starving and all. Yes, there were some lawsuits and a few peeps out of the easily distracted public and media, but overall it was a grand slam, and it earned billions. Indirectly, it also got Cheiro a largely undeserved but wildly desired vice-presidency in one of the world's largest companies.

Geur and Cheiro knew they had something. They weren't sure exactly what it was, but they knew enough to know it could be something big. They knew from two different Womansanto research and development projects that corbomite, under certain circumstances, could release enormous amounts of energy.

They also knew there were two problems with this. First, the release of the energy was never proven to be controllable. In other words, it was very likely that any attempt to harness that energy would result in some very large and uncomfortable explosions, not quite nuclear in scope but close enough to make an awful mess, close enough that no one had ever given serious thought to using it as a power source. The other problem was that you needed a lot of it, and neither the mineral nor its properties could be replicated.

What they knew that nobody else knew was that both of these problems had been solved. Womansanto researchers had discovered that certain combinations of inert gases could moderate combustion of certain compounds under certain conditions. Complicated? Certainly. As to the other problem, they had found the answer in the place they had both begun referring to as Shitbag Island. It turns out there was plenty of corbomite, enough to power the world for centuries, but found only on Shitbag Island.

So now they were the only two people in the world who knew of the existence of a substance and process that could produce energy so cheaply, it wouldn't be worth the bother to measure. What to do? What to do?

THEY COULD TRUST EACH OTHER, they knew, because they had to. They both knew they would need the resources of the company, but they both also knew that if they brought it to the company, the best-case scenario was that whether it worked or not, they would receive none of the credit for it. The worst-case scenario was that Womansanto figured out a way to bury the idea. After all, they were in the business of selling things, not making them so cheaply you could give them away. The worst-case scenario could also mean that they themselves got buried —as in dead.

History is full of would-be, dead visionaries that wanted to give things away for free, starting with Jesus and going all the way up to old what's-his-name. That's right. You never heard of old what's-his-name because he's dead, which is what usually happens when you want to do good things for everyone for free, not that these two were visionaries would actually want to give anything away for free. They were just men, after all. Money and fame appealed to them just as much as they would to anyone, maybe more so. So the problem becomes this: how do you get this far enough along without anyone learning of it, stealing it, or destroying it?

Cheiro and Geur were vice-presidents in one of the largest corporations on earth. The value of the company itself was more than the GDP of over a third of the world's countries. So the office in which they sat was nice but bland, decorated with solid woods, muted colors, a modern but dreary sort of Midwest motif.

Both men had done a little research on the island and the Bohlin, but so far the answer to the puzzle, how to secure mineral rights in one of the most remote parts of the world with a people who have no real, legal framework or need for it, eluded them. Now, the answer was right in front of them.

Usually the TV in Geur's office was on the stock market channel all day every day, but today it was on something else. It was the episode of *Friends Without Benefits* where I was pretending to be Joanie's brother from the Navy so she could get a discount on veal cutlets at the supermarket on Veteran's Day. There I was—tall, straight, white (ridiculously white), starched uniform, shiny black sunglasses, and the hat.

"That's it!" yelled Cheiro although later both would claim it was their idea. "It's him!"

"It's who? What the fuck are you babbling about?"

"The natives have this crazy religion, remember? The ships came during the war, and they thought they were gods."

"So what? That was a long time ago, and even if they still believe it, so fuckin' what!"

"Don't you get it? That's our foot in the door. We give them their god. What was that name they had for him?" He began typing furiously on his computer. "Frum. John Frum. Their religion says that John Frum is going to return on February 15th and bring the mother lode of cargo."

"Yeah, so?"

"How fuckin' thick are you? We give them John Frum. We give them cargo. We give them God. They give us the mineral rights."

At the time they saw that rerun, I was about forty years old. It was about seven years after *Friends Without Benefits* wrapped and about eight years since I had left the show. Yes, *FWB* ran one more season after I left. I'm not sure anybody missed me. I was one of the "friends" but kind of the boring one that the others persuaded to participate in their hilarious antics.

I was, in fact, the straight man in every way, actually. I wasn't particularly funny, and I am pretty sure I was the only male member of the cast who wasn't gay, so I will break a little news here about the reason I was fired. I called one of the producers "Toots." I don't know why I did it; I'm not even sure what I meant by it. I think I might very well have still been playing my character from the show, but I did say it and admitted to it when a very serious, member of the HR legal team at the network interrogated me.

He seemed surprised that I would confess. I was surprised that he or anyone else would give two shits. But they did, and nothing more was said until contract time when I was not offered a deal for the new season. I did ask—I at least cared that much—and was told that given recent events, it would be best that we parted ways.

Once again they were surprised, this time because I didn't put up any resistance. I never asked again, not because I didn't care but because I didn't care that much. I didn't *need* it. It was never my burning desire to be an actor or be on TV. It just happened, like most things. But I guess to explain, I should go back a bit.

I am the only child of Nils and Myra. At every step of the way, I was wanted, cared for, and beloved. My parents were a fairly odd couple, Nils, a nominally Catholic Swedish exchange student, and Myra, a very nice Jewish girl from Fresh Meadows, Queens. According to them, they met at the library while Nils was studying for a PhD in mechanical engineering. Myra was in her second year at Queensborough College because, in her words, she couldn't think of anything better to do.

I can certainly relate to that. Both of them were pleasant to look at in a non-threatening sort of way. Like me, my dad was about six foot, never more than 160 pounds, and had dirty blond hair. Also like me, he was fair-skinned, but no one ever guessed he was a Swede. If forced to guess, I might have gone with Dutch or German, but I was never forced to guess.

My mother was tall for a woman, almost five foot eight. She always had shoulder length, light brown hair, mostly straight, and always pulled back in a way to show off the gentle curve of her forehead and the kindness in the lines of her face.

As far as I ever knew, the two of them were ridiculously compatible. Never in my recollection was there ever a fight or even a raised voice. It is possible they fought when I was not around, and that would make perfect sense to them and for them. They both believed children learned what they saw, and it would be just like them to have kept completely hidden any disagreement or marital strife, but I never saw a hint of it. Ever.

They shared one peculiar trait, one that I also inherited. Neither of them was ever hungry. Yes, plenty of people lose their appetites for any number of reasons—grief, illness, country music— but complete, lifelong lack of hunger is very rare. Only a handful of documented cases have ever been recorded, but my parents and I have never experienced hunger. Of course, I need to eat, and I do enjoy food, but with no hunger, I have never had a problem with my weight, unlike my fellow actors on the show, all of whom had weight clauses in their contracts and obsessed over every meal, every bite.

After college my parents settled in Queens, not far from my mother's family. My father worked very hard and proudly became a U.S. citizen. He never used his advanced degree. My father, like his father, was a carpenter and had incredible technical and artistic talent with his hands. If he could see it in his mind, he could build it with his hands, so he created beautiful furniture, first as a hobby and soon after as a profession. For a time, his designs were quite popular with some of the fancy interior decorators in the city. He had a small warehouse not far from home where everything was built by hand. He created every design and made much of the furniture himself. The rest was built with never more than eight or nine handpicked craftsmen who would work with him on a rotating basis. From this he made a very good living. My mother helped him by taking care of a lot of the communication and billing, which my father found boring.

I was twenty when they died in a car accident on Union Turnpike. Several major furniture manufacturers wanting to buy his business and designs approached me. Turns out my mother had used a patent lawyer to protect everything my father had ever done. Several design elements turned out to be quite unique and patentable. She was a very clever woman, and she made me a fairly wealthy man at a very young age.

After the funeral I went alone to the warehouse. It was always oddly clean and tidy for what was essentially a factory. I had spent almost every day there after school and sometimes on weekends if my mother had somewhere to be. My father had tried to teach me as his father had taught him, although he never seemed disappointed to discover I had none of his magic in my hands nor his vision in my mind. "This—"and he would always pause after he said 'This'—"This . . . is not your thing."

And he was right. It was not my thing. And I never needed it to be. Never felt bad that it wasn't, but I really did like it. I would watch my father and the other men create things of beauty, and even as a small child, I felt as if something magical was happening, as if these men could breathe life into the inanimate. And on that day of their funeral, standing there alone in the warehouse, it felt as if there was no life. There could be no life again.

"That was God, you know," said a voice from the other side of the room. It was Tom. He was a longtime friend and sometime employee of my father. "He never said it, but your dad felt God when he was making this stuff. When he was drawing, cutting, sanding—it was like God was talking through him, making these things, using your father's hands."

"Yeah," I said. "I've never been much on this God business, especially when things like this happen . . ."

"Yes," he interrupted, "things like this happen. As far as I could ever tell, your parents were damn near perfect. Neither of them ever hurt a fly. They made some beautiful things and did at least a little bit of good. What more could you possibly ask of people? It's just plain shitty that they are gone, and I can't pretend to know why. I just know I will miss them. I'm not religious exactly, but I know we will meet again. All the souls that meant something to you in life . . ." Tom paused, choked up. "They can't ever really be gone forever . . . What the fuck can people know about forever?"

Sometimes I think about what Tom said. I lack his certainty, any certainty really, but one thing I do know. There is way more than we can possibly pretend to know, so as far as I can tell, all things are possible until you prove to me they ain't. That, I suppose, is my religion, still.

I found myself at twenty, an orphan with close to, but not quite, a million dollars to play around with. Plenty for me as even then I lacked any particularly bad habits or expensive tastes. I wasn't exactly alone in the world since I had some family in New York, and I had my dad's family, who I had met a few times on trips to Sweden with my parents, but as usual, no one I felt particularly close to. Sometimes I would go for holiday celebrations to my uncle's in Queens.

I would occasionally date. I wasn't very good at it, but I like women, and every once in a while, one of them would like me, but to this day, I have never had a relationship last more than a year. They would all end in a similar fashion. The women would say something along the lines that I lacked passion for them, that we were more like friends than lovers, that I want but didn't need.

It's hard for me to argue with that. I suppose I get lonely, but I am pretty good at being alone. After all, I was an only child of two people who were the same way but somehow found each other in what I am told is a very big world.

I fooled around for the better part of a decade. I went to school a little bit here and there. It took me seven years or so, but I earned a degree in broadcasting and was on the air quite a bit on the college radio station. Everybody seemed to like my voice, but no one ever seemed to remember what I said. Not surprising really. I never had much to say, but everybody seemed to agree that my voice sounded good.

It wasn't long before I was doing voiceover work for radio and TV. I was the voice of the Staten Island Ferry in Whitehall and St. George terminals and on the ferries as well. I even got to sing once. You might remember The Burger Putz fast food places. They lasted a few years even after my singing. The jingle went like this: "Come on down to the Burger Putz, a damn good burger without the fuss." I had free burgers there for a couple of years. They were pretty tasty. Then out of the blue, I received a call from a talent agent in California. Apparently, somebody had heard me and wanted me to audition for a sitcom pilot in Los Angeles. That agent, Mary Disir, started my career and is my good friend to this day. She is blunt and tough as nails, but there is no one better to have on your side. And she did answer one very, very important phone call, but I'm getting ahead of myself.

I had never acted. I had never thought about acting. I had honestly never needed or wanted to be an actor, but I didn't *not* want to be an actor, so I went to LA. I had an audition, which I had dutifully prepared for to the best of my nonexistent ability. I thought at the time that it had gone extraordinarily badly, but I got called back for a second audition. After that, the three producers in the room, two middle-aged men and a woman, kept looking at me in a way that I didn't really understand, like

I was an odd but interesting animal in a laboratory. Finally one of the men spoke and said what I guess I had always known. "You really are a completely blank slate, aren't you?" I will let you decide if that was a compliment or not.

So I became Joe Fray the actor for seven years. I don't know if I was a good actor or not. Reviewers and fans of the show never picked on me. They never really mentioned me at all. I would just faithfully read the script and follow directions. The various directors and other actors I worked with seemed to like working with me.

Honestly, it really is not that hard. Just show up on time, and say your lines. I saw some of my castmates and crew act as if they were working so hard, the set might as well have been a coal mine. They believed making a goofy TV show was so important, they might as well have been curing cancer. No, like everything else, it is as easy as it looks unless you make it hard.

When the gig ended, I did miss it a bit, mostly the regularity of it, the schedule, the routine. Those were things I liked. There is something to be said for going to the same place and doing the same thing with the same people. There is comfort in sameness. I liked it, but I didn't need it.

The same thing holds true for attention. I wasn't exactly the star of the show, but it was a hit comedy. Two of my castmates are now among the most in-demand movie stars on the planet. At the peak of the show's popularity, most of the cast was reliable fodder for tabloids and paparazzi. Not me. I am what they call in the entertainment media a "dry well"—no mistresses, no love children, no addiction, no horrifying stories of an appalling childhood, no sloppy, drunken acceptance speeches. Well, no acceptance speeches at all since I never won anything.

I think I am not interesting because I am not broken, or if I am broken, I don't know enough to realize I am. Or maybe I am not interesting because I am not interesting. That's okay too. It's not that I hated the attention that I did get. Being recognized in public was kind of cool at first, less so if you have to take a shit or are late for something, but why would I complain? I was on a highly rated, prime time network television show at a time when a lot of people still watched such things. I signed up for it. I didn't mind it. I didn't need it. But I didn't mind it, and when my little bit of fame faded away, I didn't miss that either.

Now that it was over, it was time for the next thing. I really wasn't blackballed or anything like that after *Friends Without Benefits*, but I certainly wasn't in demand. My agent, as I said, did take some time off, but it was not because of me, and she came back better than ever with her own agency.

I suppose there were still opportunities for me as an actor in some form. For a while I stayed in California and did some voiceover work. I even did some voice work for video games. My favorites were pornographic video games, which were just starting to become a big deal. I really nailed my role as Dick-face Luke in *Grand Theft Auto-Erotic* and followed it up with a remake of the classic *Donkey Shlong*.

After a couple of years, I drifted back to New York. I say "drifted" because it took me almost a year to get back. All I left California with was packed into a minivan, and I just worked my way across the country, zigzagging back and forth and just stopping anywhere that was interesting to me, and to me, anyplace I have never seen before is at least a little bit interesting. I settled back in New York and returned to voiceover work, which was as plentiful as ever.

As I said, Mary returned after a year off and started her own agency and PR firm. Once in a while she would call me for some type of audition or another. Occasionally, I would fly out to California and read for something but never got the part. As it turns out, passion is something directors are usually looking for. If you were to ask any of my exes, they would be happy to tell you that passion is certainly not my strong suit.

However, the phone rings one day, and a voice on the other

end says, "Is this Joe Fray?" I was a little confused because pretty much no one had called me that in years.

"Used to be," I replied. "Who is this?"

No one replied for a few seconds. I could hear arguing in the background as if someone was trying without success to cover the phone.

"Just ask him to meet with us, you dumb fuck," said the muffled voice. Now it sounded like the men on the other end were wrestling for the phone—which they were.

"I am hanging up now," I said, hoping that might help them to get to the point.

A few seconds went by and a different voice on the phone said, "We've got a part for you, the role of a lifetime. How would you like to play God?"

The men, as it turned out, had done some homework on me and knew what might arouse my interest. If they had said, "Hey, you wanna make a million dollars?" I probably wouldn't have responded. I was not and am not motivated by money. I don't need much money, and I already had a million dollars. As a matter of fact, at that point I had somewhere close to two million, and that number was always going up. Even living in New York City, I never spent as much as I was making, not that I made so much. I just didn't have anything to spend it on.

Obviously, whoever was at the other end of the phone knew a fair amount about me. They knew I looked the part. They knew that the job would interest me. They probably figured I was not smart enough to ask too many questions but smart enough to get the job done. It's hard to argue with that, so I agreed to meet with them if they came to me.

A couple of days after New Year's, I met Geur and Cheiro at a diner on Long Island. I chose the place and time because I knew it would be loud and busy. I picked a large diner at lunchtime.

I am not all that suspicious by nature, but these guys could have been anybody from scammers to lunatics or both. All I really knew was the names they told me, which were their real names, by the way. I used that info to research them a little, and that told me they probably weren't dangerous, but my research didn't offer much in terms of what they might need me for. The answers weren't long in coming.

When I arrived ten minutes early, I texted Cheiro, and he told me they were already seated. Both men stood to greet me when I arrived at the table. They seemed nervous but not overly so. Both were clean-cut, in their forties, and in decent shape. They were casually dressed but in a way that suggested they didn't know what that means. Their clothes looked new, probably purchased for this meeting specifically.

Geur spoke first. "We want you to play a part," he said, "and if you play it well, it can change the world for the better."

"And probably make us ridiculously rich," said Cheiro, interrupting.

This earned him the type of look from Geur that meant he had clearly told him not to say that.

"What?" said Cheiro. "Why not? If we do this right, we will be rich, and we'll deserve every penny."

Geur was seated next to Cheiro in a booth that was just slightly too small. He shifted uncomfortably in his seat, turned, and said. "For the love of God, can you please just shut the f . . .?"

"It would be nice," I said, "if one of you would just tell me what you want me for."

I had been looking directly into Geur's eyes across the table, just like my acting coach had taught me to do. I used a deep, serious tone, and it worked, leading Geur and Cheiro back to something resembling reality.

They spent the next hour telling me about cargo cults, about the Bohlin, and about the Island of Volavo, which is the second largest in a string of islands of the Volavo Archipelago.

What they wouldn't tell me, at least not right away, was what was on the island and why they wanted it. So I asked.

"Gentleman, I just met you. I have no reason at all to trust you. For that matter, you have no real reason to trust me, but if you want me to do this, and it certainly seems you do, now would be an excellent time to tell me exactly what the fuck you want."

They looked at each other for a second or two, and it seemed at that moment they made an unspoken agreement to go all in with me.

"We want the mineral rights," said Cheiro. "Almost nobody knows it, but a mineral that can produce almost unlimited energy simply, safely, and with virtually no pollution was discovered on that island. At least ten thousand times more of it exists there than anywhere in the rest of the world combined. All we have to do is to get their leader to sign over the mineral rights, and you will be the one to do it. You will be John Frum, their god. You will bring them cargo to prove you are real. You will promise them even more cargo, and they will give you, John Frum, the mineral rights."

"And what about Womansanto?" I asked. "What do they get?" They hadn't told me who they worked for, but they did not seemed shocked that I knew.

"They will get ninety-four percent of the proceeds," he answered honestly. "We will get two percent each, and the company will get the rest. It will be billions. It will make the earnings from Roundout look like the take from a lemonade stand by comparison."

Nobody spoke for what seemed like a long time. Finally I said, "So for argument's sake, why wouldn't we just secure the mineral rights for ourselves? Why give any to Womansanto?"

"Because Womansanto is going to get theirs anyway," said Geur. "Trust me. They always do."

He went on to explain. "Look, we need resources from the

company to pull this off, and if we were to try to keep it for ourselves, Womansanto would sue and almost certainly win and get everything."

Pausing for a moment, Geur said, "You ever hear the old saying 'Pigs get slopped; hogs get slaughtered'?"

Cheiro interrupted. "Yeah, and who's sloppier than us?"

Geur was undeterred. "This is no joke. This is the kind of thing people get killed over. This is the kind of thing armies fight wars over. It won't stay a secret forever. We need to get in, secure the mineral rights quickly, and get out. Womansanto will defend our six percent because it gets them ninety-four percent. And the best part is, we probably don't get killed."

After a few seconds of silence, I said, "Or I could not do it and not risk anything. I don't need the money, and the world will be just fine. Sooner or later, somebody puts the pieces together, and the world gets the benefit."

Cheiro and Geur looked at each other and then looked at me like I was a puppy that just did something clumsy and cute.

"Forgive me, Mr. Fray," Geur said. "I forget sometimes that not everybody understands how the world really works. There are people out there who would rather make sure this never sees the light of day, and they have the power to make that happen. You don't have to do this for the money. Honestly, I don't give a shit what you do it for, but you should do it because it's the best chance to do the right thing for humankind. How many people ever get that opportunity?"

To this day, I am still not sure what to make of those two, Geur and Cheiro. Clearly they, like me, were the product of a privileged upbringing, but unlike me, they were subjected to a set of life experiences that taught them the only thing worth working for was *more*. They were like interchangeable parts in a machine that would reward them with a life of comfort but could just as easily turn on them and spit them out.

But I had imagined at the time, perhaps naively, that they

saw this as a chance to fix a broken world, a world that had treated them well but left so many behind, or maybe I was just seeing what I wanted to see because I needed to be the "good guy," and I wanted to see something good in them.

I got my answer a moment later when I asked, "Hey, what about the islanders? What do they get?"

Again they looked at each other as if I were adorable, simple but adorable.

"They get the cargo, of course," said Cheiro as if that were an actual, legitimate answer.

"No, really. If this works, what do the islanders get? We get millions if not billions. Womansanto gets God knows how much. What does that leave for the islanders?"

"I don't know," said Geur. "What did the fuckin' Indians get for Manhattan? No, they'll be able to negotiate with Womansanto. They won't be left empty-handed."

"Who's being naive now? What chance do they have in negotiations with Womansanto? They'll be lucky to keep their cocks."

"You're probably right," said Geur, "but let me ask you this. What chance do they have if the Russians or Chinese find out first and just come and take what they want? What chance do they have if World War Three breaks out over this with their little shitbag island at the center of it? If we pull this off, it will be far from their worst possible outcome, I promise you that. If you feel bad about it, then give them your two percent. There is no other possible outcome where they do any better than that."

And you know what? He was right. At that moment sitting in that restaurant, I convinced myself there was no better possible outcome than the one that I now wanted to make happen. I would play God.

"Okay," I said. "For the moment, let's say I go along with this fakakta thing. What happens next? What's the plan?"

Geur said, "We spend about a month getting everything

ready on our end. We're going to send you in a jazzed up, World War Two era gunboat we can buy on surplus. We're going to paint it bright white and fill it with gifts for the islanders. Cargo is what they will call it."

"What kind of gifts?" I asked. "What do they want?"

"Meth and hookers," said Cheiro. "Blondes with giant tits and bad habits." Cheiro smiled and nodded as if to say, "What else could anyone want?"

We both turned and glared at him, but I have to admit he actually was funny.

Geur continued. "Well, they are not all that primitive anymore. They pretty much want what anybody wants . . . electronics, off-island foods, clothes . . ."

". . . dildos, condoms," offered Cheiro enthusiastically.

Geur went on to explain the plan so far. According to the Bohlin religion, February 15th is the day that John Frum will return to the island with the mother lode of cargo, and all of the islanders' hopes and dreams will be fulfilled. Every year on that day, they have a huge party and ceremony anticipating Frum's arrival. For the last half-century or so, they have been disappointed but undeterred and certain that the next February 15th will be the one. How they decided on that date is anyone's guess.

So I am going to arrive around February 10th with a nice load of cargo that will prove I am John Frum, Navy man, savior, and all-around nice guy. That will give me four days before the ceremony to charm my followers into signing the agreement with the understanding that if they sign, their living God will smile upon them. February 15th will be the day that all their hopes and dreams will be fulfilled—minus the dildos.

My job between now and then would be to learn everything I can about the island, its people, and its history. And, of course, I would practice my role as a god. The two assholes would go home. I would stay in New York until a couple of days before it was time to go.

They gave me a tablet that they assured me was no ordinary tablet. It was equipped with security programs that made it virtually impossible to hack. We would use it to communicate securely now and even once I was on the island.

Certain things in life seem perfectly normal at the time, but when you look back at them later, you realize they were completely nuts. This was not one of those times. As I sat in a crowded diner with two corporate stooges talking about dressing up in a uniform, going to a remote island, and tricking primitives into signing away a substance that could power the world, I knew full fuckin' well that it was nuts, worse than nuts. This was dangerous nuts.

"Okay," I said. "I'll do it".

2

SHITBAG ISLAND?

I admit I am not the most ambitious guy out there. I haven't done a whole lot, and that has always been exactly how I like it, but my saving grace, if I have one, is that when I decide to actually do something, I generally go about it thoroughly and, hopefully, competently. I threw myself into the role. As a "professional" actor, I tried to do as much background work as possible. I learned about the Navy and how a man of my rank, Captain, would conduct himself. I studied the slang, not just modern but World War Two era. Without leaving my apartment, I tried to learn as much as I could about piloting a vessel.

I knew the portrayal didn't need to be perfect. In fact, it would probably be better to play him as a better version of himself. After all, he was at least as much god as man. He didn't need to be real. He had to be better than real, lots of shine and starch, vigor and virtue.

I spent countless hours learning about the fair island of Volavo and its people, the Bohlin. I was relieved to learn that unlike the yesteryear of many of its neighboring islands, the history of the Bohlin people was relatively young. Their past covered only hundreds of years rather than thousands. There is no historical evidence of any population on the island prior to the 1400s. The record of how they got there in the first place is obscure but pretty straightforward. DNA has shown that they are a mix of Melanesian, Asian, and Australian Aborigine. It also indicates that the current population of about 24,000 all came from a relatively small group, no more than two to three hundred ancestors for the entire modern population, which also means those people arrived on the island at the same time, or close to it.

What Geur said was true. The Bohlin were nowhere near as backward or poor (by modern definition) as they were more than half a century ago. In 1995, as part of a United Nations treaty on deep sea fishing rights, Volavo received exclusive claim to an area extending 50 miles in circumference around the island. Apparently it was part of a much larger multinational treaty, and no one involved cared enough to object. That's not bad, considering the whole island itself is only about twenty miles long and less than sixteen miles across at its widest point, but the Bohlin were not fisherman by nature. In fact, they had no vessels of their own that could troll beyond a few hundred yards off their shores, but the islander who had first pulled off getting them those exclusive rights also had the wherewithal to lease those rights to foreigners as long as those foreign vessels came no closer to shore than three miles. This provided the Bohlin with enough hard currency to get along while protecting them from outside influence. Pretty amazing shit if you ask me. I liked those people already.

The island and its people had avoided colonization and exploitation through a combination of good location and good luck. Maybe there was just nothing there anybody needed, not even people. The estimated population when the Navy arrived in '43 was about 7,000. Today it's a pretty solid 24,000. It is a young population that knows nothing of the horrors of colonialism. They were barely suspicious of outsiders in a way that modern people would consider naive. What did they have to worry about? Everything they needed was either on the island or brought there by outsiders who had never been anything but friendly.

The advances they had seen had come from two main sources. First were the missionaries, Christians who wanted nothing more than to spread the gospel of Jesus. Soon after came the anthropologists, eager to study a still relatively unsullied culture and a religion very near its birth. Imagine a weather channel reporter standing outside during Noah's floods as the rains fell or tabloid headlines with rumors exposing Mary and her virgin birth. Surely paparazzi would have stalked and photographed young Jesus and his apostles as they traveled from town to town. For a cultural or religious anthropologist, there was no place better in the world to be.

Money from religious charities, research grants from governments and universities, and later hard currency from deep sea fishing rights had allowed for modest but widespread infrastructure. Power was generated and clean public water was available. More than eighty percent of the population had electricity in their homes along with indoor plumbing, low for the Western world but considerably higher than found on the rest of the string of islands. Most of those living without electricity did so by choice. The island had a decent network of paved roads and hundreds of passable dirt ones.

School was available to every child. Attendance was not required, but most would go. More schools than not were cheerfully run by the missionaries, some now part of a second or third generation. In many cases, they themselves had been born and raised on the island. They taught Christianity, of course, but they also taught English. By the year 2000, virtually every person on the island was conversant in English. Some might call this a form of "friendly colonization." I would call it a choice. Unlike most of the rest of the world, the Bohlin were offered a choice to take what they wanted from the outside world and keep that which was theirs. It seemed, from a distance at least, that they had the best of both worlds.

The more I learned about this island and these people, the more I was struck with how little I knew of the world outside of my own. As a sheltered, rich American, I knew nothing of geography. It had taken me almost fifteen minutes to find Volavo on the map. As far as I knew, it was just another tiny Pacific island just like all the others, but as I studied the map, I realized just how far Volavo was from Auckland. I also learned just how crazy far these Pacific islands were from each other.

As I learned more, I realized that in most cases the people who lived on these various islands were as different from each other as they were from me, and worse, I was beginning to have some doubts about my mission, if you could call it that. I still believed that if we were successful, it would be for the best for Volavo and its people. We are certainly not the first ones to convince ourselves that we know what's best for an indigenous people. It's especially easy to convince yourself of that when you stand to gain financially or otherwise.

I was telling the truth when I said that I didn't care about the money. So what did I need out of this that I would go across the world to lie to 24,000 people? Did I like the idea of being a god of sorts? Sure, who wouldn't? Did I want to save the world? Sure, why not? Maybe it was just that after seven years on network television, I still just wanted to prove that I could act.

A bigger question, however, was at play. The Bohlin were not the wide-eyed innocents of the 1940s. How, for the love of God, could I possibly pull this off?

The answer came as I studied further. I already knew that on February 15th every year, the Bohlin celebrate John Frum Day. They build small, fake aircraft and ships of wood. They wear makeshift uniforms emblazoned with USA across their chests and march in formation, holding sculpted sticks as their armaments. They have a ceremony on the island's main ship dock, constructed during World War II by the U.S. Navy. It has been modestly updated over the years to include a small, adjacent amphitheater with rudimentary seating for three to four hundred people and some space for spectacle. Two to three thousand people crowd the space during John Frum celebrations.

One after another, religious leaders give speeches praising John Frum. None were at all deterred by the fact that John Frum had yet again failed to return. Each man of God declared that it would be the next year that he would arrive, bringing with him cargo that would make the islanders rich and happy.

There was dancing and music. Many wore a crucifix, and the clergy praised Jesus as a just God. Others spoke of the older religions of the island, known collectively as Kastom, which ran the gamut from a belief in a god that brought the sun to a god who lived in the centuries-dormant volcano on the southern end of the island.

The Bohlin, it seems, were just doing what they always did, picking out the parts they liked and leaving the rest behind. They had no problem believing in John Frum or Jesus or a sun or volcano god. They had no problem believing in John Frum *and* Jesus *and* the volcano *and* the sun god. History had offered them a buffet, and they just ate whatever they liked. And it was John Frum that brought it all together. It was something they all agreed on because it was real. The evidence was all around them every day.

I saw a video from about 2000 where a reporter had attended the John Frum Day ceremony. He interviewed an older man who had been a child when the ships first arrived. He asked the man if he had ever seen John Frum. "I saw God himself, and I saw his men and the wonders they did," the man replied. The reporter asked, "But surely he would be dead by now. It's been more than fifty years. How do you know he will return?" The old man patiently regarded the reporter as you would a child and said, "He is the God of the world and will return when he is ready, not before. Your Christians have been waiting more than two thousand years for Jesus to return. Have they given up hope?"

Yes, this could work. If I gave the right performance, it could indeed work.

I was to meet Geur and Cheiro in Auckland, New Zealand, in order to make my arrival on the island on February 10th. I would first have to get to Auckland a week earlier. That would leave a few days for final preparations before the trip from Auckland to the island, which was a full forty-hour sea journey. So I took a flight from JFK to Auckland with a layover in Hong Kong and arrived in Auckland on January 27th. This left me a couple of days to look around a little and recover from jet lag.

The boys (I am not sure why I call them boys since they are both a few years older than me, but it always felt right somehow) and I stayed in the Hilton Auckland, right on Princes Wharf. It was the main seaport and within walking distance to where our ship was docked.

In the moment that I first saw the ship, this all somehow became real to me. It was a genuine, World War II naval gunboat, 110 feet long with a beam of just under twenty-three feet. During the war, it had featured four gunnery stations, all of which had been removed before it had been sold as surplus more than fifty years ago.

I don't know how it looked when we first got hold of it, but now it was a sight to see. It had been lovingly refurbished to what looked like even better than new. Its hull had started out a drab, almost camo-colored, dark olive. The boys had gotten it painted a shiny, bright white from stern to bow. During the war, it had been used to chase enemy submarines and stay out of sight. Now it looked like it could be seen from space. It had been designed to sleep twenty-eight, but for our mission, it would sleep only six, myself and a crew of five. There was a small galley, and the rest of the space had been converted into a cargo hold.

Apparently, the cargo itself was the source of some disagreement between Cheiro and Geur. Neither had asked my opinion, which was fine by me. Geur felt there should be an emphasis on electronics and other consumer goods. Cheiro, for some reason, was insistent on live chickens. Apparently, he had read somewhere that the islanders still raised chickens as both a hobby and a food source. He insisted that offering a live, healthy chicken is the highest honor and a sign of respect among the islanders. Not only did I never see anything like that written about this particular island, but I was also the one who had to be on the boat with them. Livestock is not exactly my specialty. And please feel free to insert your own chicken shit joke here.

Eventually they agreed on a compromise. We would bring only ten live chickens. The number ten would reflect the nine tribal leaders plus the political leader of the island, the prime minister. The cargo on this trip would be for them and only them, the idea being that John Frum would come first with gifts for the leaders to prove his worth and grease the wheels. After the agreement was signed, a mother lode of cargo for everyone would follow the announcement to the world on John Frum Day, February 15th.

We also agreed that I would have ten crisp, white uniforms, half a dozen hats, and five perfectly shiny pairs of black, patent leather shoes. I could *never* be out of a clean, white uniform. To be out of uniform would be to break the spell and shatter the illusion. I had to be John Frum, God, every minute that I was on that island. It probably wouldn't do to have me wandering around wearing a flowery, print shirt and Mickey Mouse ears. I had to be in character every minute of every day, or it couldn't work.

But I did change one thing. The Navy uniforms, at my request, were stripped of anything that would make them official U.S. Navy gear. I don't wrap myself in the flag and beat my chest, but I do love my country. I never served in the military, but I have the utmost respect for every man and woman who has ever worn the uniform and made the necessary sacrifices. I would wear *a* uniform but not *the* uniform. The boys didn't fight me on it. A white uniform with random, meaningless insignias would be good enough.

I don't know where the boys got the money for all of this. The ship, the computers and video games . . . the chickens. I never asked. I did know that Cheiro's brother was a big shot with Womansanto and probably had access to all kinds of accounts whose money he could quietly move around, but this was no small project. They had to be into this for a few million or so, no joke.

The islanders would know we were coming. The boys had reached out to the largest missionary group on the island in advance. After a nice donation, they agreed to reach out to the nine tribal leaders, promising them gifts and wonders should they appear at the naval port one hour before sundown on February 10th.

They had also contacted the political leader of the island, known simply as "the minister." He had been the leader of the island for more than twenty years and had always been extremely popular. He had been the one responsible for securing the fishing rights that earned the island its hard, international currency. He became the minister soon after, and the people simply never had a reason to seek out anyone else.

There is an election every three years, but it had been a long time since the minister had faced any serious opposition. By all accounts, he was a trusted and competent leader. Mostly, the minister attended to the affairs of the island with the ever-increasing assistance of his longtime aide and likely heir apparent, Kavu, as well as the minister's daughter, Qat. They had been notified of a visit of the highest order and had agreed to attend out of curiosity if nothing else.

Everything was ready the day before we set sail, so I took a day to myself. I didn't know what would happen when I got to the island, but I knew one thing for sure. I would be "on" and in character the whole time I was there. No, as I said before, acting isn't brain surgery, and it doesn't take a genius, but I am no natural.

Acting never came easy to me, and it's not as if I could just memorize a script. I wouldn't be facing another actor with their own script where we both knew exactly what was supposed to happen and what we were supposed to say. I would have to improvise as I went. The good news is that I had plenty of practice at that. It is pretty much how I have lived my whole life.

So I took a solo tour of Auckland. I bought a ticket for one of those hop-on/hop-off bus tours that pretty much run through the whole city. I think I saw all the touristy spots but also a lot of the "real" city with its everyday people and places.

At some point, I saw a group of schoolkids waiting for a bus. I had never given much thought to having kids of my own or not having kids of my own. That usually takes a stable relationship, if not a permanent one, and as we already know, that's not exactly my strong suit, but for some reason, it got me thinking that the world, with all the things that have gotten better, seems to be a harsher place for children now than it was when I was a child.

I have had friends and coworkers with kids, and they would speak proudly of their children and trumpet their accomplishments. There was often pride and satisfaction, but there was always weariness in their eyes and a tone in their voice that never matched their words.

It did not occur to me until that day in Auckland that they were trying to convince themselves of something, that the choice they had made was worth it. I amused myself by giving it the name "Parental Stockholm Syndrome." The symptoms made an appearance in regretful parents who convinced themselves that having had kids was a good choice in their lives.

I am a half-Swede after all, but it seems to me that the world had become hostile to parents and children. Despite all the lip service paid by politicians, parents that had to work day and night just to survive, and teachers being paid peanuts spoke much louder about just how much we actually value families or so it seems to me—not that I spend a lot of time thinking about such things.

This was a sure sign of nerves. I try not to waste a lot of energy thinking about things I can't know or control, but when I am nervous or excited, which is also unusual, my mind goes to work almost like an instinct, like I am practicing and preparing. So I guess it's not surprising that my thoughts turned to God.

As night fell, I stood in front of Holy Trinity Cathedral, a towering white building of astonishing beauty. Religion, if nothing else, always had three things going for it: art, music, and architecture. Inside the cathedral was a set of eighteen modern, stained glass windows. Unlike other churches I have seen, the windows in this church told the story of Christ as a dark-skinned man across a backdrop of palm trees, Pacific island themes, and vivid colors. The church and its stained glass windows are, I am told, examples of a style known as Pacific Gothic. Who knew? Looking at them, I had no doubt that a typical American preacher from the South would get all choked up looking at this stained glass . . . and not in a good way.

What will the islanders demand from me? What do we get from our gods? Why do we need them? It occurred to me that the face of God is usually the same as the face of the people who believe in him, and they often behave as their gods behave. The God of the Bible and those that follow Him can be petty, spiteful, judgmental, and cartoonishly violent, but they can also be kind, generous, loving, and forgiving. It is up to us to decide which God we will be.

The gods of the islanders' native religion, or Kastom, often demanded their obedience in this world in exchange for everlasting life in the next one, but John Frum was a different breed of cat. He represented the world's first truly modern religion. He demanded nothing and gave everything. He was both immortal and flesh. He would fix everything and give everything if we could just find him, if he would just come back. He is not better *than* us; he is the better part *of* us.

In that moment, it came to me. I knew exactly how to portray him. I guess you could call it Joel Osteen and Billy Graham meet Martin Luther King and Gandhi. I would sell them a not just richer but better version of themselves and just hope to heaven that it turned out that way.

By now it was dark, dark in the way that I am told it only gets in this part of the world. I walked until I found a taxi since the tour buses had ceased running hours ago. I told the driver where to go and asked him to take the long way as there were still parts of Auckland, itself a part of God's creation, I had not yet seen, angels and devils still doing battle but slowing getting ready to call it a day.

February is summertime in this part of the world, not quite as hot as you might imagine but still plenty hot, getting up into the low nineties in the afternoon. Thunderstorms were considered normal late in the day, but it was rare that they would last more than an hour or two. Tropical cyclones were always a concern this time of year, but my shipmates assured me that there was nothing lurking on the horizon, at least not as far as the weather was concerned.

We had left Auckland around midnight, not to be sneaky or

anything, just to make sure we left enough time to make our arrival on schedule with maybe a few hours to spare. We hoped to get near the island with some extra time and then coordinate the final stage to arrive exactly as promised. The sneaky part was the ship and crew, none of whom had names. Not real ones anyway. I have no idea how they pulled it off, but the ship itself had no name that I know of, no port of registry, no serial numbers, and no maritime call sign. I asked what would happen if we had any trouble since we were an anonymous vessel and had filed no manifest. Would there be anybody out there to help? I was assured there would be, but there would be a lot of explaining to do afterwards.

The six of us sailing aboard the mystery ship had single names. There were two crewmen who called themselves Smith and Wesson. They were there to provide some security, I guess for me, once we reached the island.

When we met, Wesson told me, "Just call me Wes." He was a thin, serious-looking man in his early fifties. He and his partner both had the look of men that had just taken early retirement from the FBI and had all the good humor of J. Edgar Hoover. They were men of few words. In fact, they were men of no words. We were twenty-four hours into a forty-hour trip, and neither had spoken a word since we left Auckland. You would think they would be curious about what we were up to, but I never saw the slightest hint of curiosity out of either of them. I can only presume that they were being paid big money to work a couple of weeks silently and efficiently while minding their own business. They seemed used to that, comfortable with that, and that is exactly what they would do.

The other two crewmen were lawyers. They did help the captain a couple of times when he requested it, but they were there to create the documents. A couple of hours into the trip, I met with them privately as instructed. They introduced themselves as Bert and Ernie and then assured me they weren't a couple, as if I could give a shit. Their job was to create the documents we would hope to get signed. Bert was a specialist in international and maritime law. Ernie was an expert in matters related to geological finds, mineral rights, and land grants. Each worked from a very high-end laptop, hooked up to a very high-end printer, all linked to a very secret satellite, which provided them better internet access than I had at home. They both looked a bit paunchy, well-to-do, and more than happy to be there. Despite that, Ernie found plenty to complain about. Unlike Smith and Wesson, Bert and Ernie had arrived in Auckland just a day before we sailed. Ernie didn't like the food. He didn't like the water. He even didn't like the way water in the toilet swirled in the opposite direction when he flushed because it was different from what he was used to.

I was always to be called John Frum—not John, not Mr. Frum, not "Hey, fuckface." No, only John Frum, just in case anyone was listening. They didn't even know my stage name. None of them seemed to recognize me, or if they did, they didn't let on. Bert and Ernie assuredly knew why I was there, but nobody knew who I was.

The captain was called "Captain," which worked out nicely since he was, in fact, the captain. He had arrived in Auckland before any of us and had overseen all the loading of the cargo and all of the final preparations. He didn't say, but I didn't get a military feel from him. He was thorough, professional, and friendly in a formal sort of way. He was clearly the youngest of us, but when it came to the ship, his manner left no doubt that he was in charge. All of us except Captain were clearly American. Captain, I would guess, was Greek or Italian, but his English was perfect with just the slightest hint of an accent.

So here we were, six strangers on a ship without a name, halfway between New Zealand and Volavo—with chickens, of course.

It was time for me to get some sleep. I wanted to schedule

my sack time so I would wake three or four hours before it was time to dock, before it was time to see what waited for us on what the boys called Shitbag Island, but even then I knew better. I have never had trouble sleeping, and it was no different here. My nerves about the coming days had settled into acceptance of any and all possible outcomes. In minutes I had drifted away into the inky black of sky and sea.

3

QAT . . . AND DOGS

I am Qat. Exactly. Just Qat. In English it is pronounced "Cat." I am a daughter of the island of Volavo though some might say "first daughter." My father Karbina is the political leader of the island though he is known simply as "the minister." He has retained that title for more than twenty years. He has held power, but I have never noticed in him any actual desire to exercise that power unless it was to protect our island. I have always thought that was why he was good at it. My father is not an old man, but in the last few years, he has relied on Kavu and me to share some of the responsibility.

Kavu might as well be my adopted brother. He came to live with us when he was nine years old after his parents were killed during a cyclone that struck the island. Between us we handle the more mundane tasks of administration for an island of almost 25,000, and we advise my father when asked, which has grown more frequent over the years as we have matured and learned.

I cannot say that I am a typical Bohlin. I was born and raised on the island, but I spent five years in the United States. While there, I traveled when I could and learned, I think, a great deal about the remarkable country and some of its people. Like almost all of us on the island, I speak English. Unlike most Islanders, I speak English with almost no accent.

I have seen with my own eyes just how big the world can be, so it was not surprising when my father asked us what, if anything, we should do about a peculiar request. Sara, a missionary, teacher, and lifelong friend of the family had been contacted by a man who said there was going to be a big event on the island. Whoever contacted her knew that she would reach out to us. Whoever this man was, he was quite coy about exactly what would be happening but asked if we could arrange for my father and all nine of the tribal leaders to attend. He told Sara that on February 10th, a ship would dock an hour before sundown, and he assured us we would want to be there to greet her.

Whoever made that call had to have known a little bit about the island. It was a good guess that afternoon rains would have subsided by dusk. He may also have known that it would take some time to arrange for the attendance of all the tribal elders. He even seemed to understand that an hour before sundown would be two hours before the men would congregate for the customary evening ritual.

Almost every man on the island participates in what I call "Bohlin Happy Hour." In many parts of the world, that means alcohol. On Volavo, that means *kava*—and quite a bit of it. Kava is a root from a type of pepper plant that grows on the island. It is made into a drink that soothes, relaxes, and turns every conversation into an interesting discussion.

The use of kava has always been at the center of social life on the island. The evening ritual itself is a men-only affair, but unlike many other islands where the kava root grows, women are permitted to consume and many do. I myself will indulge on occasion. The point is that if they had planned this event even one hour later, they most certainly would have been all alone when they arrived at what we call Port John. Absolutely nobody would have attended.

As it was, it was no small task getting all of the tribal leaders to agree to attend. Transportation was not an issue, and there were no current petty squabbles going on between any of the tribal leaders. Fortunately, each elder was curious to some degree, and of course none wanted to be left out, so they all agreed to attend albeit most of them begrudgingly. After all, John Frum Day was only a few days away, and they, like us, seemed to sense something.

I guess I should probably explain why John Frum means something to us, to me. It is said that you can know a people by the stories they tell. That is especially true of my people. The story of John Frum is known and shared by virtually every islander and told to our children when they are old enough to understand. This is one of our oldest stories, and it says a lot about who we are.

At long last, the farmer brought his young son to begin a life of bringing fruit from the earth. Like most dutiful children, the young boy was eager to help and learn the ways of his father. It was soon time to plow their small field. The father used a switch made of a whittled tree branch. With it, he would often whip their ox as it plowed the field. The child could see the pain in the eyes of the beast with each blow from the father's switch.

"Must we hit him?" he asked his father, tears forming in his eyes. "Is there not another way?"

The father replied with a kind smile. "I don't know," he said. "Maybe you should ask him," as if to say that whipping was the only way to tell the beast what was needed of him.

But the boy was not comforted. "No father. Why must he suffer?"

The father was not a cruel man, but he knew the ways of the world and said, "Son, without the food from this field, we will have nothing to eat and nothing to trade. I have no wish to harm this animal, but we need these things."

The son paused for a moment, pondering. Finally he said to the father "Our need brings his pain. It is not fair."

"No, son. It is not fair, but it is the way of this world. Where there is need, there is always pain."

Okay, I admit it's not the most exciting tale, but it tells our own story perfectly. If need brings pain, then less need brings less pain, and as a people, we always keep our needs few and thus our pain, and the pain of others, tolerable. In this way, the legend of John Frum fits like a glove. He is a powerful god who showers us with gifts. He takes away all of our need and, in theory, all of our pain. All of our beliefs sit side by side on the island like books on a shelf. Taken together, they are known as Kastom. The Jesus brought to us by our missionary friends has its own place on the shelf as do our kava rituals, as do our volcano and sun gods, as does John Frum, as do our dogs.

Dogs? Yes, dogs. Volavo is home to a single breed of dog that exists nowhere else in the world. Their existence on the island predates any human population. Kastom teaches that these dogs were sent by God to protect the island until the arrival of the Bohlin and to spare us from loneliness once we arrived. They are without exception friendly to people and, like us, have no fear of strangers. We have never had a reason to fear, and neither do they.

Physically, they look like large Chihuahuas but with a slightly elongated snout. They are either black or black and tan. A very few are born black, tan, and white with the white almost always on their feet or lower leg. Males are usually thirty-five to forty-five pounds while the females are just a bit smaller. They are curious and playful and bark only when given a very good reason to. They are excellent and enthusiastic swimmers but poor watchdogs in that they lack the suspicious nature present in many canines. The breed is unique and ancient, but their name is contemporary. They are called the goon'do by all of us. The name came from the days when John Frum and his Navy men walked our shores. Seeing the dogs everywhere, the men called them "good dog," which we copied to the best of our ability at the time, calling them goon'do. We are an island without many laws or need of them, but it is a crime of the highest order to harm any goon'do, and no one does.

The goon'do live among us however they wish. Many live in packs in the jungles where they are perfectly capable of fending for themselves though they will often turn up at a village for a snack or if they are sick or injured. Many live independently within the villages where they are fed and cared for collectively and sleep in huts called domes, which are built by the villagers. Only the nine village leaders, the tribal elders, keep an individual dog of their own that resides within their home. It is considered a special privilege for the elder, that is, not necessarily for the goon'do. Though all of our goon'do live as they wish, it is generally the dog that chooses the elder rather than the other way around. As part of Kastom, the prestige of the village is represented by the quality of life provided to the pack that resides in the village. This results in some very happy and sometimes very fat goon'do. It also sometimes ends up as a comical arms race of sorts with each village trying to outdo the others, building ever bigger and more elaborate domes for their resident goon'do.

An elder will go nowhere without his goon'do, so on the day of the arrival, the only presence at Port John was me, my father, Kavu, the nine village elders, and nine patient and pampered goon'do.

So here we were, waiting as promised, one hour before sundown on February 10th. And as promised, a beautiful white ship appeared in the distance. We watched as it grew closer and larger. As it approached, we could see that it appeared to be a military vessel but without the guns. Markings were curiously absent from the craft. For all appearances, it might as well have been a ghost ship, but it was not. Soon we could make out two men on deck, then four. Within minutes it was dockside.

It was a fairly large ship, but we were quite accustomed to ships this size or even somewhat larger. What was different was that it had much of the appearance of a military vessel, and no military vessel had ever been to this island during my lifetime. We were neither frightened nor concerned. That's simply not our style. There was nothing to be afraid of. The ship appeared to have very few crew and no visible weaponry whatsoever. It was definitely not military or threatening. In the minutes it took for our dock crew to secure the vessel, we simply took our seats and waited.

We were situated as we would be to greet a visiting dignitary or person of some importance. We didn't know what to expect, but my father had insisted on some type of reception, and he was right. If we were going to be there anyway, what harm could it do to be polite?

There was a small, low platform equipped with a lectern and microphone. Just a few feet in front of it were three chairs, one in front and two set slightly behind it. My father now sat in the front chair. Kavu and I sat just behind. Ten feet behind us was a semicircle of nine chairs. In them sat the nine tribal leaders, and next to each leader sat a goon'do as patient and calm as their companions.

Soon the ship was docked and a gangway secured. Four middle-aged white men emerged. All were dressed in beige khakis and a black polo shirt. I laughed to myself and thought that if Ralph Lauren fashioned a navy, this would be their uniform. They carried large baskets, so large in fact that it took two of them to carry each one. Silently they came and went. They first placed a large basket in front of my father, then in turn in front of each of the leaders. I glanced over my father's shoulder to see that the basket contained a laptop computer, an iPad, and plenty of other electronic devices. Many of the items were beautifully packaged foods. The food, of course, got the attention of the goon'do, but they remained patient and calm. However, it didn't stop them from looking and sniffing from a distance.

Once again I realized that these men had done their homework. They knew full well we were a somewhat modern people and that these items were familiar to us, but they also understood that we did not have easy availability to them and that their gifts would provoke our interest and curiosity, if not our appreciation.

I almost changed my mind about their knowledge of us when the men returned from the ship with their final gift. A single, live, caged chicken was placed at the feet of each of the nine elders and my father, breaking the silence and challenging the patience and curiosity of the goon'do.

The men completed their work with all of us still in silence, not particularly awkward silence, but silence. Only the chickens made a sound as if all of us, including the visitors, were waiting to see what might happen next. The four men retreated up the gangway. Then a figure descended. He was tall but not overly so. He was dressed to match the ship. He wore a clean uniform starched brilliantly white with a Navy captain's hat to match and shiny black shoes. Like the ship, the uniform was devoid of identifying insignia. It could be described as military-ish.

I rose from my chair. I received a glance and a nod from my father and walked up to the gangway to greet our guest. Over my shoulder, I could hear a few of the leaders saying a single word—Frum.

As I grew closer to him, I could see that he was also a middle-aged white man. He was thin and pleasant looking enough. He actually looked a little familiar. Our eyes met, and I silently gestured as if to say, "Follow me," and I led him to the lectern.

. . .

HE STOOD in front of the microphone and looked comfortable in doing so. He raised the microphone to a suitable height, and in the process, subtly tapped it in a way that would tell him its volume and modulation. He had definitely done this before. Well, obviously not exactly this. Most people don't dress in a faux uniform and sail to a remote island in a fake military ship to drop off a fruit basket, but he was clearly comfortable speaking and most likely with himself. He had an ease about himself that some might describe as almost boring or possibly soothing. Finally, he spoke.

"I . . . am John Frum. I have returned. I bring you greetings and gifts from your gods . . . and from America. I am here to tell you that a glorious new day is about to dawn for the Bohlin people and for the beautiful island of Volavo.

"I hope you enjoy these gifts that I have brought for you, the noble leaders of this island, but just a few days from now, on my day, John Frum Day, will be the day that all of the people of your villages have hoped for, have prayed for. There will be gifts for all and not just for that one day, great as it may be. From that day forward, all will have everything. All will have what they want. All will have what they need. And I, John Frum, will be the one to bring it to you."

He then stepped away from the microphone and took two steps toward my father. Extending his hand, he said, "Minister, my greatest thanks to you for being here to greet me today. I promise you, you will not disappointed."

My father, meanwhile, had risen from his chair and also extended his hand. The two men shook hands, and my father said with a smile, "So, what's with the chickens?"

John smiled as my father continued.

"Thank you for these gifts. This is a great day, and there is much to discuss and consider, but for now, my friends must return to their villages for the evening ritual."

The men had risen from their chairs as well and stood behind my father.

"And we all know that nothing can keep us from our evening ritual," he said with a laugh, "not even God himself."

He now spoke directly to John.

"For tonight, please return to your vessel. You may stay docked. Tomorrow you will come, and we will talk."

He turned to the leaders and said, "Thank you all for coming. I will learn, and then all of you will know what I know. On this you have my word."

My father did not need to make that promise. The men promptly left for their villages. Indeed, they were thankful not to be late for the evening ritual. My father's word, coming from a man who lived a lifetime of honor, meant that the men had no worry that my father would take any action without their knowledge or counsel, and whatever he might learn would be shared when the time was right.

Now alone, my father asked, "You have sufficient food and water aboard your vessel?"

"Yes, sir," came the response.

"If you are what you say you are, then it is I who should call you 'sir,'" said my father. "Please stay on your vessel tonight, and come back down tomorrow morning. Qat will be here to greet you at ten," he said, gesturing toward me.

Without another word, John simply nodded and did an about-face, returning to the ship.

Now alone, the three of us stood on the dock. Finally, my father looked at us and said, "What in the world just happened?"

"God is here," I said as the three of us together started the short walk home.

"I am glad you asked him to remain on the boat," Kavu said,

"Yes," said my father. "I don't know what it is, but he wants something. Until we know what he wants, it won't do to have him wandering around the island in that costume. Even the gods don't come with chickens," he said with a laugh. "We will find out soon enough."

4

UNDERWHELMED

"So how did it go?" asked Geur.

I had returned to the ship and was talking to him on our super-duper spy tablet. "Well, not bad really —" I said.

He interrupted eagerly. "So it was good?"

I could see his face, and I could see Cheiro in the background. He was shooting balled up paper, presumably at a wastebasket.

"I don't know," I said. "They were polite, respectful, and very quiet, but all in all, I would say it was—"

"What? What?" he said eagerly.

"Underwhelming," I said. "I don't get a sense that they think I am God, so to speak, but they are curious. Nothing much happened, but all the leaders showed up, and I am going to meet with the minister tomorrow morning . . . I think."

"He thinks?" said Cheiro from across the room. I could see him come closer. "Listen, God, you're not on vacation. Every minute that goes by is a chance for this to get out, especially now that you are there, all white and Navy-ish . . ."

"He knows; he knows," said Geur. "It's pretty much what we expected."

"True," said Cheiro. I guess we didn't expect them to blow him."

"Yeah. I guess I didn't know what to expect, and it wasn't terrible. But I'll tell you, these people are no dummies. That's for sure. They watch and they listen . . . and that puts them way ahead of most people I know, present company included," I said, looking at Cheiro. "Oh, and by the way, asshole," I said to Cheiro, "they hated the chickens! They had no idea why we brought them chickens. They don't mean a damn thing to them other than a meal."

Cheiro laughed. "I know. I just thought it might be fun."

THEY HAD WATCHED, and they had listened. I needed to be very careful, not that they would hurt me or anything like that. It was more like I would speak only when I had to so I wouldn't offer any information that didn't fit. I genuinely liked these people, even more so now. The minister had all the attributes of leadership. He spoke softly and confidently. He had a full head of short, mostly gray hair and a closely cropped beard to match. I would say that he almost looked a little like Nelson Mandela, but the comparison was as much about his bearing as his appearance. His advisor Kavu had sat with the minister's daughter right behind him. He had not been introduced and had not spoken, but I assume it was him. Our research had revealed that he was an adopted son of the minister, and he was taking on more of an active role as the minister aged. While the minister had worn cotton trousers and a thin white cotton shirt, Kavu was dressed more traditionally with a loincloth, but he also wore a Nike T-shirt. To complete the outfit, he wore a traditional penis sheath known as a *namba* under the loincloth.

Yup, it's just what it sounds like, a cloth wrapping around the penis but much longer. The tip of the fabric is then tucked into the waistband of the loincloth or shorts or belt as some of the tribal elders wore, forming a triangle of sorts. When standing, it is either fully visible, or might as well be, since it lifts whatever fabric is in its path. As this was something of a formal occasion, most of the elders had been wearing a namba but also mostly Western style trousers, T-shirts, and shorts.

And then there was the minister's daughter, Qat. She looked to be in her early thirties. She was tall by island standards and wore her jet-black hair long and straight. She had on a simple white dress and a small, plain yellow headdress. I considered her beautiful, but I learned long ago that my taste in women was nothing close to typical. Three of the actresses I worked with on the show were widely thought to be some of the most beautiful in Hollywood, but they had always underwhelmed me. They were pretty, and they were nice enough and had beautiful, well-practiced smiles, but they never seemed real to me. To me, what is real is what is beautiful. What is real is what is sexy. Qat, though I had yet to even hear her voice, was real.

I spent the night on the ship along with my mates. This was no punishment. We had plenty of supplies and comfortable enough accommodations. It was even better now that the chickens were gone. Smith and Wesson went about their business and kept to themselves, never once asking me anything about what happened after they had returned to the ship, not that there had been much. Bert and Ernie had asked halfheartedly if there had been any progress, but they knew the gathering hadn't been anything but a greeting. Captain stayed to himself. Unless there was an emergency, he would be staying on the vessel for the duration.

I was calm and comfortable, absorbing the day's events. It had been pretty easy so far. I knew it was likely to get less so with each coming day, but I was ready, even eager for more. If life is an adventure, then this was life to the fullest. I remember that when my father was happy, which was usually when he'd see the finished product of one of his designs, he'd say, "This is life. The rest is *smorja*." He was right. The rest *is* crap.

I stood on deck for a time. From the dock I could see the modest lights of Gothen, the capital city of the island. Odds were I would get to see it for myself tomorrow. I returned below to my quarters and quickly drifted off to sleep, the sleep of the still pure.

Morning came quickly. I rose at eight, and I could smell coffee coming from our makeshift galley. I found Bert and Ernie having breakfast. They had documents laid out on the table but quickly scooped them up, making a place for me.

"Have some breakfast," said Bert. "Smith and Wesson made the coffee, and they made some eggs. Not too bad actually."

Smith and Wesson had risen before everyone and made breakfast for all of us, then disappeared silently back to their quarters. These were men who clearly liked to be of use and earn their money.

"I'm not hungry," I said, "but I will definitely have some coffee." There was no point in explaining to them that I am never hungry. That always leads to a ten-minute explanation, incredulous looks, and at least one person saying, "I wish I had that problem!"

I returned to my quarters with the coffee and took my time getting into uniform. I appeared at the top of the gangway at exactly 9:55 in order not to risk being late, and I certainly didn't want to appear to disregard the minister's request.

Qat was already standing on the dock. She nodded to me as I came into view as if inviting me down. She stood alone, which actually made me think I had accomplished one thing yesterday, at least. They did not fear me. The minister trusted his daughter would be safe to come meet me alone. Yes, there were workers and a few other people scattered within view, but her presence was still something.

The gangway was stable and not steep, so I was able to keep my gaze on her as I descended without fear of falling or stumbling. As I reached her, I slowly extended my hand. She reached out and received my greeting by grasping my hand gently while looking sharply and directly into my eyes as if searching for clues to my character, or perhaps because my eyes are dark blue, they were a curiosity. Blue eyes, I have read, are not part of the gene pool in this part of the world.

"I am John Frum," I said as our hands touched.

"I know," she said. "I am Qat. My father wishes to welcome and meet with you. Please come with me. It is not a long walk."

We walked together through the amphitheater adjacent to the dock, then past a couple of port administration buildings that were Western in style and construction but were probably built during the war. They were old but clean and well maintained. We exited Port John and traveled west at a leisurely pace.

We arrived in Gothen, the capital of Volavo, in only a few minutes. The city itself had no legally defined border but was a section of the western shoreline of the island. It was basically five modern, paved streets arranged vertically. The westernmost road hugged the shoreline and almost completely encircled the oceanfront of the entire island. The other four roads remained adjacent to each other for about a mile, and then each of them curled inland at a different angle, making almost the entire island passable by road. The city part of each road was no more than a half-mile while they were still adjacent to each other.

All of the city life on the island was in this area. There were six hotels ranging from exotic to Western traditional. The largest and most modern was known as The Frum, of course. It was a squat-looking, concrete, three-story hotel with most modern amenities.

Volavo had not seen a tremendous rise in tourism as had occurred in other parts of the region for a variety of reasons. Probably the biggest reason was that they didn't need tourism or seek it out. They didn't mind tourists, and they were friendly to visitors, but tourism was not their life's blood. The best numbers I could find were that Volavo received between 5,000 and 7,000 tourists each year. Almost all of them came during the dry season, which ran from May to October when there was no worry of tropical cyclones.

Downtown Gothen was home to an assortment of shops and restaurants of a surprising variety. There were several kava bars serving watered down but still potent versions of the ritual drink that was so important to the islanders. There were plenty of homes and offices along the five main roads, becoming more sparse as each trailed off into a jungle landscape as the city receded.

One section of the road, the one that was next to the ocean-front route, was reserved for several official-looking government buildings. However, one structure stood out. It looked like a two-story, wood-framed home except for the thatched roof. The home would have looked familiar to any American. This served as the home and official offices for the minister, Qat, and Kavu.

We didn't speak much during the ten-minute walk. I made one attempt at conversation when I asked why there were no dogs around, not even with the people we saw in the streets. After seeing a dog with each of the elders yesterday, I expected them to be everywhere. Qat explained to me the origins of the goon'do and how the dogs are revered on the island. Turns out they basically live wherever they want, and not many want to live in the city. She said they have everything they need on their own terms in the jungle and the villages and have no need to approach the relatively crowded city area except perhaps out of curiosity.

As we arrived at the family's home, she asked me to wait outside. She would go in to make sure the minister was ready to receive me, and I found myself waiting alone for several minutes.

There were a few cars on the street, and none went more than fifteen miles per hour, which was the speed limit within the city for two reasons. One, the streets were shared with pedestrians, and two, no one here was ever in much of a hurry. There were cars, trucks, jeeps, and even a few golf carts. Some looked ancient. A few looked more modern. They had no traffic laws to speak of and not a single traffic light. They simply didn't need them.

I waited at the end of a short sidewalk that led to the residence. In front was the flag of the island, indicating the home of the minister. The flag had a definite American influence. It was blue, albeit a pale blue. In the upper left corner was a red box. Below the box was a larger circle with a smaller white circle within. The right side of the flag displayed one white star with nine smaller white stars further to its right. I learned later that the large circle represented God while the smaller one within represented his children, the Bohlin. The stars represented the minister and the nine elders. I never did find out what the red part was about. Maybe it was just to make it look more American.

Soon a young man came from the house to escort me in. He was dressed in pseudo-military garb including camo-style trousers and a button-down shirt. He gestured for me to follow, and I entered to find what could have been a museum replica of an American middle-class home of the 1970s.

Two old but very clean sofas were arranged facing each other about ten feet apart, each flanked by a plain, wood end table. At one end of the room were two large La-Z-Boy chairs arranged next to each other. Each had a TV tray in front of it. At the other end against a wall was a simple wood cabinet with an old-style tube television on it and photos on either side. I expected to see Archie and Edith Bunker walk in. We walked through a similarly appointed dining room that led to a door.

When we walked through the doorway, we magically advanced a couple of decades. The minister's office had the appearance of a modern office—if it were 1989. The minister sat at a large desk. Behind him on either side stood Qat and Kavu. Behind them was draped a very large U.S flag. It was a bit frayed and faded but had clearly been treated with care. It was the 48-star flag that was last used in 1959. The minister silently gestured for me to sit in the chair in front of the desk, and I did.

"Please forgive our formality," said the minister, "but if you are who you claim to be, then this is a historic day indeed. I do not know if you are God or man or perhaps both, but I know that you must come from America and at great expense. I think even God himself might have trouble finding a World War Two era gunship that he could put his hands on."

He paused for a moment, chuckling a bit at his own joke. Qat smiled.

"You say that your arrival will bring us riches and happiness, and I do believe you, Mr. Frum, but there is something that tells me there is a price to be paid, so I ask you, who are you? What is it you want?" He sat up straight in his chair and looked directly at me as he stopped speaking as if to say, "Okay. Your turn."

"I am John Frum," I said. "Whether I am God or man, I cannot say. The truth will be known as the reality of my promise comes to pass, but your wisdom, sir, cannot be denied as you are correct. I will ask something of you in return.

"On your island is an ancient volcano. The caves formed over millions of years by this volcano contain a mineral like no other. We can use this mineral in a way that can benefit every man, woman, and child on this planet. I will ask only that we can extract it so we may make the world a better place."

Kavu first looked to his stepfather for approval before speaking. "You must think us foolish children, dressing up in that costume and sailing here."

The minister raised his hand to silence Kavu. "Forgive me," he said. "I did not properly introduce my daughter Qat or my son Kavu, who will someday soon relieve me of the burden of leadership.

"Kavu," the minister said, looking at his son, "he comes to us as John Frum because he knows that most on the island will be eager to accept him as a god. Whether he is god or man is of no matter. It only matters whether the goal is worthy and the result a good one. As the leaders of this island, it is our job to learn if that is so."

He turned back to me. "Tell us more. I do not expect you will tell us all, so do not fear. Simply tell us what you can."

Holy shit, I liked this guy! At that moment, I would have voted for him for president of the United States. I wanted to be him when I grew up! It didn't matter squat to him who I was. All he cared about was protecting his people and doing as much good as he possibly could. He knew that it didn't matter whether he believed me or not. The people would. He also knew that by now, word of my arrival would be spreading throughout the island, and it was, so he did what a good deci-sion-maker does. He gathered information and bought time.

I did as he asked. I gave him as much information as I possibly could. I didn't mention the mineral's specific use as energy, and I didn't dare yet mention Womansanto, but I gave him what I could. I told him truthfully that the rocks could be mined easily and without disruption since they were located in a remote and uninhabited section of the island. I said that at any given time, there would be from two hundred to three hundred people involved in mining operations, but they could live on ships offshore and simply shuttle back and forth. Not only would they not bother the islanders, but the islanders probably wouldn't even know the miners were there unless the islanders went looking for them.

When I finished speaking, the minister sat silently as if to digest everything I had to say.

"I have no answer for you at this time," he said.

"I did not yet expect one," I responded.

"This is not a dictatorship," he said. "Something of this importance requires the agreement of each of the elders as this would affect us all. For now, please let my daughter Qat show you Volavo. I am sure there are already many here that are quite eager to meet you. You will come to me again tomorrow. Today you will learn more about us, and we will learn more about you."

From his tone, I could tell this was the end of the conversation, and I rose from my chair. "Thank you," I said.

"And thank you," he said, smiling. "It is not every day I come face to face with God."

Qat had come around the desk, and we were walking together to the door when the minister stopped me and said coyly, "Oh, and Mr. Frum, tomorrow you may bring your legal documents."

Now I smiled.

"Surely you have come with legal documents. Tomorrow you may bring them to me. We will look at them."

"Yes, sir," I replied as Qat and I turned again to leave.

5

GETTING TO KNOW YOU

My father had arranged to have a jeep out front and ready to go for us after the meeting. God and I walked to the jeep where it was waiting with a driver. I dismissed the driver and jumped into the driver's seat and gestured for John, which is what I will call him, to sit in the passenger seat. In his eyes I could see he was surprised that we just assumed he would come, but my father knew. He always knew what people were going to do before they even knew it themselves.

My job was to learn as much as I could about John Frum while showing him around the island. Really it was more about showing him *to* the island, the elders, and the people. Whatever John Frum wanted, he definitely was not going to get it unless the people and the elders were along for the ride.

Kavu had already reached out to all the elders to let them know to expect a visit. John didn't know it yet, but he was going to be the guest of honor at a kava ritual this evening with four of the elders. Each village usually has its own ceremony, but on special occasions, some villages will combine with others at a single location. But that was much later.

John jumped in. Our transportation was an old, slightly beat-up but very capable jeep, white, open-air with a perfect, uncracked windshield. At some point, someone had hastily rigged up an eight-track player under the dashboard, and it held a well-worn tape wedged into position with a folded up matchbook cover.

I started up the jeep, and it growled to life, simultaneously and loudly playing the tape. Hearing Julie Andrews singing "Getting to Know You" from *The King and I* had me smiling to myself at how perfect the song was for the situation. After all, that is what I was doing—getting to know him.

"Do you like the beach?" I asked as I started out onto the road. It was probably not the first question he was expecting, but he didn't seem fazed by it. Now that I think about it, he hadn't seemed fazed by anything so far.

"I like to look at it," he said. "I like to walk on it, but I don't really like to lie in the sand or swim in the ocean. I kind of figure that whales and dolphins don't often bother us much on land, so I can return the favor by staying out of their neighborhood."

I laughed. "I'm kind of the same. I like the beach as long as I am clothed, dry, and with no sand between my butt cheeks."

He hadn't asked where we were going, but I figured I would tell him anyway. "We're going to take a tour of your island, Mr. Frum," I said with exaggerated formality. "You'll need to show your face to each of the elders at some point, and we might as well get started.

"We have nine main villages, each with its own elder. We've got some smaller hamlets scattered around, too, but even those are loosely affiliated with one of the larger villages and its elder."

"Sounds good to me," he said. "How long do you think it's going to take?"

"It will take as long as it takes," I said. "Definitely all of today, and you can probably count on tomorrow too."

"So where to first?" he asked.

"To our largest village, though it probably won't look so large to you. It won't be long now."

He became silent after that, and I realized he was listening to the song from the eight-track as *The King and I* continued. This time it was Yul Brynner's turn. I listened as he sang about the conundrum of trusting others, both people and nations. He sang of the dangers and the rewards. He sang of his own uncertainty. No wonder he found so much of life a puzzlement. I did too.

"You know, I didn't have any actual expectations, but I was pretty sure that I wouldn't be listening to show tunes on Volavo. Is Broadway a big thing here?"

"My father likes them, especially *The King and I*." I didn't tell him that because of my father, I had practically grown up on show tunes, and I knew every word of every soundtrack.

We had traveled about three miles out of town on the outermost road when we arrived at our first stop. Well, our stop was actually a short walk away. I pulled the jeep off to the side of the road where about a hundred and fifty feet of dry sand stretched to the ocean. On the other side was fairly dense jungle foliage with a small clear-cut walking path.

"I hope you have comfortable shoes," I said as we walked to the opening of the path.

"Good enough," he answered as he followed.

As we walked, I told him that he was about to visit Kepal, a town of about 1,600 people who lived in and around the village. Its elder was also named Kepal though he was the only elder to share the name of his village, as was their custom. He was one of the oldest and kindest of the elders. He would simply want to see John. I wasn't even sure that he would want to talk to him. It would be just like Kepal to adopt the attitude that if this was

God, then he should not speak with him because he believed a man should not know his gods on that level.

The foliage gradually gave way to a large clearing. In the center was the dome for the goon'do. A small group of them had already detected our presence and had run to greet us. Most of them were familiar with me and greeted me warmly but offered no less of a warm greeting for the tall, white stranger in uniform. They wagged and wiggled their way over to him, clearly presenting the best places he should scratch and the opportunity to feed them if by chance he was carrying anything tasty.

John smiled and gave them what they wanted, pats and scratches. He apologized for not having brought anything to eat. I swear he was considering getting down on the ground to play with them, but he appeared to think better of it so as not to soil his brilliant white uniform.

Soon a group of children followed, shouting my name and excited by the stranger. There were mumbles of "Frum," evidence that word of his arrival had predictably spread.

"Where is Kepal?" I asked the children who had now surrounded poor John, laughing and pointing as he played with the goon'do.

All around the clearing was a curved line of homes, many of which were attached to each other. Some were of plywood construction. Many were made of *tegel,* a form of brick that we made on the island from mud and sand. It was the color of chocolate and almost as durable as conventional brick but a bit lighter.

Every home was similar in that all of them had a thatched, pitched roof with the traditional tiki hut look. Kepal emerged from one of the homes and headed in my direction. A small crowd of men and women had gathered nearby, but John was busy with the dogs and children and did not seem to be aware of the crowd, nor did he notice as Kepal greeted me.

. . .

We spoke for several minutes. He laughed when he said that he had planned to serve his gift of a chicken to his goon'do and asked how my father was feeling. I told him that all was well and that my father seemed preoccupied, as he should be, with the appearance of John Frum.

We looked up to the sound of loud laughter from the children. There stood John, still surrounded when one of the children stepped forward.

"Pull my finger!" said John. The child pulled his finger, and John made the loud sound of a fart. He immediately started waving his hand in front of his nose as if to wave away the odor, then pointed at one of the goon'do. "Stop that!" he yelled. "That's disgusting."

The children roared. Another child stepped forward with the same result, except this time he pointed at one of the shy children in the back of the pack as being guilty of the offending smell.

Shaking his head, Kepal looked at me with a wry smile and said, "This is our new god? I guess it could be worse. I have no need to meet him. Tell your father that I trust his judgment, and he may proceed as he wishes."

We said our goodbyes, and Kepal turned and walked across the clearing, returning to his home. John had been oblivious, but he saw Kepal turn to leave and reluctantly walked over to me with the children following.

"Hey, doesn't he want to meet me?" he asked.

"He's satisfied," I said. "What he is satisfied about I don't know, but he's satisfied. You made quite an impression."

John laughed. "I was just having fun. I didn't insult him or violate some custom, did I?"

"No, no. It's fine," I said. "I think he likes you."

We wandered around the village for a time. A few of the

children remained, and John selected one of the children, a small boy, to act as our "royal guard." The boy took the role seriously and walked a few paces ahead of us, fending off nonexistent dangers both large and small.

The grownups, for the most part, were curious but kept their distance. Sporadically, they would approach John in pairs, offering greetings and sometimes making specific requests for certain goods when he brings the giant load of cargo.

John would smile broadly, promising only that they would be very happy when that day came. We made our way back to the jeep with our small entourage in tow. John wanted to take a walk on the beach, so we made our way across the sprawling stretch of sand to the ocean's edge.

Here he was, probably thousands of miles from wherever he came from, completely alone among strangers, and yet for all appearances, perfectly at ease. Maybe he really was a god, or maybe he was just a very good actor.

And then it hit me. Now I realized why he looked familiar. I had seen him on television. He *was* an actor. He had played a role for a long time on an American comedy show.

I wasn't sure what this meant. It's not as if I really thought he was God and was shocked that he was a man, but this meant one thing was certain—deception. Still, as my father would say, what matters is the result. For the moment, I would keep this revelation to myself.

We walked along the water, and John asked, "Why is the oceanfront so empty? No one is swimming."

"I guess they don't like the beach either," I said.

"Oh, yes," he replied, "that whole sandy butt thing."

"Actually, a lot of people do go in the water, just not in this area. This section of oceanfront is called Banyu Cepete, literally 'fast water.' We call it 'The Rush' because the power of the waves and current of the water rushing to shore make swimming almost impossible and very dangerous. It is a big part of the legend of how the Bohlin came to live here. Every islander knows the story by heart, so you should know it too."

I told John the story as it was told to me, as it was told throughout our history.

A great wooden ship traveled by night in the dark of a vast sea. Clouds formed above her as the sea heaved and swirled beneath her. The master of the vessel, knowing the ship was in grave danger, told the people that the ship could not survive unless half of them jumped into the sea so the others may live.

Though they loved their lives, half did jump. Whole families— men, women, and children—threw themselves into the ocean so that the others may live. As soon as they had jumped, a great bolt of light- ning burst from the sky and struck the vessel, breaking it in two and sending the ship and those who had remained aboard to the bottom of the sea.

Those who had jumped found themselves swept up in a giant wave, which soon brought them to the shores of Volavo. The four- legged gods awaited them on the shore to offer them comfort and to lick their wounds.

"That is why we are called the Bohlin. It literally means 'the children of the brave.' The four-legged gods, of course, are the dogs we now call the goon'do."

John looked thoughtful for a few seconds as if pondering the story. "It would not surprise me if at least some parts of that story are true," he said. "From what I know about this island, something like that could have happened five or six hundred years ago. It makes sense. At that time, probably nobody could have found this place except by accident."

I stopped walking and turned to face him. "I believe every word of it, and so does virtually every person born on this island! We *are* a brave and virtuous people. We have many beliefs, some old and some new. Some of our beliefs even conflict with each other, and that's okay. You know why? Because we don't take any of them too seriously, including and especially you, Mr. John Frum, especially you, but who we are and how we got here, that we do take seriously. That we do believe."

I wasn't actually angry, but part of me needed to make him understand. Part of me wanted to shake him up a bit, see if I could get underneath his calm, well-rehearsed exterior.

I turned around and started to head back. He hesitated for a moment as if he were going to say something and then quickly caught up. We walked silently until we reached the jeep.

I leaned over to turn the key in the ignition. Then I stopped, turned to him, and said, "So, uh, do you want to have sex?"

He sat straight up in his seat, and then he hesitated. I think he realized what I was up to.

"What, you mean with you?" he asked.

"Yes, of course with me," I said.

"Just like that?" he asked.

"Just like that," I answered. "Well, there's more to it actually. If I were going to have sex with God, there would have to be a whole ceremony. We'd need flowers, of course . . ."

"Of course," he agreed, getting into the spirit of the thing.

"And soy sauce. We will probably need a rabbi and some non-dairy creamer . . ."

He was laughing now and shaking his head. "This is what passes for humor on my island?" he asked, laughing harder.

I couldn't hold back any longer, and I started laughing hard too.

"Should I ask what we'd do with the non-dairy creamer?" he said.

"I am sure we could think of something."

By now I was howling, and I could barely get the words out. I had started to drive away but had to stop the jeep because I could not catch my breath. I calmed down a little and pulled the jeep back onto the road. The sounds of our laughter blended with the melodies of *The King and I,* still playing on the eight-track.

"Where are we off to now?" he asked after we had both settled down a bit.

"We are going to do some sightseeing around the island. After that, I will take you back to your ship to rest up a bit for tonight."

"I thought your father wanted me to see all of the elders," he said.

"Tonight you will be meeting with four of them at once as part of the kava ritual. Believe me," I said, "you're going to want to rest up for that. Oh, and you should probably have something to eat. Have you ever tried kava before? I know you can get it in the states now."

"I've heard of it but never tried it."

"That's probably for the best," I said. "I can't imagine it's any good after being shipped around the world. It should give you a mild buzz, but it affects everyone a little differently. It makes me really relaxed and alert at the same time, and I absolutely cannot shut up. After two or three shells, I am convinced that I am the most interesting person in the world."

"You are interesting," he said. "I don't know you that well, and I don't know what else you might be, but rest assured, you definitely are interesting." He smiled.

At that moment I was flooded with the feeling that this man, while no god, was a man with a kind soul, and he, at the very least, meant us no harm, but I also knew he was an actor playing a part. It was his job to persuade us, and he himself might not even know the true motive.

We circled the island. The oceanfront road held beautiful views almost everywhere but not a lot more than that. The villages are all located a little inland, and there was almost no real commerce outside of Gothen. Every couple of miles, there were small stores we called *fosalos.* They mostly serve the stray tourists that happen by. The fosalos have cold drinks, some packaged snacks, and some towels and sunscreen for the unprepared. All the merchandise is shipped in from Australia or New Zealand.

We stopped at one for some water. I took John for a short walk across the road and a little inland to the place we call The Lookin. The Lookin is perched at the highest point above a gentle slope. It's only about forty feet from the top down, stretching out a mile or so in every direction. Except for the volcano, the rest of the island is mostly flat. If we made postcards of Volavo, they would probably have a picture of The Lookin on them. We stood looking down at the top of a seemingly endless forest. It was ridiculously beautiful.

As we continued our tour, we would pass an occasional small group of goon'do. Once in a while, we would see another vehicle or see some villagers walking along the road. John got in the habit of offering a smile and a crisp salute. The islanders would point and laugh.

"How do you keep this place so clean? John asked. "Not that I expected it to be filthy, but I haven't seen a hair out of place since I've been here."

"A place is as clean or as dirty as the people choose to make it, and we have always chosen to keep it as God made it."

"It shows," he said. "It definitely shows."

We made it back to the ship, and I dropped him off at the entrance to the port. I would be back to pick him up at seven o'clock for tonight's festivities. I hoped for his sake that he was ready for it.

6

IT'S KAVA-LICIOUS!

I had a couple of hours until Qat was going to come back to get me for the kava ritual. I was actually looking forward to it. My own history with drugs was not much to speak of. I was not much of a drinker. One or two beers was a heavy night for me. I've smoked weed just often enough to know that I don't like it. It's not awful, but it definitely does not make me feel good, so what's the point? I have had opioid painkillers a couple of times after dental work, and I did enjoy that. In fact, I think I enjoyed it too much. The drug didn't cause the pain to go away as much as it made me not care about it, but I'm pretty mellow to begin with, so if you take me and add Percocets, I become way too chill.

Most drugs actually scared me enough to avoid them. I'm not saying completely though. Trust me, if I had surgery, I'd be the first one asking for a morphine drip, but that's about it. I would say coffee is the closest thing I have to a drug habit.

I checked in with Geur and Cheiro, telling them of the progress I had made. And there really was progress. They would at least listen to us. That's a start.

Geur and Cheiro, of course, were their usual nervous and

impatient selves. Bert and Ernie had prepared the documents for me to present to the minister the next day while Smith, Wesson, and Captain were still on the ship but nowhere to be found.

I took the time to rest. I tried to completely clear my mind and not think about anything, but it was fleeting. This island, these people . . . they were a world of their own. They had almost a mystical quality about them and a kind of innocence, but it was not an innocence of ignorance. It was as if they had the wisdom to allow the outside world in but only just enough, enough to enjoy the benefits of what it had to offer without having to endure its pressure and dysfunction. It may have been egotistical of me to even think it, but I would not allow anything to change that.

I took my time getting cleaned up and dressed. I broke out a clean uniform. I'm not sure which one, but either Smith or Wesson had already hand-washed, dried, and pressed the uniform I had worn yesterday. It was like new, neatly folded and left on a chair right outside my cabin. As I said, those guys love being useful.

At 6:55 I went on deck. I was surprised by the little jolt of happiness I got when I saw Qat. The feeling was not something I was used to.

She was standing at the bottom of the gangway, looking up at me. She was dressed all in white, including a white head-dress that was pulled back on her forehead and covered all but the longest strands of her hair. The headdress did not cover her face but framed it in a way that made her look very different than she had only a couple of hours ago. She was beautiful indeed. I didn't think I had a visible reaction, but she seemed to notice my gaze.

"I haven't changed anything," she said, "except my clothes. I have to represent for the ladies."

I wasn't sure what she meant by that, but I would find out soon enough. We walked together back to the jeep.

As we drove, Qat filled me in on the evening's plan. "As I told you earlier today, we're going to meet four of the elders at one time at the kava ritual. They are Ola, Vanu, Manko, and Barun. Barun likes to be called Barry, though, because he's a fan of Barack Obama. They're each around forty and all fairly modern in their ways and outlook, but don't be surprised if they are wearing dick tents tonight because they might see this as a formal night since you are going to be there."

I worked very hard not to look surprised when she said that, but I am pretty sure I failed. "Excuse me, but did you just say 'dick tent'?"

"Yes, dick tents," she continued casually, "the ceremonial penis sheath that they wear sometimes. It's called a namba, but I call them dick tents because that's what they look like.

"Don't tell me you didn't notice. Kavu was wearing one yesterday. I swear, sometimes the wrapping is bigger than what's underneath, if you know what I mean."

She smiled brightly, innocently. She knew full well what she was doing.

I recovered enough to say, "You know, it's a shame you are so shy and reserved. You should probably try to open up more, learn to just say what you feel."

She laughed. "Anyway, they will expect you to match them shell for shell, so I hope you ate something, or the kava will give you one hell of a tummy ache. They are hoping you are John Frum, the god, so you can expect them to ask you to prove it somehow. Good luck."

"How do you know I'm not?"

"Not what?"

"God," I said. "How do you know I am not your god?"

"Well for one thing, I'm pretty sure god wouldn't be so gullible.

Honestly, I don't care if you are God or not. It doesn't matter. Even if you aren't God himself, who's to say you are not the hand of God working in mysterious ways or something? It makes no difference."

She had a point, but I was pretty sure it would matter to at least some of the elders, and I should try to be pretty damn godlike if I wanted this to work.

It was almost dark as we left the city, and the road we took curled inland. The well-paved road gradually gave way to a route that was never quite level and was riddled with dips and small potholes. The already sparse lighting of Gothen had become the nearly pitch-black of the jungle. The surrounding branches and leaves practically enveloped the road like a canopy. In some parts it felt like we were driving through a living tunnel, making the moon and stars invisible. The only light came from the glow of the dashboard and the thin beams of the headlights.

Qat, of course, was used to the darkness and seemed completely comfortable. I, on the other hand, was not and realized that I was crouching in my seat to avoid the random branch, palm frond, or exotic night-feeding jungle creature that might find me, but none came.

Qat noticed me crouching and said, "Don't worry, tough guy, nothing's gonna get you. We'll be out of this thick stuff in a minute."

She was right, of course. Not long after she said that, the canopy opened up, and the stars returned.

"I don't blame you," she said. "It takes some getting used to."

Minutes later the road came to an end at a fairly large clearing. In the center was what looked like a large yurt but with the type of thatched roof that I had seen earlier in the day. Behind it were two more structures that were slightly smaller but similar in design. A scattering of tiki torches provided enough light to see the ground, but the torches were electric, providing light not heat.

There were no people in sight, but voices and music could be heard coming from the buildings. Qat had told me earlier that this was like a community center of sorts for four of the villages, all of which were nearby. Obviously they were within walking distance, as there was not another vehicle in sight.

Qat stopped the jeep but did not get out. "Okay," she said, "you're going to be on your own for a while. The kava ritual is a men's only affair and we women have our own gathering next door.

"See that building? It's for both men and women, and some of the people gather there after the ritual is over. It's sort of the after-party, mostly for the unmarried men and women, but there aren't a whole lot of them. We still get married young here and tend to stay married. Arranged marriages still exist on the island, but they are becoming something of a rarity."

It looked like I would be on my own with the men for a while. I knew the ritual would sometimes last three hours or more, and meanwhile, Qat would be with the women.

"I don't come here often, but as the minster's daughter, it's still my responsibility to attend every month or two. Regardless, I always receive a warm welcome.

"Okay, are you ready?" she asked as she jumped out of the jeep.

"I don't know. You tell me. Am I ready?"

"You'll be fine . . . I think."

I didn't know what to expect. I now knew enough about these people to know that whatever I might expect would be wrong. A couple of days ago, I might have expected a solemn ritual, but that did not seem to be their style. When I was a boy, I might have imagined an old movie scene with a vat of boiling oil and me being slowly lowered into it to be prepared as a meal, but they probably wouldn't boil a god, even a fabricated one. What I never imagined, although it made perfect sense in hindsight, was what I found when I walked through the door.

The big round room was a time capsule. On the walls were Americana of many varieties. Posters of American film actresses adorned the walls, as bygone as Betty Grable and as recent as Demi Moore from *G.I. Jane*. There were U.S. flags of various sizes and ages, and there were other movie posters —*Earthquake, Goodfellas,* and *The Bridge on the River Kwai*— among others. Old U.S. military uniforms from all different branches and ranks were displayed. The most modern item in the room was a large poster of Barack Obama with the presidential seal as the background. The floor held dozens of rubberized mats scattered over dirt and sand beneath.

On one side of the room was a long bar with more than a dozen rickety bar stools, a simple wood construction that would have looked at home in an officers' club, which is exactly where they had come from decades ago. Scattered throughout in no particular pattern were folding chairs and a few old couches and loveseats. There was a very old jukebox that was just for show, but there was music coming from a more contemporary boombox perched on a chair. Yes, the music blared show tunes but ones I couldn't identify. On one wall was even an old, hole-ridden dartboard with a few men competing.

In the center was indeed a large vat, not boiling but warming with a very small controlled fire below. Behind the vat stood three boys who were probably twelve or thirteen years old. Each had a small table in front of him and a basket full of dry kava root next to him. From what I could tell, there were two types. The first looked like a tree branch. The boys would use a small wood-handled paring knife, carefully stripping the top layers. This left a thin pulpy stick about ten inches long and an inch or two around. The other type looked like a clump of thin roots. The boys would use a longer, serrated blade to chop these roots. Once properly prepared, the boys would take them and drop them into the vat. This was a steady, ongoing process.

About sixty men filled the room, all but a few in trousers and T-shirts. All except me were barefoot. A few wore nambas. They were in groups of three or more, and everyone was holding either a bowl or a coconut shell, and virtually everyone was talking. This barely changed when I walked through the door. A few stopped their conversations and turned to look, but most simply went about their business, and at the moment, their business was filling their bowls or shells from the vat and guzzling down the contents in one giant swig. This was a "ritual" in the way that Moe's bar was a ritual for Homer Simpson —except the bartenders were underage.

I stood by the door for a moment just looking around. Two men approached. I recognized them from yesterday as village elders. Both men were in their mid to late thirties and wore shorts and flowery print shirts with no sign of a namba. One had closely cropped hair and a mustache. The other was shaven bald. By appearance alone, they may as well have been vacationing accountants from New Jersey. Only their voices, which spoke grammatically perfect English with a trace of an island lilt, would suggest otherwise.

The bald one spoke. "You are the one who calls himself John Frum. Whether this is true or false, real or imagined does not matter tonight, for you are an honored guest. We welcome you."

He extended his right hand while still holding a coconut shell in his left. I shook his hand and then turned to shake the hand of the other man.

"Thank you for this most gracious reception," I said.

And so I met Ola and Vanu.

They walked over to the vat of kava in the center of the room. Ola raised both his shell and his voice shouting, "This is John Frum, our god from America. He has come once again to make us all rich and happy! Shall we share our blessed kava with him?"

"Yes!" came a resounding roar from every man in the room.

"Then who will be first to bring him a shell?"

Instantly bowls and coconut shells came at me from every direction, and I chose one.

Ola leaned over to me and whispered conspiratorially, "You ever try kava before?"

"No," I whispered back.

"You'll be fine, but you have to drink. Try to drink it in one gulp," he said quietly.

Then he yelled, "It is time to drink! And we will drink like men!"

All the men came to the vat and filled their bowls. I reached over and filled mine. It was lukewarm, and I have to be honest. It smelled like dirt. Oh well, as far as I know, nobody ever died from this. They all seemed pretty healthy, at least.

Vanu now raised his shell with both hands, and every man in the room did the same. "We, the children of the brave, give thanks for this gift. May we be forever worthy of it!" He put the shell to his lips and drank it in one mighty gulp.

Every man in the room did the same—except me. It took me about five to seven seconds to drink what was about the size of a bottle of beer. Not bad, I thought, but it was a very long five to seven seconds with every eye in the room upon me. A cheer erupted in the room as I drained the last of the liquid into my mouth. It tasted pretty much like it smelled, like dirt.

The only immediate effects were that my lips and tongue began to feel numb, kind of like novocaine as it was wearing off. There was also the slightest buzz as if I were fully awake.

I turned to Vanu and asked, "Is there normally a whole speech and prayer every time?"

"Nah, usually we just drink it. That was for you."

He turned back to the crowd once more, saying, "And again!"

He filled his shell. We all did the same. The second shell went down quicker and smoother than the first, and I didn't spill a drop. The numbness in my mouth increased, but I could still talk.

Vanu once again filled his shell and addressed the group. "And just one more . . . for now!"

Again we filled our bowls and drank.

Each one went down easier than the one before. My mouth was still a little numb, but rather than get worse, it seemed to level out to a slight tingle. I can only describe the feeling as being a clear kind of alert pleasure. I felt I could taste my breath as I filled my lungs. It was nothing like alcohol or painkillers. I have never used cocaine, but I don't imagine this is anything like that.

The rest of the men dispersed around the room, and another two men approached us. It was Barun and Manko.

"It's an honor to meet you. Thank you for allowing me to join you in this ritual."

"Call me Barry," Barun said, but I already knew his preferred name, thanks to Qat. Barry, like most of them, had never been off the island. He had a lot of questions about the United States and hoped to visit one day. The five of us stood together and chatted as if we were old friends. Occasionally one of them would fill their bowl and drink, but no one pushed me to do so.

I couldn't help but notice that I was eager to speak, answer questions, and converse. I wasn't shy normally, but no one could ever call me a great conversationalist. But now, with three bowls in me and more to come, words came easily and everything was interesting.

Other men would come and go from our group, joining and leaving the conversation. They would ask me about my ship or my uniform or my home in New York, where I had honestly told them I came from. No one asked me if I were god or man. Either they were being polite, or maybe it just really didn't matter to them. They had many gods, and except for the occasional cyclone, the gods had always treated the Bohlin pretty well. They expected I would do the same.

Over the next hour, I had three or four more bowls. Each gently intensified the effect, but the numbness in my lips and tongue had actually dissipated to the faintest of tingling.

No one had entered or left since I had gotten there—until now. Through the door walked Kavu. He was alone and casually dressed, no dick tent for him today. Everyone in the room turned to look at him as he came in, but talk and activity continued. No one seemed surprised at his entrance.

Acknowledging no one, he marched directly to the vat. One of the boys handed him a shell. He drank one, then another and another.

"I can see I have some catching up to do," he said to no one in particular.

He downed two more shells, one after the other, and then turned to address the crowd.

"I have come to see the great god, John Frum!" he yelled.

This quieted the crowd and got their attention.

"He has told us that he comes to make us rich and happy, but we already have everything we need that makes a man rich, and"—he paused to drink another bowl of kava—"as you can see, we are already happy."

He turned to me but spoke to the crowd. "So tell me, John Frum. Surely you can tell us how next year's kava crop will be. Tell us, God. Will it be bountiful?"

There was a curious lack of tension in the room as he spoke. Maybe it was the kava. Maybe it was simply just how they were.

I paused just long enough to let the echo of his words ring their last. Then I said in the biggest, loudest, fullest voiceover-announcer intonation I could muster, "There will always be more than enough kava to fill *my* shell . . . and if there is any left over, we shall fill yours as well."

No one spoke or moved for what felt like forever but was probably no more than two or three seconds, and then the sounds of laughter filled the room with none louder than Kavu himself. He moved toward me, his hand extended. We shook hands and pulled each other together in a quick, firm hug. "I am glad you are here," he said in my ear, "no matter who you turn out to be."

We quickly separated, and the conversations continued with Kavu as an eager participant. He was, not surprisingly, a clever young man. I took note of the tactics in play. That is, either Kavu's tactics or the minister's.

They waited for me to get five bowls deep into my first kava buzz before testing my reactions. Clever indeed. I was also not surprised to learn that Kavu had visited the United States, more than visited, in fact. He had spent a year in school in Virginia. He spoke well of us but also with some sadness for what he saw as the sorry state of our souls.

About twelve of us stood together with Kavu. He told us that the Americans were a great and kind people, but almost all served the twenty-two balloons. All the men nodded and seemed to understand instantly.

By now I was about ten shells in, but it wouldn't have mattered. I had no idea what that meant. Kavu saw my confusion and explained. "We are a people of many stories. This is the story of a man who went mad, spending his days keeping twenty-two balloons in the air, running from one to another in terror, lest one touch the ground. Every Bohlin knows the story. It reminds us to keep our needs simple and our masters few."

I asked about the boys who still stood in silence, preparing the kava root that would go in the giant vat. The men explained that in the old days, only boys younger than fourteen were considered pure enough to be trained and entrusted with the duty of preparing the sacrament of the kava root. Now it was more like a familiar tradition than a religious duty, but it was still considered an important rite of passage for boys, all of whom were trained to prepare the root. After passing all of the requirements, boys became men at the age of fourteen.

"You will learn of another of these tests tomorrow," said Kavu coyly.

I knew better than to ask what that might mean.

Vanu asked, "How do you like the kava? Are you enjoying the ritual?"

It seemed important to him that I felt welcome, and I did. "Kava," I said, "your hospitality is very much appreciated."

"And the Kava?" he asked. "How does it feel?"

I answered by once again filling my shell. I raised it to the sky and then down to my lips without spilling a drop. I drank it in a single gulp and proclaimed in my big announcer's voice, "IT'S KAVA-LICIOUS!"

The men roared in agreement.

Roots were still being prepared, shells were still being filled and quickly emptied, but men were leaving now, many stopping to say goodbye to Kavu and me. The ritual was winding down, but no one was staggering or stammering. All were in full control of their wits and senses. There had not been a single fight or loud disagreement of any kind. The men just wanted to talk and play while enjoying each other's company. Kava, it seems, is a gentle beast. It offered only a warm glow, relaxation, and a keen sense of alertness. Finally, Kavu himself said goodnight to everyone who remained.

Clearly, as they say, I did not have to go home, but I couldn't stay here either.

7

TOMMORROW IS ANOTHER DAY

I was waiting for John in the jeep. The women had all gone home half an hour ago from what had been a pleasant evening. The kava and conversation had flowed as always, but there was a different feel in the room than there had been the last time I had attended. Everyone wanted to know about the stranger who had come as John Frum.

They knew he was next door, and a few had waited around, hoping to catch a glimpse, but most had children or parents or something else waiting at home that would require their attention. In this way, island life was not much different than in the West.

The most important duties still fell upon the women, but unlike in the West, the woman of Volavo had created a clever way of managing the demands of children and family. Women with children or elderly parents would basically pair off in a form of social contract and serve as caregivers to each other's kids or parents every other day, more or less. This had other benefits too. The arrangement built bonds of trust within the community and gave Bohlin women free time that always seemed impossible to find in other parts of the world.

The men, of course, had their ritual every night and still pretended that it was a sacred, solemn affair. We all knew better, but it's always best to let them think they are keeping something secret. It helps to keep them out of trouble. Women felt no need to create any religious pretext. We just enjoy kava, and it is a harmless part of our social life on the island.

The women had heard or maybe concocted all kinds of rumors about John. He was the tallest man on the island, they said. He wasn't. He was a little taller than my father, who is only a little above average height for the Bohlin men. He had piercing pale blue eyes, they said, that could look right through you. Yes, he had blue eyes, I told them, but dark blue like the sea.

"Why did he bring chickens?" one woman asked. "Ours never shuts up."

"That I don't know. I guess he thought we wanted them," I answered.

This went on for quite some time, but then, as Bohlin women are prone to do, they got around to asking the important questions:

"What does this mean?"

"What does he want?"

"What is your father going to do?"

I answered as best I could. "We will watch and learn. I know my father's wisdom will prevail as it always has."

It was cool on the island that evening, maybe seventy degrees or so, and there was always a slight breeze no matter where you went. I sat in the jeep but left it off. Only a couple of tiki lights remained on, and sounds of life still came from the men's ritual, but I had seen many of the men leave. Kavu himself had said goodnight and departed minutes before.

So I waited and enjoyed the darkness of the sky and the brightness of the stars. I had always loved the stars above Volavo, but my own five shells of kava certainly didn't lessen my appreciation any. Kava affects everyone a little differently. For me, it seemed to sharpen my eyesight and hearing. Colors appeared brighter, and music seemed richer and fuller. There was no telling how it might affect John, especially with this being his first time. No doubt the men had given him a bellyful.

Out he came minutes later with Barun and Manko on either side of him. I was not surprised to see that they looked like they might well have been lifelong friends, the three of them.

"We hereby deliver him to you, dear lady, unharmed," said Barun with exaggerated formality.

"Oh, worthy chaperone of the gods," said Manko.

John just smiled and said "Hi" sheepishly.

"Gentlemen," John said. "It was my pleasure to attend your solemn ritual, and I hope I didn't embarrass myself too much."

All three laughed. I played my part and just stared at them as I would three naughty boys. Barun and Manko said goodnight and headed back inside. John threw himself into the jeep heavily as if with his last ounce of energy.

"I cannot tell you," he said, "when I have ever been this tired, which is weird because half an hour ago I could not imagine ever being tired at all."

"Kava affects everyone differently. In the same night, it can make you wide awake yet sleep like a baby just a little bit later. How many shells did they give you?"

"I'm not sure," he answered. "I stopped counting at ten . . . maybe fifteen, twenty . . . you know? After a while, it kind of stops tasting like dirt. I kind of like it."

I wasn't surprised.

As we drove, I told him about my night with the women and some of the crazier things they had been told about him. "You know, a few of them actually believe you are the original John Frum from the 1940s."

"That would make me about a hundred and four. I've aged well."

"You have," I agreed. "You don't look a day over eighty."

"That's funny," he said, "but probably just kava funny. Don't bother putting that in your stand-up routine."

We were back where the jungle closes in and the stars disappear. I turned to him to offer reassurance that we were perfectly safe, and I was not surprised to find him fast asleep. Do gods snore? This one does. Maybe it was my own kava buzz, but I found his snoring to be endearing, cute even. "All behold the god who snores!" I said aloud to no one, and soon we were back at Port John.

"Are we home already?" he asked groggily as I shook him awake.

I parked the jeep and walked with him to the gangway. There is no such thing as kava drunk. John, as tired as he was, was still steady on his feet and needed no help, but I walked with him anyway.

"By the way, be ready at ten o'clock tomorrow morning. I'll be back to pick you up."

As he started up the gangway, he turned to me and said, "Thank you."

"For what?" I replied.

"I'm not sure exactly . . . but thank you."

"You are welcome," I said.

He looked like he was about to say something else but then paused as if he thought better of it. "Tomorrow is another day," he said.

I agree. Tomorrow is another day.

8

SHIT, MEET FAN. PART ONE

Geur and Cheiro are nervous people to begin with. I think it's one of the professional hazards of the world they chose to live in, but they were even more nervous than usual. Each of them had found an envelope on their desk when they arrived to work that morning. No one knew where the envelopes had come from. They contained an invitation, more like an order actually. Geur and Cheiro were to be in Cheiro's office at exactly 1:00 p.m., just the two of them. It was from Grant Barnwell, CEO and chairman of the board of Womansanto. This, they knew, could only mean one thing.

Neither of them had ever met Barnwell in person. They had received group e-mails and an occasional memo directed to all the vice-presidents, and once, he had appeared on a livestream to wish everyone in the company a happy New Year, but that was it.

Barnwell had been running the company well before either of them ever worked at Womansanto. His public reputation, as well as his reputation within the company, was that of a charming and kind man, but Geur and Cheiro both instinctively knew better. No one in their world could take and hold that kind of position of power without a dark side. It simply was not possible.

Barnwell was sixtyish but didn't look anywhere near it. He usually maintained a low profile but had been through a very public divorce about a decade earlier. He had been linked romantically several times with prominent, sometimes even famous women. Generally those women were little more than half his age, but he had not remarried.

Under his direction, Womansanto had gone from being a Fortune 500 company in a mature and stagnant industry to a Fortune 100 company with tentacles that reached into technology and aerospace and utterly dominated its core, the chemical business. In short, this was not a man to fuck around with.

At 12:30, a man neither Geur nor Cheiro recognized arrived wheeling a 50-inch TV on a rolling cart. He was silent as he attached a webcam at the top and placed two chairs in front of it. By the time he was done, he had set up a conference call where they would be able to see the chairman, and he would be able to see them. He then handed each of them a headset and offered them a set of very brief instructions.

"Be seated in those chairs, wearing these headsets with the door to this office locked no later than 12:55. Make sure all other electronic devices in the room are off. We will know if they are not."

The man left. Complete privacy, of course, was the point.

"What the fuck did you do? Who did you tell?" yelled Geur at Cheiro, who for some reason already had his headset on and couldn't hear a word of it.

"What?" he answered.

Geur leaned over and pulled the headset off of Cheiro. "WHAT THE FUCK DID YOU DO?" he yelled again, pausing between each word for effect.

"I didn't tell anybody anything. Why would you think it was me?" Cheiro asked.

"Because you are a putz," came the answer. "You probably babbled the whole thing to some waitress or that Russian girl you have the hots for at the dry cleaners."

Cheiro denied telling anyone, and he was telling the truth. Turns out there are two kinds of employees at Womansanto: the ones who either worked for Barnwell and Womansanto or the ones who worked just for Barnwell, personally.

Nothing like our plan could ever happen without Barnwell knowing about it. He had actually liked the idea. He also liked that by letting it happen in the dark, he could always claim he had no part in it if it didn't work. If it blew up in someone's face, it wouldn't be his.

He had been tipped off almost from the moment Geur and Cheiro conceived the plan. They had thought they had maneuvered the money and resources deftly and secretly, but Barnwell had been watching. He was giving them just enough time to get things in motion. Smith and Wesson, Bert and Ernie, Captain—they all worked directly for Barnwell, and they knew it.

The only one who didn't know it at the time was me.

At 12:55 the two of them sat fidgeting in their chairs, headsets on in front of a dark TV. At exactly 12:59 the TV came on showing a large close-up of a very empty, very upscale desk. Behind it was an American flag on one side, hanging on a stand. On the other side was a flag with the Womansanto name and logo. We all knew the logo, a rugged looking farmer in overalls holding and gazing lovingly at an ear of corn.

At exactly 1:00 p.m. Barnwell stepped into the frame, seating himself in the giant chair behind the desk. "Good afternoon, gentlemen. My name is Grant Barnwell. I am the President, CEO, and Chairman of the Board of Directors for The

Womansanto Group Incorporated, the company that at the moment employs you."

Geur and Cheiro knew that Barnwell had no real need to introduce himself. They knew damn well who he was, and Barnwell knew that too. It was simply a way for men like him to apply the full weight of their power to men like them. It works.

"The two of you have been very busy, I see," Barnwell said as he looked down at a piece of paper he held in his hand. "Forgive me, but I have found that if I write everything down, I don't forget anything, but please, don't think for a moment that you do not have my full attention." He hesitated a moment, still reading. "My full attention indeed."

Geur and Cheiro glanced at each other nervously. Neither knew exactly where this would go, but both knew for sure it wasn't good.

"Okay," continued Barnwell. "I'm going to try to keep this really simple for you. From what I know about you two, I think it's my best bet, so try to follow along. I know what you are up to on that island. Every person on that ship that you think is working for you is actually working for me—except the actor. He's working for me too. He just doesn't know it yet. The rest of them, Smith and Wesson, Bert and Bernie or whatever the fuck you are calling them, they do know it. None of them will forget that, and neither should either of you. Would you like to know why?"

Geur and Cheiro looked at each other, unsure whether to respond or if the question was rhetorical.

"Would you like to know why, gentleman?" Barnwell said again, with even more force.

"Um . . . why?" asked Cheiro.

"Because the process that will make those rocks into power . . . It is *my* process! You and the people that you thought worked for you on that island . . .they *and* you are *my* people! And those rocks in that cave on that godforsaken island will be *my* rocks because it is *my* world! You will get those contracts signed, and those rocks will be the wholly owned property of this corporation. Whatever you need to do to complete this cockamamie plan of yours, you will do. You will make this happen."

He paused for a few moments and then continued with a softer tone. "And when you succeed, you will be rewarded handsomely. Each of you will receive five million dollars if you pull this off, and our shareholders and I will be very happy to give it to you. If at that point you wish to continue with the company, you will have your choice of any position you want, except mine of course. Naturally you won't be required to perform any of the actual duties of those jobs because as we all know, you are morons. You are two utterly ordinary men who lucked into prominent families and cushy jobs, none of which was deserved. But you are also a couple of quite clever and sneaky fuckers. You are not altogether stupid, and so I believe .. . I believe with all my heart that you can pull this off."

He paused, smiled, and then slowly got up and walked around to the front of the desk and leaned on it with his back to it. He loomed large on the screen as he now looked down at them.

"Now, let's ponder the impossible, shall we? Let's say for argument's sake that this does not work out. We don't get the mineral rights. We don't get the rocks, so to speak. The important thing to remember here is that I am in no way threatening you. I am absolutely not saying that your dull, pointless careers with this company will be over. I am also in no way saying that you would be brought up on charges of embezzlement and fraud for your activities in preparing this mission. And there is no way on earth that I would possibly suggest a threat to your very lives with the terrible power of this company, its bloodthirsty and relentless security force, or God himself. Never."

Once again, Barnwell paused and took a couple of deep breaths before he returned to his chair. "Now I know, and even you two idiots must know, that the process we have for turning that mineral into an almost free energy source is easy to duplicate and impossible to patent, even for us.

The only way we are going to make money is by controlling that mineral. We need to control that mineral. We deserve to control that mineral. Will we control that mineral, gentlemen?"

Geur and Cheiro had fallen into a nearly catatonic state of awe mixed with terror, so it took them some time to respond. Barnwell was patient and then asked again, this time warmly and kindly. "Will we control corbomite on Volavo, gentlemen?"

"YES!" they shouted in unison.

"Good," said Barnwell. "I knew we could come to an understanding. The man you met earlier will have further instructions for you. Thank you."

Immediately the screen went black.

Geur and Cheiro stayed seated in the chairs as if Barnwell were still watching them or as if he might jump through the screen at any moment. This had all become very real, very fast.

They had been working on this plan for weeks. They had acquired and refit a ship. They had moved accounts, filed purchase orders, and made countless other arrangements, but now and only now did they fully understand the sheer scope of what they were doing and just how vast the potential consequences could be.

They understood something else too. Grant Barnwell, one of the most powerful men on the planet, was scared, and they knew why. The Womansanto method for safely producing energy from corbomite had been a breakthrough, but once known, anyone could do it. Geur and Cheiro didn't understand the science, but they knew there was nothing proprietary or patentable about it. Simple, small, and cheap plants could be built anywhere and produce almost unlimited electric energy.

It would truly change the world. It would turn darkness to light the world over. It would produce almost zero emissions and once implemented would dramatically reduce pollutants from other energy sources everywhere.

No one could own the process, but what you could own were the rocks that made it all possible. The Bohlin people of Volavo were the only ones that had them, and they had enough to power the planet for hundreds if not thousands of years.

Barnwell had to own the minerals. You may think of Womansanto as a chemical company or a seed company or a maker of high tech equipment, but like every other corporation on earth, their real business was money. Their corporate charter did not say "We exist to make better seeds so everyone gets yummy things to eat" or "We exist to supply cheap, clean energy." No, they and every other corporation on earth exist to "enhance shareholder value." In other words, make money.

If that meant selling seeds, great. If that meant selling Roundout, which was responsible for mass starvation, great. If that meant clubbing baby harp seals to death, well, great. In other words, the gods of economics demanded that Grant Barnwell, in order to be worthy, must make untold billions from something this huge, this game-changing, and truth be told, Womansanto did deserve to profit from this. How much they should profit is a question for greater gods, but in any scheme of ethics, they must deserve something.

However, Grant Barnwell could never settle for something. It was his duty to get everything, and that is why he was scared. Like it or not, his fortune and reputation were now tied forever to two blueblood putzes and a washed-up actor. He'd be crazy if he weren't scared.

The man returned to remove the TV. When Geur and Cheiro handed him the headsets, he said, "You will contact Mr. Barnwell with any further developments. You will use the tablets you have already procured."

The man left the office, and Geur and Cheiro still sat. Finally, without saying anything, Cheiro got up and returned the chair to its original place. Geur just stared at him as he came back and looked as if wanted to put the other chair back too. Geur got up and made a gesture towards the chair as if to say, "Okay, asshole, take the chair." He did.

The two men finally got their wits about them when Cheiro said, "Well, now fuckin' what? What the fuck do we do now?"

"Well, first things first," said Geur with surprising confidence. "We talk to Bert and Ernie and find out what those contracts are going to look like. You can be damn sure they won't be what we told them to be."

He was right. I'm sure Barnwell had actually laughed out loud when he heard that Geur and Cheiro thought they were going to get two percent each. What did they think they were going to give the islanders? Nothing? Some green stamps? Blankets with smallpox like the Spanish did to Native Americans? Even Barnwell would never think to try to fuck the Bohlin that hard.

No, Barnwell would give the islanders ten percent however they wanted it—cargo, cash, gold. It made no difference to him. Barnwell believed this to be not just necessary but fair. Then again, Geur and Cheiro thought what they were going to offer was fair. The one thing no one had thought to do was to ask the people of Volavo what they thought was fair. That, of course, is never a consideration when creating deals between the large and small, rich and poor, white and black.

For me, it had been the longest day of my life, not a bad day but a long one. Kepal . . .Kavu . . .kava . . . all swirled around in my head as a blur but not Qat. She was crystal clear.

I didn't dwell much on whether the day had been successful or not. I knew it was not a disaster, but I also knew that the Bohlin had no illusions of me as a god and probably never really did. It was a bit of a relief actually. I was still playing a part, but I could now afford to be more myself. It was less of a strain, and there was no need for me to speak in grandiose terms or parables. Besides, the islanders seemed to have the market cornered on parables already. Oxen, people jumping off ships, crazy people with balloons—the islanders had a story for everything, and the last thing they would need from me is to teach them right from wrong.

I had returned to the ship to find everyone asleep and my uniform from the daytime once again neatly washed and folded on a chair outside my quarters, no doubt courtesy of Smith and Wesson, my security and drycleaners. I headed to the galley where macaroni and cheese had been left in a bowl in the microwave along with a small note taped to the window saying I should heat it for one minute. Apparently, Smith and Wesson were my chefs as well. I wasn't hungry, of course, but I heated it and ate it while struggling to keep my eyes open. It tasted like home.

It occurred to me that kava might be a genuine wonder drug, if it could even be called a drug at all. No doubt I had consumed a huge amount of the most potent kava in the world with no ill effects, just a clear, alert calm that was about to give way to peaceful sleep. I made my way back to the cabin and was asleep the moment my head hit the pillow.

I awoke the next morning around eight o'clock to the sound of Ernie knocking on the door. "John," he shouted through the door, "we need to talk."

As it turns out, that would be a bit of an understatement. I had woken up pretty sharp, which was always a little tricky for me. Usually getting out of bed is the worst part of my day. I am not generally prone to dark thoughts or pointless negativity, but if either were going to happen, it would be when I first woke up. On this day, however, I was energetic and ready for action, so I practically jumped out of bed. I found out later that the islanders had a name for this. It was called "kava fresh," and I sure as shit was.

I got dressed in a clean uniform and went to the galley. Bert and Ernie sat at the table, which was covered in neatly arranged piles of documents. Smith and Wesson, as usual, were nowhere in sight but had made coffee.

"So what's up?" I asked them as I poured myself a cup.

Bert said, "Okay, I won't bury the lead. The contracts have changed."

He went on to explain that the new contracts would have ten percent of the proceeds from the sale of corbomite going to the islanders and the rest to Womansanto. He said that if successful, I would receive five million dollars instead.

I think he expected me to be upset. In his mind, getting only five million instead of untold millions would be disastrous. I couldn't have cared less. In fact, I felt better about the deal. If the original deal was good for the Bohlin, then this deal was great. No problem here.

When I asked what caused the changes, they explained Barnwell's involvement. I think their account was honest.

"We now work directly for one of the most powerful businessmen on the planet," said Bert.

"Hell, one of the most powerful men of any kind," added Ernie. "John, this is no game, and they are not playing. If you didn't understand just how serious this was then, I hope you do now. It would be best for all of us not to disappoint Mr. Barnwell."

Well, so much for my kava fresh. I had understood. Mostly I thought about what cheap, clean, and plentiful energy would mean to the world. That had not changed. What had changed were Bert and Ernie or maybe it was just how I saw them. They hadn't exactly been a barrel of laughs before, but now they seemed just a little bit afraid as if just conjuring up the name Barnwell held a dark magic of its own.

But my mission had not changed, and at 10 a.m. a beautiful woman was coming to get me for what promised to be another long day of adventure.

As usual, I had no idea of what was in store.

9

SCRABBLE

Kavu and I had also woken up "kava fresh" and walked together to the ship to get John. Kavu had asked to come along, saying that John had done well the night before and that he liked him, but I knew Kavu too well. I could practically see the wheels turning. He had something on his mind. Neither of us held any illusions that we were dealing with a god. We never really had. I already knew he was an actor, and we had a friendly little surprise waiting for him back at the house.

But we also knew there were big decisions to be made. It could only help to treat him with respect, play for time, and make the best decisions possible. Besides, who's to say he is not the hand of god? I don't know if I believe that, but it's a safe bet that at least half of my fellow islanders do.

Unlike yesterday, John stood on island ground at the base of the gangway. He held a small pouch that I assumed contained the documents. He smiled and waved as we entered the port. We exchanged warm greetings and began our walk back to the house.

"Are you getting tired of wearing the same thing every day? It's not exactly island wear," Kavu said.

"It's a bit warm, but the good thing is I don't have to figure out what to wear every day. I was able to pack light." John smiled as he said this.

Everyone agreed that we had a good time the night before, and John commented that if kava ever became popular in the West, there would be some pissed-off companies in the drug and alcohol business.

"Who in the world would want to get drunk, throw up, and have a hangover when you can drink kava, have a blast, and wake up feeling like this?" He raised his hands and gestured to the sun and sky above him.

We certainly didn't argue, and soon we reached our home. We entered to find my father sitting in the living room in one of the easy chairs facing the TV.

"Good morning," he said and gestured for each of us to find a seat.

Kavu sat in the chair next to my father. John and I sat next to each other on the couch. My father seemed to make a mental note of that as he waited for us to get settled before continuing.

"I hope you don't mind the less formal setting today as we have something to show you."

My father held a remote control in his hand and without fumbling turned on the TV. He then grabbed a second remote and again without delay pressed a couple of buttons. An image popped up on the screen.

It is a small thing, but it is testimony to my father's professionalism and preparedness that he had practiced using the two remotes for much of the morning so when the time came, the result would be seamless. It was respect for himself and his job that he would master such a detail. He also would not have wanted anything to distract from what he now brought onto the screen.

It was an image of John, of course, in an episode of *Friends Without Benefits*. In the scene, John's character had solicited a prostitute but not for sex. They are together in his room. He explains to the baffled woman who speaks broken English that he wants to play Scrabble with her. He explains that he has been playing with his roommates all day and has lost every game. Nobody will play with him anymore, but he can't give up without winning at least one game, so he called her. He pulls out the Scrabble board and nervously begins setting it up. The scene fades to black and is replaced with a commercial. I don't remember too much about it except it featured a beautiful woman selling small pills that promised to make you "All man, all day."

Real-life John looked like he wanted to say something, but a quick glance from my father told him to be patient. My father wanted to watch a bit more.

The show returned as the camera cut to John and the prostitute playing Scrabble. There is a sudden loud banging, and two uniformed police officers barge in about to arrest John for soliciting prostitution. When the officers realize that both are fully dressed and playing Scrabble, they cannot arrest John, but they do stay to help the woman play. John loses yet again. Everyone says goodnight and leaves John alone, pondering who he might be able to play next. The credits roll. My father freezes it at the point where the name Joe Fray appears on the screen.

Nobody spoke for a few seconds until my father broke the silence.

"It seems you very much like to win, Mr. Fray, but I suppose that, too, is a stage name. I would ask what your real name is, but we all know that it is of no matter. More importantly, we can now be sure of who you are not. You are not John Frum."

John started to speak, but my father once again waved him off. "It is a deception, Mr. Fray, but an understandable one. I will choose to see your elaborate arrival as a clever form of introduction rather than as a pandering insult to our intelligence." He paused for a moment, offering John an opportunity to respond.

"Minister, I hope you know that I meant no insult, and I think it is clear that if anyone's intelligence should be in question here, it should be mine."

This response seemed acceptable to the minister, and he answered. "Then I will permit you to continue. I will accept your documents for our review. Today you will continue to visit with our elders, and we will meet again tomorrow to discuss the contents of these agreements."

He paused for a moment before adding, "On one condition. . . In the name of your parents and whatever god you hold in your heart, you will swear that you will offer us only complete honesty from this point forward."

Again there was a pause. At least fifteen seconds of silence passed before John realized that my father had not been speaking metaphorically. His words had been meant quite literally. He expected John to make a promise, out loud.

John leaned forward on the couch and then stood, his gaze moving from the minister to Kavu to me and back again. It was awkward, and in all honesty, it was the first time I ever saw John look ill at ease, nervous, or unsure of himself, but again I found it somehow endearing. I felt like I was witnessing the transformation of a false god into a real man.

John finally spoke. "Minister, located right here—and only here—is a mineral that will change the world, beginning with this island. That will be true no matter what you or I do. The change will happen no matter what. There will be vast and far-reaching consequences. The real question is will it be peaceful? Will it be orderly? Will this island and its people benefit or suffer or both? The truth is, as you will see from the documents, I have come here as the representative of powerful men and a powerful company. It will be up to you to determine if this agreement is right for Volavo and its people. As far as I am concerned, I believe I have already fulfilled my responsibility to those who enlisted me. I have delivered this agreement to you."

He paused for a moment while handing the pouch to the minister and then continued.

"I am the child of Nils and Myra who were honorable and honest people. I like to believe that I have thus far led an honorable life, that as you say on the island, I have kept my needs simple and my masters few. I cannot honestly tell you that I have any of the gods in my heart, but in the name of my parents, I can promise you this: From this point forward, I will offer you nothing except honesty. My goal will be to serve you in the hope of reaching the best possible outcome for this island and the Bohlin people. I will assist in any way that you may wish. On this you have my promise."

John sat back down. My father smiled whereas Kavu looked doubtful.

"Well said, young man. My daughter did tell me you are a pretty good actor."

Kavu and I chuckled.

"It is okay," my father said. "I'm joking with you. I will accept your words as truth, and I look forward to proof through your actions. I will review these documents, and we will meet again tomorrow. You may as well get started. I am sure our island has many more surprises for you today."

We took that to mean that our meeting was over for today. John, Kavu, and I rose. John shook hands with both Kavu and my father and added, "Thank you."

My father responded. "You are welcome. I know you will not disappoint us."

John and I left while Kavu remained behind.

Once again the jeep was ready for us outside. We jumped in, and I turned to John and said, "Well, at least we don't need to deal with any of that John Frum God business anymore."

"Yeah," he answered, "but I am still going to wear the uniform."

"Why?" I asked.

"I didn't bring any other clothes," he said laughing.

"I'm sure we could find you a dick tent if you need one in an emergency," I said.

He started laughing again which got me laughing. It was funny but not that funny, so finally I asked him what he was laughing at.

"I am trying to imagine a dick tent emergency," he said, still laughing. "We have a problem, and the only way to fix it . . . is a dick tent," he said in a very serious voice.

I chimed in too. "There is no problem that cannot be solved with a proper dick tent," I said in my own best, deep, and serious voice.

"Let's face it," he said. "No offense to the custom, but dick tent is just funny."

I interrupted him. "No! No! You know what would be funny? You wearing a dick tent—a red, white, and blue one!"

He answered with mock piety. "I'm not sure that's a proper use of the stars and stripes. Besides, I doubt you have one small enough for me!"

"Remember," I replied, "it's not the size of the dick tent that matters. It's what's underneath that counts."

"Is that an old saying?"

I couldn't help but laugh again. "Nah. I just made it up."

By now we were on the road heading toward the village of Baku. John had finally stopped laughing and had gotten around to asking me where we were going.

"You, sir, are going to attend land-diving practice."

"I'm sorry, but did you just say 'land-diving'?" he asked. "Land-diving practice?"

"Yes," I answered, "land-diving."

He didn't reply for a few seconds but finally said, "Land-diving. Yes, that sounds perfectly safe."

I had been right. Kavu was up to something. I knew he and my father would spend hours reviewing the Womansanto contracts. They were lengthy and detailed, but the premise was quite simple. Womansanto would provide everything and everyone that was needed to properly mine the mineral. They would also make sure that those involved in the operation remained restricted to that specific section of the island. The workers would be housed in offshore ships and ferried back and forth to work each day.

In exchange, Womansanto would earn ninety percent of the net proceeds from the sale of the mineral. Volavo would receive ten percent. By Womansanto's projections, which they claim were very conservative, the proceeds would be massive, as much as $4 billion the first year. Years two and three would be in the $5 billion range as the project reached scale, and the technology spread throughout the globe. From that point on, proceeds of at least $6 billion per year could be expected.

The company had provided a written summary of the proposal, explaining that these numbers could be realized without price gouging. Even though the island would most likely remain the sole source of the mineral, a fair price would always be asked, and any future price adjustment would be based on a widely accepted measure of global inflation.

At least at first glance, it appeared to be a reasonable approach that would result in very cheap and clean energy worldwide and an almost unimaginable bounty for the Bohlin although Kavu had expressed to my father that there could be no long-term guarantee. Once the contract was signed, and there were boots on the ground, Womansanto would always have ultimate control of the mineral and Volavo. Over time, Womansanto would gain even more power and influence.

My father said, "We still have some time."

Kavu asked, "Time for what?"

"Time to think," said the minister.

Kavu decided it was time to find out what more there was to think about. It was February 12th. He knew the situation, and he knew my father as if he were his own. He knew a decision would be made before the John Frum Day celebrations on the 15th. The more information he could gather, the better.

He knew John and I were going to Baku and would be gone for hours, so he made his way back to the ship. He figured that at least some of the brains of the operation might be there, and he was right. Bert and Ernie had written the contracts personally. Of course, they were written at the direction and approval of Barnwell himself, but Bert and Ernie were pros, and not a single word was out of place.

As Kavu walked up the gangway, two men waited for him on deck. It was Smith and Wesson, of course. Both men were dressed in the same khakis and polo shirt as before, proud members of the Ralph Lauren Navy. The two men made sure that they could not be perceived as threatening in any way when Smith addressed Kavu.

"Is there something we can be of assistance with, sir?"

"I am Kavu, advisor and first assistant to Minister Karbina, the duly elected leader of this island."

"Yes, sir. We know who you are. What is it we can help you with?"

Kavu permitted himself to answer with a hint of annoyance in his voice. "The minister has sent me to request further information about a potential agreement. Can you assist me with that?"

He was lying. My father had not asked him to go, nor did he have any knowledge of it.

"No," came the flat reply from Smith, "but please wait here for just a moment."

Smith went below deck while Wesson remained with Kavu.

He returned with a surprised looking Bert and Ernie. They invited Kavu to the galley. Smith and Wesson seemed satisfied there was no threat to security and disappeared.

Kavu introduced himself to the men though he now knew no introduction was necessary. Kavu chuckled when the men introduced themselves as Bert and Ernie. Like most of us, he too had grown up watching *Sesame Street*.

Kavu said, "I understand your desire for anonymity, and I welcome you to our island. Thank you for sitting down with me. I have some questions that I hope you can answer.

"By the way, it is not necessary for you to remain restricted to the ship. We have suitable lodging, and you may stay as guests of the minister."

Bert thanked him but explained that the terms of their employment dictated that they remain on the ship for the duration of their visit.

"Thank you for the offer," said Ernie, "but we are fine here. We have everything we need, but that is most gracious of you. So how can we help you?"

Bert went on to explain that they were attorneys representing Womansanto, and for the most part, what they could say would be limited to what's already in the proposal.

Kavu said that he understood, but he really had just one basic question: "Why should we agree to this?"

That, of course, was *the* question, and seconds passed as Bert and Ernie pondered their answer.

Bert spoke first. "Peace, wealth for your people, stability both here and for the rest of the world."

Kavu listened intently but did not answer or interrupt, knowing his silence would prompt the man to continue. Kavu had learned a great deal from my father.

Bert continued. "I don't think I need to tell you that this is a big deal. What happens here in the coming days will result in changes that will affect the whole world for decades, maybe centuries."

Bert paused but Ernie continued. "But because there is so much at stake, it is difficult to predict what could happen. If you sign this deal, Volavo will be protected."

Kavu finally spoke. "From what?" he asked.

Again both men paused to consider their answer, and this time, Bert responded. "I don't know how else to put this, so I will just say it, and please understand that I am not trying to scare you, but this is reality. With great opportunity often comes great peril."

Over the next half hour, they explained to Kavu everything that could go wrong—and it was a lot. Kavu was no dummy and definitely not naive to the ways of the world, but he sat in shock as he listened.

The biggest problem was that any of the world's military powers could become convinced that controlling the supply of corbomite could be the only way of securing what they might see as their national interest. Any one of them, including Russia, China, or even the U.S., could invade and occupy the island and then dare the rest of the world to act to remove them. Volavo would be ground zero in such a scenario. It would be disastrous for Volavo and its people. A contract with Womansanto would not make that scenario impossible but much less likely.

There was also the possibility of corporate sabotage. Almost free energy would disrupt any number of huge, powerful corporations that make their money selling oil, gas, and coal among others. These industries were legendary for using hard-ball tactics to cut the legs out from any emerging technology that might replace them or cut into their profits. Those forces, explained Bert and Ernie, were capable of anything from polit-ical assassination to outright destruction of the mineral itself. These were all real possibilities. Womansanto had the resources to protect them from these threats, and they would out of shared self-interest.

"Kind of like the devil you know," said Ernie.

"It is funny how talk of John Frum, the god, has turned so quickly into talk of Womansanto, the devil," he said, more to himself than to them.

They went on for a bit but slowed as they realized they were, in fact, making a very good case and a very big impression on the young man. They were lawyers, but both Bert and Ernie had a bit of salesman in them. They both understood the first rule of sales: once you have convinced the client, it is time to shut up. If you keep talking, you can only un-sell them.

So they did just that. They shut up. To their credit, everything they had said was true.

Bert added one last point. "From what I know of your history, the Bohlin have somehow defied the odds and have always controlled their own destiny. In the coming days, that will be challenged no matter what you decide. We believe we offer you the best chance to determine your fate."

Kavu, despite trying hard not to, looked a little shaken. Only now did he truly understand what a huge responsibility we faced and how dark were some of the possible outcomes. He also felt a pang of guilt for not having consulted my father or me before coming here. He now fully understood that this should have involved all of us.

He gathered his resolve and asked if negotiations were possible or if the offer was take it or leave it. They answered that it was not within their power to make any changes, but if there were a counteroffer, they would present it to the CEO.

They also offered one more word of caution. Time was indeed short, and no one could know how long this would remain secret from the outside world. Anything that was to be done would need to be done quickly.

Kavu thanked both men warmly. They returned the thanks

and wished him and my father well. None of them knew at the time that Smith and Wesson had been listening and recording their conversation. Grant Barnwell would hear every word that had been spoken. In fact, Barnwell had heard everything said on that boat since before it had even left Auckland.

10

LAND DIVING OVER WATER

Ah, land diving. Just the sound of it fills one with a sense of warmth and safety. We were on our way to land-diving practice, which Qat explained was actually done over water. For some reason, that information gave me little comfort. Also according to Qat, the practice of land diving was the inspiration for bungee jumping. Apparently a tourist from New Zealand was one of the first non-islanders to witness the practice, and it gave him the inspiration.

The online encyclopedia has this to say about land diving:

"The Bohlin people of Volavo have developed their very own peculiar ritual. Land diving is said to have started with an overly amorous husband. Years ago, a village woman was trying to escape what she saw as her husband's excessive sexual appetite. She fled his advances and took refuge by climbing up a tall tree. In the throes of lust, her husband Tamalie climbed up after her. To his surprise, she jumped from the tree, presumably to her death. He followed her in either shock or perhaps an attempt to catch her. What he didn't know was that she had tied vines to her ankles, so she survived the fall. Tamalie, on the other hand, did not."

Later, as it became part of the island Kastom, land diving had changed to jumping from towers rather than trees, and it became part of *Nechani*, the Bohlin rite of passage for boys into men at the age of 14. There was a time when land diving was dangerous and deadly. These days, Qat assured me, it was only dangerous, and here's why: In the old days, the boys would jump off the platforms, each leg tied to a vine secured to the structure. The idea was that there was just enough line that the boy, with his head tightly tucked in, would glance off the tilled and softened soil below with his shoulders or neck. Even the slightest miscalculation could lead to crippling injury or death. The modern Bohlin ritual required only that the boy fall close enough to touch the ground, stretching out his arms as he plunged and slapping the ground at the bottom. Make no mistake, it was still pretty hardcore, but it had been decades since a death had occurred. Broken bones in the wrists, shoulders, and ankles were still possibilities, though, averaging about one every year or two.

The village of Baku was on the northern side of the island. Qat had taken a bit of a scenic route. The oceanfront road probably would have been faster, but we went that way yesterday, and she wanted me to see a bit more, so she had taken the third road inland, which the islanders, always practical, called road three.

We headed northeast on the road, but as it started to move more inland, we turned off onto a series of smaller connecting roads. These roads were narrow, with way more dirt and gravel than asphalt, but they were level, and it was daytime. It was way less intimidating than the drive to the kava ritual the night before.

Baku itself was more like a spread-out series of hamlets than a village. Before turning off the other way towards the lake, Qat pointed down a road and said that Baku proper was that way. There were no homes in sight, but Qat assured me that they were all around, always just off the road and just out of sight.

A few minutes later we arrived at a lake. It wasn't a huge lake, but it was probably about a hundred and fifty yards to the far side. From where we were, there was a clearing of about eighty- to a hundred feet leading to the water with only an occasional palm or Banyan tree dotting its landscape. The rest of the lakeshore was surrounded with trees and foliage right up to the water's edge.

About twenty-five boys and six men, all wearing only shorts, either stood on or around a sort of scaffolding that had been built on a concrete base right next to the water. At its highest point, it was probably about sixty feet but had two platforms jutting out over the lake. One was at the top and the other at perhaps forty feet. The platform at the top was at least six feet longer than the one below, presumably so jumpers from the top would not crash into the lower platform. Both platforms were supported by what looked like a makeshift array of vines and branches. The platforms looked sturdy enough, but there was certainly a bit of bounce to them.

Everyone had turned to look when we pulled up in the jeep, but no one stopped what he was doing. Qat and I approached a group of two men and six boys. The boys were seated on the ground in a circle. I recognized the two men as the elders who had been at the port on the day we arrived.

"Good afternoon, gentlemen," said Qat. "I am sure that at this point he requires no introduction, but this is John Frum."

I extended my hand in greeting and was introduced to Ishka, the elder of Baku and the surrounding hamlets, and Kolai, the elder of a nearby village. Both seemed cordial but standoffish, a far cry from the boisterous welcome I had received at the kava ritual. I couldn't help but think that if I dumped about ten shells worth of kava into these two, this would go a lot more smoothly.

Qat had offered no warning about them, but I definitely got the sense that these two were pretty firm traditionalists, at least by the fairly mellow standard of almost everyone else I had met. And it made sense. They were the boys' trainers, not just for their own villages but also for all of the boys on the island. They were entrusted with the second most important part of the boys' rite of passage, land diving. This was serious business, and these were serious men.

All this being said, they were still polite, almost friendly and more than happy to explain whatever I wanted to know about the ritual. There was a set of two level benches nearby that looked a lot like bleachers. They invited us to sit and watch for as long as we liked, so we did.

What we saw was really cool. On each of the two platforms was a man whose job it was to prepare the boys for the jump. Obviously jumping over water did not have the same risk as diving into solid ground, but Qat explained that the preparations were identical. They were just as careful in practice as they were on the day of the actual ritual, which would take place in April.

The vines they used came from the Banyan trees, which were all over the place on the island. It was the same tree that the woman in the legend climbed and provided the vines that had saved her life.

I listened as Qat explained the varying length, strength, and texture of the vines depending on the height and weight of each boy. To me it looked like they were being very careful, painstaking even, but still, there were no measuring tools and no precise weights. There was nothing I saw that would indicate that this was an exact science.

It wasn't. The men would prepare the boys by wrapping a vine around each foot. Qat explained that they used a knot that would not tighten on the foot. Rather, it would remain as a closely fitting loop around each ankle.

We watched a boy approach the edge of the platform. He took part of the vine and draped it over his right arm, which was held upright in front of him, cradling the vine. He walked to the end of the platform so only his toes were over the edge while the balls of his feet rested on the ledge. What happened next was not so much a dive as it was a fall. The boy, slightly bent at the waist, simply leaned forward until inertia and gravity took over. He plunged toward the water. As he approached the water, he extended his arms. He reached the end of the vines, which allowed the slightest bit of give. His outstretched hands touched and then quickly slapped the surface of the water. This slowed any side-to-side swaying motion at the bottom though there wasn't much swinging to begin with. The boy then reached up to loosen the grip of the vine, just enough to remove his feet and lower himself into the water. He smiled broadly as he made his way back to land. It had been a perfect dive.

Everyone turned to look at me because I was wildly applauding. I was the only one applauding. I couldn't help it. It was fucking awesome.

Qat looked at me with a smile and agreed. "It is pretty amazing, isn't it." It was not a question.

We watched as the boys dove again and again, some from the upper platform, some from the lower. I noticed for the first time that they had one of the men stationed close to the landing spot in the lake. He watched every dive and would be there to help if a boy was injured or couldn't free himself from the vines. So far, none of the boys had required his services.

Ishka approached and said to us, "It is quite remarkable, is it not? It is one thing to hear about it or read about it and quite another to see it with your own eyes."

I agreed.

"It is even better to see the real thing on land," he said.

I replied, "That would be exciting to watch, but it might be too much for me. I would be worried for the boys' safety."

"Don't be," he said. "In the modern ritual, there are few injuries and even fewer serious ones." He hesitated for a moment before asking, "So what about you? Are you ready to try it?"

Qat reacted immediately and turned to glare at Ishka.

I thought he was kidding and said, "Yeah, right. Do you have anything higher? This looks too easy for me."

He continued to look at me, and it took me a few seconds to realize he wasn't joking.

"Don't worry," he said, his tone mocking. "We will take care of you. It wouldn't do if the great god John Frum twisted his ankle or, heaven forbid, broke a fingernail."

Ah, I thought, there it was—dumbass male machismo, Pacific island style. He was trying to goad me, and truth be told, it was working. I'm no tough guy and never claimed to be, but I am a man. I kept the irritation and anger off my face and out of my voice, but he had gotten to me exactly as he had intended.

Qat reacted first and violently. "Cut the shit, Ishka!" she said. "He is not a circus animal here to perform for you! You may think and do as you wish, but he is a guest of my father, and he is here out of respect to meet you and the other elders. You will treat him with respect!"

I had been looking at Qat as she spoke, but when I turned to look at Ishka, I found him looking at me with a look of surprise.

"You are shocked?" he said, still looking at me. "What is it that shocks you, that I would mock your manhood? No, that isn't it at all, is it? No, you are shocked that a woman would dare speak to me as she has just spoken."

The truth is, again he was right. The manner in which Qat had spoken to Ishka *had* shocked me. Somehow, even though I knew the Bohlin were in no way a backward people, it still stunned me that in a place like this, a woman could speak to a man that way without fear. It was a bias for sure, now fully exposed.

Ishka sensed it and continued. "So you think us savages. Surely in your mind, I would beat her like an animal for reprimanding me in front of you like that." He shook his head "Oh, great God Frum, you still have so much to learn about our people, but I will help you."

"The Bohlin have lived in peace and harmony with each other for centuries, and it is precisely because we respect and revere women. We know that women are at least as smart and as strong as we are. Do you think any woman would be stupid enough to jump onto solid ground? Of course not. It is men who must do this so they may prove their worth to women. Women need not provide such proof of their worth.

"No one on this island can remember even one time when a man raised his hand to a woman. It is unheard of. No, John. Despite what you think, we are not *less* civilized than you. We are *more* civilized than you!"

It wasn't fun to hear, but he was right. Old habits, old thoughts, old prejudices die hard, and I realized at that moment that despite all the evidence to the contrary, some small part of me still thought of them as savages, uncivilized . . . black . . . savages. It sucked to know it. And it sucked to have to face it, but the truth is that it was in me, like it or not. All I could do, all anyone could do, was to try to rise above these mindsets and not pass them on to future generations.

Qat was still fuming that Ishka would try to goad me into a dangerous stunt. The truth is, it really isn't that dangerous, but I am a full-grown man, taller and heavier than any of the boys who had jumped. If I did dive, it would not be without some risk.

Meanwhile, Ishka had ended his barrage but continued in a softer, questioning tone. "You come to us, if not as a god, then as what? One of us? If you wish to be one of us, then is it not too much to ask that you complete this part of the ritual? It is still much less than we demand of our own. So what do you say, John? Want to try it?"

I rose from my seat and removed my hat, which I placed on the bench. I began unbuttoning my shirt.

Qat was still angry and said, "John, you don't have to do this! Ishka, tell him he doesn't have to do this!"

Ishka just shrugged and said, "He knows he doesn't have to."

I had taken off my uniform shirt and was neatly folding it, saying, "I know I don't have to do anything."

I pulled my undershirt over my head. At this point, almost everyone had heard the commotion and stopped what they were doing to witness the whitest man in the known universe disrobe. At that moment, I suddenly had an urgent, slightly panicky thought. Underwear. I was stripping down to my underwear to do this dive.

In planning this mission, we had tried to think of everything. That included making sure I had plenty of uniforms for as long as I might be here. The one thing we had not considered was underwear. I usually wear boxer briefs, a tight fitting version of a brief that provided generous coverage, but I had also brought a few traditional "tighty-whities." As much as we had tried to plan for every eventuality, the idea of stripping had not been considered.

As I prepared to unbuckle my belt, my mind raced. For the life of me, I could not remember what underwear I was wearing. As I unbuttoned my pants, I found to my relief that I was wearing navy blue boxer briefs that were fairly loose-fitting and from a distance might pass for shorts—but only from a distance.

"I know I don't have to, but you know, it is kind of warm out, and this uniform is pretty hot," I said with exaggerated, cocky confidence. "I could do with a little swim, cool off a little."

By this time, Ishka had started walking toward the scaffolding and beckoned for the men and boys up top to come down. I turned to Qat and quietly asked, "Are there any piranhas or other scary shit in that lake I should know about?"

"Not that I know of," she said, still annoyed, "but you might have thought about asking that question before you started taking your clothes off."

It then occurred to me that I was standing there practically naked in front of Qat. In general I am neither proud nor ashamed of my body. I am thin and not particularly muscular, and I am a man of almost forty. Some things were situated a little differently than they had been when I was in my twenties.

Still, I was not embarrassed and neither was Qat. She just looked me up and down without hesitation but with bewilderment that I would be stupid enough to do this. It was her "boys will be boys" look, and I was getting used to it. Meanwhile, Ishka had climbed to the upper platform and called for me to come up.

Qat and I stood alone, looking at each other. I tried to think of something cool and macho to say, but instead I said, "You should know how lucky you are. Normally I charge a lot of money to strip."

As I started off, she just shook her head and yelled, "Try not to die." I just waved without turning around.

A group of the boys, laughing and happy, gathered around me as I walked to the scaffolding and began climbing. There were vines and cross supports, and it really wasn't difficult, but it was high. I'm not exactly afraid of heights, but let's just say I have a healthy respect for them. The more I climbed, the farther away the ground began to look.

None of the boys had climbed behind me, and I could see everyone gathering around to watch the spectacle. I reached the top platform where Ishka alone awaited me. His demeanor now was actually friendly but also serious as he began to prepare the correct vines for such an unusual diver. Finally, he was satisfied with his selection and turned to me and asked me to sit. I did.

He carefully tied a vine around each foot and made a peculiar type of knot. He said, "Don't worry. The last thing I want is for Qat to be mad at me if I let you get hurt. You won't."

"Thanks, Ishka," I said.

Ishka replied, "She is quite something. If you ask me, she should be in charge when the minister retires."

That was nice of him. I think he was trying to keep my mind busy so I wouldn't think too much about the dive. It worked.

He asked me to get up and hold out my right hand. When I did, he draped the vines across my arm as I had seen the boys do. "This keeps the vines from getting tangled. Do you need instructions? Just don't push off the platform. Move the top part of your bodyweight forward until you fall."

I just nodded in agreement and walked toward the edge of the platform. Everything looked small from up here except the distance down. From my towering position, I could see beyond the lake. I could see villages beyond the trees and the ocean in the distance. I looked down and tried to find Qat. She was there, looking up at me. It was reassuring to see her. It was also reassuring to see that the lake looked plenty deep.

I stepped forward and placed the balls of my feet on the edge as I had seen the boys do. Without hesitating, I began slowly leaning and moving my head forward, and just like that, I was falling. And also just like that, I immediately knew that something had gone wrong.

I didn't have a chance to think about too much as I plunged headfirst toward the water. I had let the vines go and had my hands outstretched above my head. I was waiting to feel the water on my hands and the tug of the vines on my feet.

I did feel the water on my hands, and then I felt the water on the rest of me as I plunged completely into the surprisingly cool water. There had been no pull from the vines. Ishka had chosen vines so long that I had plunged straight into the water as if the vines weren't there at all, but they were, and this was definitely not a mistake.

As I turned upright and stuck my head up above water, I saw a man swimming over to me. One at a time, he loosened the vines on my ankles. I sputtered a bit and looked to the shore to find everyone laughing uproariously, including and especially Qat. I started laughing as well. It had to be funny, this white and blue bullet plummeting into the lake. I looked up at Ishka as I swam to shore.

"You said you needed a swim to cool off!" he yelled and was rewarded with another wave of laughter.

"Thank you!" I yelled back as I now stood dripping on the shoreline.

Qat was now at my side as I called to Ishka again. "That won't do! If I am going to do it, I want to do it right!" Qat didn't say anything, but I can't imagine she approved of another attempt.

I immediately made my way around and started the climb back up. Ishka started preparing another set of vines. I reached the platform, and this time, even Ishka was trying to talk me out of it.

"You don't have to do it again," he said. "At your weight, you will get a pretty good jolt at the bottom."

"I trust you as I would trust myself," I replied, and I sat down, awaiting the vines.

Ishka took his time finding just the right vines before he once again began securing them to my ankles. The laughter below had long since abated. Ishka finished his work, and I rose from the platform. I draped the vine across my right arm as I had been shown. I moved quickly so I wouldn't have time to think about it too much. I walked to the edge, positioned my feet, and leaned forward.

The fall felt different this time. Once again, I stretched out my hands above my head. I felt the water touch my fingertips and then my hands. I felt the very harsh tug across both my ankles simultaneously. I quickly pulled my hands back and even more quickly slapped my hands across the surface of the water. I felt a kind of satisfaction as I heard the sound of my hands smacking the water. It had sounded just like when the boys had done it right, when they had received the approval of their instructors.

I reached up to remove the vines from my ankles but realized that no one had shown me how. The same man came over to assist me in taking them off, but I waved him away. I got them off. It wasn't easy or particularly graceful, but I did it—by myself.

This time my dive was greeted with applause from everyone, and yes, with some laughter mixed in. I swam back to the shore and took a couple of tentative steps. Both ankles were sore as if they had been slightly sprained, but I wasn't going to show any signs of pain. It took some effort, but I walked normally over to Qat. As I approached her, it seemed to me for just a moment that she wanted to throw her arms around me. She then seemed to think better of it and instead offered me a seat back on the bench. "You did well, John," she said simply. Just those four words meant a lot to me, much more than any applause from the studio audience back on *Friends Without Benefits* ever had. I didn't stop to think about why.

Meanwhile, everyone had gone back about his business. We sat watching from the bleachers as I dripped and dried in the sun, wondering for the first time why there weren't any towels. I really didn't want to drive back to town in my underwear, or worse, without underwear, so we decided to hang out long enough for me to completely dry so I could put my uniform back on.

I somehow felt different now than I did before I arrived on the island. I even felt different than I did when we first arrived at the lake. It's probably silly to say, but in some way, I felt a sense of belonging and no small sense of accomplishment. Did I do it to impress them? Did I do it to impress Qat? I am still not sure, but I just knew I had to do it, and having done it, I somehow felt closer to all of them. It was a feeling I can't remember ever having before.

When I was dry enough, I began putting on my uniform. Ishka returned, and he did actually pull me in for a hug.

"You will have my approval as an elder," he said.

"And you will always have my thanks," I replied.

"For what?"

"You have shined a light on a part of me that I have kept hidden even from myself, a part that I hadn't even known existed." Both he and Qat understood what I meant without further explanation.

As we prepared to leave, I saw that everyone else had gone back to their routines. I completed getting dressed by pulling my white Navy hat smartly over my mostly dry hair. We walked away, and I turned to yell goodbye to everyone. "Thanks, guys! It was fun!" Many of them stopped long enough to wave goodbye as Qat and I climbed back in the jeep.

11

WALK THE WALK, TALK THE TALK

Johohn was mostly quiet as I drove him back to the port. Gone was the cocky guy who had jumped from a tower into a lake, not once but twice. I am pretty sure he didn't realize just how easily that could have gone wrong nor how bad the result could have been if it had. Those towers and those vines were meant for children, not a full-grown man-child. He could have easily broken an ankle or even both ankles, or worse, had he panicked, he could have become tangled in the vines as he dropped. No, he didn't realize it, and there was no point in telling him now. Ishka and God had protected him, and for that I was grateful.

"Let's head back to the ship so you can clean up and change. Then I'll come back to get you so we can visit downtown. You've only been to our house in Gothen and haven't yet seen our shops and restaurants and our local hotels."

The proposition seemed to perk him up a bit.

"May I buy you dinner?" John asked. "After all, it's the least I can do after all the hospitality you've shown me."

"Thank you, but no. It's our custom to take care of our

guests, and we could certainly have dinner, but there will be no bill.

"It's about four o'clock now. How about if I come back to pick you up around six?"

"If it's okay with you, I'd rather walk to your house to meet you. Would you mind?"

"Not at all. I'll see you then."

Even though he was now fully dry, he still seemed soggy and rumpled as he got out of the jeep looking like a tired little boy at the end of a long day.

I was a little tired myself when I got back to the house, and as I entered, I found my father and Kavu seated in the chairs as they had been earlier today, but the other two people in the room were unexpected guests, Maru and Goriko, two of the elders.

John had met all of the elders except them. As far as I knew, the seven elders John had met had offered no objection to his presence, nor had they objected to whatever decision my father might make on their behalf. They would defer to his knowledge and wisdom since my father had always, without exception, proven worthy of it. I sensed this was somehow different.

My father acknowledged me and gestured that I should stay. As I listened, the situation soon became clear. The two men were the most traditional of all the elders. They were not unreasonable people, but they felt the greatest connection to Kastom and the old ways. Both were about my father's age. They felt strongly that John had come as a god but was now here as a man. If he wished to be heard, then he must abide by our ways. To them, that meant he must complete the rite of passage to be a man before he could be considered a man or be heard as one.

While the elders spoke with my father, Kavu quickly brought me up to speed with all he had learned from Bert and Ernie, and it was evident that my father already understood the dire implications. All of the perils that Kavu had learned about from Bert and Ernie were already fully understood by my father. He knew how big this moment was. He knew just how great the dangers were. He also knew, however, just how great the opportunities were.

He was aware of how easy it would be for us to be crushed by the world, be it colonially, economically, or militarily. Volavo had always thrived in the sweet spot of being nowhere anyone needed to be and having nothing anyone needed to take. We all understood that was about to change drastically.

I turned my attention back to my father as he made his case for John. He did not disagree with the elders but stressed that time was of the essence, that events could quickly escalate out of control if we did not act quickly.

The men listened carefully. They reminded my father that he could act without their approval, but I recognized it as a bit of gamesmanship on their part. Both men knew damn well that he wouldn't act on his own. He would always seek consensus. The two elders had effectively cornered him, so my father simply asked them what it was they wanted. With four parts to the Bohlin rite of passage from boys to men—Land Diving, The Walk, The Request, and The Gathering—I already knew, and I think my father did, too, which of the rites the elders would choose. Both elders chose The Walk.

Land Diving didn't occur until April, and Maru and Goriko had already heard that John had completed the two dives out at the lake. They were satisfied with that.

The Request was a ritual where every woman and girl in the village would assemble in one place. Boys who had successfully completed the other parts of the ritual would appear before them one at a time and formally "request" the privilege of protecting them, as men. The ritual of The Request varied a little from one village to another, but all were performed during late April or early May.

The Gathering was also village specific. I called it the Bohlin Bar Mitzvah. It was basically a celebration of the boy's passage from boyhood to manhood. Everyone in the village would attend, and of course the village goon'do would come to the party. The kava flowed, and men and women fourteen and older could drink their fill. Only on this day did the men of the village prepare the kava for the new, full-fledged men.

The Gathering also played a big part in courtship. Arranged marriages were announced at the gathering although there were fewer every year, and rarely were there any that were truly forced on anyone. For the rest of the boys and girls, this was the first day that the boys could show interest, at least publicly, in any young lady they may have had their eye on. Needless to say, it is always quite a party. I should know. As the daughter of the minister, I was expected to attend The Gathering at every village. The gatherings always took place in the second week of May.

Since the traditional times for these rites were still months away, that left The Walk, a fifteen-mile journey from Banyu Cepete to the summit of the volcano at Mount Garak. The trek was a symbol of the path and courage of the Bohlin people. Each boy, as part of the rite of passage, must complete the challenge alone. It begins at Banyu Cepete, where we believe we first came ashore as a people, and finishes atop the cone of Mount Garak, the so-called dormant volcano.

Dormant is a scientific term, but I can assure you that the gods within our volcano are patient and gentle but most certainly alive and well. The Walk ends with the boy completing two trips around the cone atop the volcano and then returning from the summit on the opposite side from which he climbed. This symbolizes that the youth ascended the volcano as a boy but descended as a man.

The elder from his own village would await the boy at the bottom of the summit to congratulate him and bring him home. Nowadays, the elder would be waiting in a jeep and drive the exhausted and grateful boy back to the village.

The Walk takes at least eight grueling hours from start to finish. For John it would probably take longer. Assuming he didn't get lost, he would still have to negotiate difficult terrain and wet and slippery conditions.

And then there was the mountain itself. The good news for John is that the slope of the mountain is gentle, and no vegetation, trees, or plant life hinder a climber. The bad news is that it is still over eleven hundred feet up, and the climb doesn't even start until the participant has already been walking for six hours or more. Thankfully, the cone at the top is only about a quarter of a mile around.

According to Kastom, the boys must perform the walk alone, wearing only a namba. They are also barefoot, and the only companion they may have is a willing goon'do who wants to come along. John could not possibly complete the journey barefoot. No one could unless they were already used to going barefoot.

As the conversation continued, I was relieved to hear that the two elders did not expect John to do the walk barefoot or without clothing. As I said, they are reasonable men, but the namba was not negotiable. He must wear a namba. I chuckled to myself at the thought of John with his very own dick tent.

Finally, the terms were agreed upon. In exchange for our consideration in signing the contract, John must first complete The Walk. The two elders considered it a matter of respect, both the respect to our ways as the Bohlin people and the respect John would earn if he were able to complete the journey. Maru and Goriko would meet us at ten the next morning at the starting point at Banyu Cepete. They would also await John's arrival at the journey's end on the far side of the volcano on the shoreline.

The men thanked my father and said goodbye, and I was

glad they left. I was supposed to be getting ready for this evening, and John would be here soon. My father and Kavu intended to break the news to John when he arrived. I excused myself to get ready.

I was almost done getting dressed when I heard John enter downstairs. I was able to hear Kavu greet him warmly. I could even hear that bit of mischief in his voice as he invited John to have a seat while he waited.

I knew that Kavu liked John. He may have even trusted John to a great extent, but even so, I am sure that Kavu couldn't wait to break the news. He, too, thought that John in a namba would be hilarious. Just having John try to put one on would be priceless, but he restrained himself and was dutiful, as always, and waited for my father and me to descend the staircase together to greet John.

I noticed John's eyes as he rose and watched me come down the stairs. I couldn't help but feel pride as I realized his eyes were locked on me. I did look damn good, if I say so myself. I wore a flowing, white cotton dress that was not at all see-through but somehow still offered that promise. I wore white sandals and no headdress of any kind with my hair pulled back simply, flowing behind me to my shoulders. John, of course, wore his uniform.

John had bounced back nicely and looked clean, starched, and refreshed, no small trick after today's adventure, but when he stood, I noticed that he seemed a bit stiff on his feet. No doubt his ankles had to be sore.

When we were all comfortably seated in the living area, my father, ever the tactician, began speaking.

"We have agreed to sign the contract with Womansanto. After a great deal of consideration, I believe my people may benefit greatly from this momentous discovery. I also believe it will provide the best chance for our people to determine their own destiny and keep their way of life. Understand, the choice was not easy, and I am still worried about the outcome, but waiting is not an option. We know that could be very dangerous."

He cleared his throat before speaking again. "There is one condition, however. You will have to perform The Walk, or there can be no deal."

John raised his eyebrows, but he listened with interest as my father took him through the entire rite of passage, explaining that John's practice dives at the lake were accepted as fulfillment of that requirement and applauding his courage for having done so. He told him that he would once again have to summon that same courage.

Without providing too many details, and he was way too dignified to broach the subject of the namba with a Westerner, he concluded his explanation. By now, John must have a pretty good idea of what he was in for.

More quickly than we expected, though none of us was surprised, John agreed to the terms. We were surprised, however, when John asked, "Do you think I *can* do it? Do you think I can successfully complete The Walk?"

We were paying him a great compliment, because it had not even occurred to us that he might try but fail in his effort. After all, the trek was certainly not easy. Some of our own boys fail on their first try, and this is their island. Maybe at the end of the day, all of us really did believe, at least subconsciously, that this was God's will.

Again, my father's wisdom prevailed. He knew John needed reassurance. He looked directly at John and said in a strong, calm voice, "You will not fail. We believe in you as a man." Kavu and I solemnly nodded our agreement.

I could see that the answer bolstered John's confidence, and he asked many questions regarding the trek. When John had learned all that he could about the upcoming ritual journey, he thanked the minister for the great faith he had shown in him.

Now that the hard part was over, my father asked us where we were heading, and John explained that since he had not yet seen the city, I was going to show him Gothen. We were going to a restaurant where he would finally get a chance to sample some island cuisine. John politely asked Kavu and my father if they would like to join us.

I have to admit that I hoped he was just being polite, and I felt a wave of relief when they declined the invitation. There was still much to be discussed and plans to made, both for tomorrow and for John Frum Day, which was now only three days away.

John and I headed out to the mostly quiet and lightly traveled streets of our island's only city—or the closes thing we had to one. As we walked, I asked what I thought was a pretty normal question.

"Are you hungry?"

"No," said John, "but let's eat anyway."

His response sounded a bit odd, but I didn't question it, hoping he might elaborate, and he did. He told me about his very unusual condition. I guess you would call never being hungry a condition.

"Huh," I said. "I've never heard of anything like it."

"That doesn't surprise me," said John. "Very few people know of it. It's pretty rare."

"Almost everyone I ever met in America would be thrilled to have your problem, and even quite a few here on the island probably wouldn't mind".

"I'm not complaining," he said. "It is what it is. I just have to be careful to make sure I eat. There have been a few times that it became a problem. Back when we were shooting the show, I would sometimes be there for sixteen hours and forget to eat even though there was food everywhere. I still need food, or I get lightheaded. One time I passed out."

Maybe it was a dumb question, but I asked it anyway. "Do you like food?"

"Very much. Do you have somewhere in mind? I'm at your mercy."

"There's a place I know of. It's probably the closest thing we have to a diner on the island. From any table in Sisko's, you can see the sunset over the ocean. It's big by our standards and has a huge menu. You can get Western style items like burgers but also island specialties like seafood, pork, and at least ten different kinds of yams.

"Did you know yams are a staple on Volavo? They grow everywhere. You can hardly stop them from growing. Pound for pound, we grow as much in yams as we do in kava. That should tell you we love our yams."

We made our way to the restaurant, passing a few closed shops along the way. It was not tourist season, and most of the shops and restaurants kept sporadic hours at best, but Sisko's stayed open year round from eight in the morning 'til eight at night. It was one of the oldest businesses on the island and had been run by the same family for almost thirty years.

I could see the owner's daughter standing by the door. I've known Vera my whole life. She is a beautiful and very bright woman only a couple of years older than me. She runs the restaurant with her father and husband. With few tourists this time of year, she was dressed in Western style jeans and a T-shirt. During the season, she might have been wearing something a little more traditional for their benefit.

She greeted me with a hug, and I thought I caught a glimpse of a knowing look as she saw John, handsome and tall in his starched, white uniform.

"You must be the great John Frum," Vera said with just a touch of sarcasm. "We have all heard so much about you! It's funny we've heard not a word yet from the daughter of our minister." She turned and smiled at me. "I think maybe she likes to keep some things all to herself."

John just smiled as she took us to our table for two facing the window and the sunset. I was relieved there was a waiter, and Vera would not be the one taking our order. We now sat facing each other across the small, square table covered in a clean white tablecloth.

The waiter came over with a pitcher of water containing a few lonely cubes of ice swirling around. "Filtered and clean," he announced as he set it down. This was the standard saying of waiters at every restaurant on the island. It was meant to put tourists at ease.

John filled both of our glasses and handed me one. "Cheers," he said.

"Cheers," I replied as we touched glasses and drank. "So what do you think?" I asked, looking around the mostly empty, still sunlit restaurant.

"I've been thrown out of worse places," he said.

I proposed that we order four different items, two Western style and two island specialties, and share them all. This way John could get a taste of the island but wouldn't be obligated to consume an entire meal he may not like. After what he had told me, I wanted to make sure he ate. Of course he agreed and asked that I do the ordering.

To give John the experience of our island fare, I ordered a cheeseburger cut in half with a side of baked yam slices. I also ordered chicken breast in onion gravy, served over mashed yams. Then I added ground pork meatloaf, served with yam fries. Finally, I ordered fruit bat soup.

Yes, fruit bat soup. Aside from yams, fruit bat is the most popular and plentiful food on the island. Fruit bats are everywhere, but you'd hardly know it. They live their lives clinging to the sides of trees, usually near the crown. Even when they are low enough to see, they aren't noticed because they have evolved to look like part of the tree itself unless you look very closely. And yes, there are bits of yam in the fruit bat soup.

I chose fruit bat soup because it was probably the most palatable to a Westerner. It sounds cliché, but fruit bat soup does indeed taste like chicken soup although the broth looks more like American-style wonton soup. Fruit bat soup can be ordered with the entire bat floating in the soup. That is called whole fruit bat soup, but I was merciful. What I ordered had shredded fruit bat meat but not the whole bat.

John did an admirable job of appearing comfortable when I ordered it. The waiter disappeared, and John sat quietly for a few moments before asking, "Fruit bat soup?"

"Sure. The best way to know a people is through their food. When I lived in America, I made it my business to try as many different foods as I could. I have to tell you, though, I was really disappointed with my first McDonald's hamburger. After watching all their commercials, I was expecting a juicy, perfect work of art. Instead, I got a squished grey disk with yellow goo dripping from between the buns. It was okay, but I never had one again."

Instead of serving everything all at once, restaurants on Volavo bring out food as each item is ready so each selection can be enjoyed at its best. The waiter returned with only the meatloaf. He gave us each a small, empty plate and set the meatloaf down between us.

We were not shy. I immediately loaded some onto my plate, and John followed suit right away. He might never be hungry, but I sure was. The cheeseburger and chicken breast weren't far behind, and the waiter was able to make just enough room to fit the plates between us. I knew the main attraction would take a little more time. The broth for the soup was already prepared, but the bat itself was always fresh and always took a little while.

We didn't talk much while we were eating. It was as if we both needed a little time out. John had only arrived three days earlier, yet in some ways, it felt like a lifetime ago. I could only imagine what it felt like for him. Once in a while he would comment on the food, and he really did seem to enjoy it, but for the most part, he appeared content to just eat, relax, and enjoy the sunset outside our window.

One way or another, the world was about to change, and we were right at the center of it. I knew that very well, but at the moment, I was just happy to be here with John, enjoying a few moments of peace.

I also enjoyed when the waiter cleared away some of our now empty dishes to make space for the main event, the fruit bat soup. I felt a moment of mischievous regret that I hadn't ordered the whole bat. The waiter placed the generous bowl between us and gave us each a large spoon shaped like a ladle. Fruit bat soup was meant to be shared.

John looked down at the soup and then looked me straight in the eye. "Am I going to like this?" he asked.

"You mean the soup?" I replied, knowing damn well he meant the soup.

"Yes, the soup," he said. "I already know I like you. The soup. Am I going to like the soup?"

"That depends," I said. "Do you want to like it? If you want to like it, you will."

He laughed and tentatively dipped his spoon into the bowl, trying to get only broth.

"You know," he said, "not everything has to be deeply philosophical. It's just soup."

I watched his face as he tasted it.

"It tastes like chicken," he said.

Of course it did. Everything tastes like chicken.

As we ate from the bowl, John tried some of the shredded meat and found it to his liking. When the waiter came to clear the table, John ordered a beer.

"I'm not much of a drinker," he said, "but sometimes only a

beer will do." He was not surprised when I said I would join him and ordered one for myself.

By now the sunlight in the room had been replaced by candlelight. John said, "You know who I am. You know I was an actor, and I am guessing that as resourceful as you are, you probably know a lot more."

I nodded a bit in agreement.

"But I have been hanging out with you now for two days straight, and I know next to nothing about you. I know you are the minister's daughter. I know you have spent some time in America. You have a better command of the English language than my father ever had, but that's it. That's all I know. Oh. And you are a beautiful woman with a wicked sense of humor."

I can't lie. I felt flush when he said that. I knew I was attracted to him, and I was pretty sure he felt the same way, but I reminded myself that this was not the time to become involved. The stakes were too high with so much still to be done. I ignored the compliment.

"So you want to know about me?" I asked.

"Yes," he answered, "but not too much. Start with the day you were born, and finish with the fruit bat soup. That should just about cover it."

I laughed. "That's all? Just my whole life?"

He nodded.

Three days ago, I didn't know this guy at all except as an actor in an old sitcom. Now I was about to tell him my life story, but I silently resolved to finish the tale by the time we finished our beer. It's not that I don't think I am interesting, but we are slow drinkers, and that should provide more than enough time for the story of anyone's life, so I began at the beginning.

"I spent about five years in America. A missionary teacher, a friend of the family, saw how curious I was at an early age and had taken charge of my education. She made sure I had every-thing I needed to attend college in America. She arranged a full scholarship to an Evangelical Christian College in Northern Virginia. I know that sounds like it would be crazy culture shock, but it really wasn't that bad. I never felt like an outsider. I already spoke almost perfect English when I got there, and within months, I don't think I had even a hint of an accent. That wouldn't have mattered anyway. Everyone at the school, without exception, was good to me. I was included in any activities I wished and even made a handful of friends, both with other foreign students and with the locals. I never felt like an outsider.

"There were always student groups that traveled together during the summer months, and I did that every year, so I saw a lot of the huge and beautiful country that is the USA. One summer, I even made it all the way to Alaska. If you add it all up, I visited thirty US states plus Washington, D.C. "

John had been listening, occasionally taking a sip of his beer. "I've never actually added up the states I've seen, but I think that's more than I've been to. He then surprised me by asking, "Did you date anyone while you were there?"

I laughed a little at the memory that question conjured up before answering. "It was a Christian school with a lot of rules regarding dating among the students, but there were plenty of kids who found a way around it. There was one boy who had started out as a friend, but I felt a special connection with him. One day he comes to me and tells me that he has feelings for me and wishes our relationship could be more. Before I could even answer, he went on to tell me that it could never happen because his parents would not understand if he had a relationship with a black girl.

"Just so you know, I don't even understand the use of the word "black" in the description of a human being. There is no such thing as a black person. There are black souls. There are black thoughts. But there are no black people. There are, however, brown people and whitish-pinkish people and yellowish people. Where I came from, there was no need for this distinction based on such trivia.

"But I wasn't naïve. I had seen with my own eyes what race meant in America, and for the first time, I felt that impact in my own heart. Truth be told, I am sure the college would not have approved either.

"It was an odd duality I couldn't understand. All the people I met at school, even that boy, were welcoming and accepting. Yet I was not blind to the bizarre and hateful public statements of American Christian leadership. I still don't understand it. These were people as pure and kind as any I had ever known back home being led by people who spoke as if their souls were truly black.

"Anyway, I went on to earn two bachelor's degrees, one in anthropology and one in world history."

"Why those subjects?" asked John.

"Simple. World history so I could begin to understand the world beyond the shores of Volavo, and anthropology so I could understand how the world views us.

"I had expected my parents to make the trip to attend my graduation ceremony. Two weeks before the event, I got a phone call from my father. I knew it could only be bad news. My father never speaks on the phone, so I knew there had to be an important reason for the call. I thought he was going to tell me they couldn't come to the graduation for one reason or another. The news was much worse. My mother had passed away from cancer that morning.

"I remember being so angry with my father, I couldn't breathe. He told me only then that she had been sick for months.

"Why hadn't he told me sooner so I could come home? I mean, I know why he did it. I know why he chose not to tell me. He wanted me to be happy for as long as I could. He wanted to bear the burden of her illness and death himself. He wanted me to finish my work and earn my degrees, but in my mind, that changed nothing. I wanted to see my mother again. All I would ever see was her simple gravestone and a handful of photographs."

I am not usually an emotional woman, but I had not told my story to anyone in years. I was a little teary-eyed as John listened and knew he must surely see the pain in my eyes and hear the sorrow in my voice. He reached out across the table, his thumb gently stroking the back of my hand.

I could hear the tremor in my voice as I said, "If I were to tell you that I feel closer to you right now than I have to anyone in a very long time, would you make fun of me?"

He smiled. "Probably."

I answered with a slightly embarrassed laugh through my tears. "Okay, let me finish. You're almost done with your beer."

"What does that mean?" he asked.

"Never mind," I replied.

"Before that phone call, I had been trying to figure out how to break the news to my parents that I intended to stay in America for a while after graduation. I had already lined up a job and a roommate. I was going to share an apartment not far from the school. My visa was good for another eighteen months, and it was very likely I could get permanent residency in the U.S.

"I don't know if I had intended to stay forever, but I knew that I wanted to stay for a while, at least. Nonetheless all of that went out the window. It was time to return home. To this day, I have never told my father of my plans to stay in America. I would never want him to think that he was my burden or the cause of any regrets I may have had. He is not. I know he needs me.

"Within a week, I had returned to my father's home filled with the ghosts of my mother. In most ways, my father seemed the same as always. Kavu and I resolved to be his companions and helpers. Over the years, it has become more of an official role.

"In my third year at school, Kavu had come to America to begin what was supposed to be a three-year degree program, but he had returned home with no regrets after only one year. He had been happy to have the experience, but he knew where his home was. And now, so do I."

John drained the last sip of beer out of the bottle and said, "One more?"

I felt oddly satisfied as I nodded in agreement.

"Last one!" he said as the waiter brought the second round. "Apparently I am going to be walking four hundred and seven miles up a volcano tomorrow, so it's probably better if I am not hung over. Cheers!"

We touched bottles, and I wondered when we might touch hands again.

"Okay, " I said. "Your turn." Although he had said we knew a lot about him, in truth, we actually knew very little. How does one go from being a working Hollywood actor to climbing a volcano on a remote South Pacific island? How does that happen?

I asked every question I could think of. I could say that my curiosity came from my role as the daughter of the minister and that I was gathering information for the benefit of Volavo, but by this point, I had already admitted to myself that my interest in John was more personal—very personal.

He seemed surprised when I asked him if he was married, as if the thought of marriage had never occurred to him. It turns out there was no wife, no ex-wives, no recent girlfriend, and no kids ever. If it were anyone else telling me this, I might have thought they were gay. I think he may have sensed that, so he explained.

"Maybe I'm weird, but I don't need a relationship. I like girls. I like sex. I like companionship, but I don't need it. Oh, and I really hate kids!" he said with a laugh. "They're like drunken midgets, and they smell funny!"

I laughed and replied, "No, you don't. Don't bullshit me. I saw you with those kids in the village. They loved you, and you liked them. And it wasn't an act. Trust me. You are not that good an actor!"

He laughed and agreed, and then he explained his comment.

"I actually do like kids, but that's not a reason to have them. Most people have children for all the wrong reasons. Either it's an accident, or it's because people think it's what you are supposed to do. I believe you should only have kids if you are going to make them the centerpiece of your life, if they're going to be the most important thing to you. A lot of women have kids because they are taught it's their only reason for being, and their lives would be meaningless without them."

"Not here," I said. "On Volavo we practically try to talk women out of it. I think our attitude is different because we have always understood how small Volavo is, and it can only support just so many souls. Half of our women never have kids even though most marry, and it is also very different here than it is in the West. In some ways, we see all the children on the island as being our own children. We all share in the success of all of our children."

"And you?" he asked. "Do you want children?"

"I might," I replied. "Since I returned to the island, I've been focused on taking care of my father. I still have some time on my biological clock, so I'm not worried."

I turned the subject back to him. I needed to know more.

"What about your parents?"

"I lost them in a car accident years ago. I was twenty."

He didn't say it, nor did he need to. Losing both parents at twenty had changed him in ways that I don't think he fully understood to this day.

"I kind of wandered after that. I went to school and fell into a career. That career was what brought me to Volavo. Now here I am—with you."

All in all, his words felt like those of a visitor, always the welcome guest in his own life but never at home. Maybe it was the loss of his parents. Maybe it was just who he was, but I couldn't help feeling that the only home he ever knew was lost on the day he lost his parents. He had been wandering ever since.

By this time, both of us had finished our second beer. John held up his empty bottle and sort of shook it a bit as if to say, "Should we risk it? Should we have just one more?"

A third beer would equal the amount of alcohol I had had in the last six months, but we both agreed that this was a special occasion that warranted one more.

I was never a big fan of the taste of beer, but I had to admit, the third one was starting to taste better than the first two. That might explain my surprise at his next question.

"Are you a Christian?"

After all, I had been educated by missionaries and attended a Christian college for five years. Had anything stuck? Had I found Jesus?

"Not exactly," I said. "Like most of us on the island, I value Jesus as a holy man and prophet, not unlike John Frum. The missionaries on Volavo have become more like us than we ever became like them. Most of the missionaries here are now second generation. Many have been born here, and like us, found that honoring Jesus was completely compatible with our other beliefs and our Kastom."

I got the distinct feeling that he had brought this up because he really wanted me to ask him about his beliefs, so I did.

"Oh, well thank you for asking!" he said sarcastically as if I had walked into an obvious trap. I do think he was just a bit drunk.

"You know, I have been on this island for three days, and in just three days, I have found that Volavo loves its stories. Don't get me wrong. They are nice stories with nice lessons. The ox, the balloons, the ship . . . but I think it's time for me, the great John Frum, to tell one of my own.

"By the way, you still haven't even asked me what my real name is. It's been so long since I've used it, I don't remember it myself. Something Swedish, I think. Anyway, I learned this story just recently when I was researching this island. It's not from Volavo though. It came from a different island in the Pacific, even smaller than Volavo."

He wasn't drunk, but he was buzzed just enough to really enjoy dragging this out. The truth is, I was a bit buzzed myself and enjoying his performance.

"It's from a very small island, but it's a really good story, and it perfectly sums up my views on God and religion. Hold on a second. Okay, I remember now. Two villages right next to each other. They believe in the same gods of peace and plenty. Is that right?"

I interrupted him. "What's the name of the story? All the best stories have a cool name."

"Yes," he answered, "a very cool name, the coolest name. Actually, I don't think it had a name, but I am going to give it one. I, the great John Frum, am going to give the cool story a cool name, the coolest name. It's called . . . 'The Sword and the Shield.'"

"Very nice. That's a very fine name for a story." I hoped my response encouraged him.

"Anyway," he said, "the two villages battled over . . . something. It was terrible. Both villages burned to the ground, a bunch of dead pigs . . . not good."

"Sounds awful," I said. "What were they fighting about?"

"I don't remember," he said. "Who could remember with all these interruptions? It was something about spelling, something about how to spell God's name or say his name on a Thursday. I forget, but here's the point..."

"Oh, there's a point?" I asked in my silkiest and most sarcastic tone.

"Yes, and it's a good one, or I wouldn't have carried on like this."

Suddenly his playful tone was gone, and he became serious. "The point is that religion provides us with a shield. Faith is a shield that protects us from life's questions and disappointments and provides us comfort, but faith also gives us a weapon that can be used to hurt those who believe differently than we do. Faith wielded as a weapon gives some people a certainty that can cause great harm. Faith is a tool that can be used as either a shield or a weapon. You can never have too many shields, but even one weapon is too many."

He continued. "You, the missionaries, and your friends from college use faith as a shield. Leaders too often use faith as a weapon. That is the difference. If anything, my religion is the shield—never the sword."

We were both quiet for a few seconds before I broke the silence. "Well, that got serious in a hurry. No more beer for you, John Frum—or whatever your name is."

We both laughed. We were the only remaining customers in the restaurant. Outside our window was a dark, barely moonlit night. We finished the last sips of our beer in quiet candlelight.

I knew we both had a long day ahead of us tomorrow, especially him, but I didn't want this day to end. I had to force myself to tell him that it would be best to call it a day.

"It's time to get your drunk, white ass home," I said in no uncertain terms.

"Excuse me, miss," he answered, "but I simply will not tolerate racism in any form."

"Oh, please do forgive me," I replied, "but I meant nothing of the sort. I was referring to your white uniform."

"Really?" he asked. "So I suppose that means my white ass is part of the uniform?"

By now we had risen from the table to leave, having long ago settled the bill.

"That's a good question," I said, "but I'm not sure. I haven't looked."

By now we were back on the street and heading toward the ship. He was laughing quietly to himself.

"What's so funny?" I asked him.

"Of course you looked. You saw me in my underwear. I can only imagine what a spectacle I was, stripping down to my underwear and jumping—not once but twice!

"It was funny, you know, but it was also a bit scary. Are you okay?" He looked like he might be a bit sore, but he wouldn't admit it.

I still don't think he understood how much danger was involved. Maybe it was because the boys made it look so easy.

We were back at the port now, making our way to the ship. When we arrived, he turned to face me and once again gently took hold of my hand. He leaned close, gave me a very soft kiss on the forehead, and simply said, "Thank you."

I wrapped my arms around him and pulled him in, gripping him tightly as he put his arms around me gently. I could feel the warmth of his hands at the base of my back. I pulled my arms around to his chest and gently pushed off, putting a little bit of space between us.

He said, "I would offer to show you my gunship, but I think I have a pretty busy day tomorrow."

I turned and started to walk away, saying, "Oh, is that what you're calling it now?"

He shook his head a bit and chuckled.

"I will be here at nine thirty. Be ready," I said as I walked away.

At the time, neither of us noticed the man on the deck of the ship, nor did we see the camera he used to photograph us as we embraced.

12

WALK THE WALK

I wasn't lying to myself anymore. I was done trying to convince myself that I wasn't attracted to Qat. She was beautiful and smart, but there was something more. I had known many smart and beautiful women, but there was something about her that was different and special.

The only way I could come close to describing it is to say that she knew who she was, and she was more comfortable with that person than anyone I had ever met. I'm not completely dense. I could tell she had at least some feelings for me, but what felt different was that she didn't need me in order for her to know who she was. That, for me, was the sexiest thing imaginable, that she might want me for myself, but she didn't need me in order to be herself. Had she had marched up that gangway with me, there was absolutely no way I could possibly have said no to her.

I returned to the ship to once again find everyone in their cabins. No one came out to greet me or ask any questions. There would be time for that in the morning. It occurred to me that I had not even seen Captain since the day we got here. Smith and Wesson were also pretty scarce, but once again, my uniform from the day before had been washed, pressed, and neatly folded, waiting for me on the chair outside my cabin.

I was exhausted, and Qat had been right. My ankles were killing me. I was relieved to find no swelling when I removed my socks and shoes. Good thing, too, because there was no ice available on the ship. It took everything I had left to strip down to my underwear and climb into my bunk. I closed my eyes and could see her face, feel the touch of her hand in mine. Sleep came quickly.

I awoke at eight to the sounds of activity in the galley. I threw on an undershirt and found Bert and Ernie waiting for me. I am sure they were expecting a progress report, and I was ready to give them one. I hadn't talked to Geur and Cheiro yet, and I was in no hurry to do so. There was no need. I knew that Bert and Ernie would pass along whatever they needed to know.

What I didn't know then was the involvement of Grant Barnwell. As far as I knew, this was still Geur and Cheiro's baby. I had never heard of Barnwell and wouldn't have known him if he bled to death on my front lawn.

There was coffee, toast, and instant eggs that Smith and Wesson had whipped up. As usual, they disappeared when their job was done. I was starting to think of them as helpful ghosts. I ate and had some coffee, knowing I would need the energy.

I started giving Bert and Ernie the rundown. I told them of the minister's intention to sign tomorrow morning if and only if I was able to complete today's journey. I explained that they had concluded I was no god, but if I completed the rite of passage, I would prove I was trustworthy in word and deed, as a man.

"Wow, sounds great!" said Bert. "How's it going to work? Where? When?"

"The signing will be tomorrow morning at the home of the

minister. You are both expected to attend, explain each document, and oversee the signing. The public announcement will be made the following day. It's going to be part of the John Frum Day pageantry and celebration, but as I said, it's only going to happen if I'm successful today."

I knew it was not a foregone conclusion.

Neither of them made mention of Kavu having come to the ship or of their conversation. I don't suppose it matters. It certainly didn't hurt, and it might have helped. For better or worse, the Bohlin were going to sign.

Smith and Wesson appeared, holding a small box. Smith said it had just been delivered for me. I knew it could only be one thing—the namba I was expected to wear during the walk.

As I opened the box, I began to explain to them what it was and what was expected of me. It was the first time I saw Smith and Wesson laugh or show any emotion at all, for that matter. All four of them were laughing, and I couldn't help but laugh too.

"What the fuck are you laughing at?" I yelled, still laughing. "I don't see any of you walking across an island and up a damn volcano!"

"Is that what you're doing today? In that thing?" Smith asked

"Yes. Yesterday I jumped off a goddam six-story platform with vines attached to my ankles, not once but twice!"

They were still laughing.

Ernie said, "You really are a dedicated actor!" Their laughter became louder.

"He does his own stunts!" added Bert.

Soon I returned to my cabin to get dressed. The namba was shaped almost like an ace bandage. It was about thirty inches long in two attached sections. Both sections were striped in shiny gold and black. The bottom part was supposed to be wrapped around the penis and was fairly soft. The top part was more rigid and was supposed to be tucked into a waistband, which they had not provided. It wasn't needed. Since I would be wearing pants, the top part of the namba could be tucked into the waistband of my trousers or my belt. That would create the triangle shape that Qat so enjoyed calling a "dick tent."

There was just one problem. I had no idea how to put it on. As a matter of fact, I was pretty sure that even if I did know how, it wasn't meant to put it on oneself.

I opened the door of my cabin, and before I could even step outside, I heard Wesson say, "You can't put it on, can you?"

My helpful ghost had of course anticipated my problem and was there to help, not that he was happy about it. Wesson just shook his head and came into my cabin. If I were wrapping a man's penis in a ceremonial sheath on a remote island, it would almost certainly make me question many of the life choices that had brought me to such a moment.

I noticed no such introspection from Wesson. He quickly and efficiently completed the task as if he knew what he was doing. He even made small talk.

He noticed my discomfort and asked, "So you think you can do this? You look like you have an injury, like you can barely walk."

Of course with him, even small talk would relate to the mission at hand. "Of course I can, and I will. The whole mission depends on it."

That's just the type of thing he liked to hear and nodded his approval as he finished his work. "Okay," Wesson said, "put your pants on. Let's see how this works."

He had created a perfectly triangular dick tent. It soon became apparent that the only way I would be able to walk was to have my fly open with the triangle jutting first through the gap in my underwear and then the unzipped fly. I can't say it was a flattering look, but it wasn't going to work any other way.

I thanked him, and he wished me luck. Quickly, he

vanished to wherever helpful ghosts go when they aren't needed.

Qat appeared at the bottom of the gangway at exactly nine thirty as promised. This time, she had driven the jeep right up to the pier and sat in the driver's seat looking straight ahead as I descended the gangway and sat next to her. I heard a man singing, "*Oh what a beautiful morning!*" and looked down to find that *The King and I* had been replaced with *Oklahoma!* in the eight-track player. The tape was held in place by the same folded-up matchbook cover.

Qat began to drive slowly out of the port without saying a word or even turning her head to look at me. Finally I asked her if everything was okay to which she said that everything was fine, still without turning her head.

Okay, I can play that game too. So we sat, silently, both looking straight ahead as she drove toward the starting point of The Walk. After about ten minutes of silent driving, I could see two men in the distance, standing by the side of the road. I could also make out a handful of dogs with them, certainly goon'do.

Qat saw them, too, and stopped the jeep abruptly. She said more to herself, I think, than to me, "I guess I might as well get it over with."

She turned to look at me. She looked in my eyes. Moments later her eyes trailed downward—and then the laughter began. She was laughing so hard, I thought the men down the road might hear her, but they didn't, just me.

Even seated in the jeep, the triangle of the gold and black namba stood out prominently from the fly of my very white trousers.

"Go ahead. Get it all out," I said. "I am glad everyone is enjoying this. If I had gotten this many laughs when I was on TV, I would probably still have a job."

This just made her laugh harder. Finally she calmed down

enough to put the jeep in gear and drive the rest of the way to where two men stood with six goon'do sitting patiently behind them.

They were Maru and Goriko, the elders I had not yet met and the ones who demanded I complete The Walk. We got out of the jeep, and the men noticed the namba. Both nodded approvingly.

Both men introduced themselves, Maru speaking first. "Welcome to our island, Mr. Frum, and welcome to The Walk."

The other man was a bit more talkative. "I am Goriko and this is Maru. You honor us with your respect for our ritual and your willing participation. In turn, you become worthy of our honor. While you are not the god of our fathers, we hope that your presence will result in even greater happiness on our island."

Clearly they had rehearsed those lines, and now they stood quietly, awaiting my response. I thanked them for allowing me to participate in these rituals. Qat had told me that she could think of no other outsider that had ever been asked.

I surprised myself with what I said next and was even more surprised as I realized that I meant every word of it. "The greeting that I have received from you and the people of this island has touched my heart in a way that I have never known before. It is as though I have found a family I never knew I had. My only hope is that I may complete this walk and prove myself worthy."

Goriko responded first. "You prove yourself worthy with the attempt. You will prove yourself strong with your success."

Maru added, "We will await you at the end of your journey."

I had expected these guys to be rather formal. That was their reputation and, after all, they were the ones who had insisted that I complete the ritual. What I had not expected was their kindness, but I should have. Kindness was something these people seemed to have in abundance.

They began giving me instructions. The boys who performed this ritual got no advice because they didn't need it. I did. After all, it was only fair. Fairness was another thing they had in copious amounts.

Maru and Goriko told me that a single goon'do usually accompanies each boy on their journey, but they were not sure that any would choose to walk with me since I was new to them. If a goon'do did choose to go with me, they would not stay the whole walk as they lack the stamina, but another may turn up along the way. Furthermore, and this was the really important part, no matter how thirsty I might get, I should not drink water from anywhere along the way unless the goon'do drinks first. Not all of the water on the island was safe to drink, and only the goon'do could be trusted to know if it was harmless or not. Pollution and chemicals were not the problem, but there were natural hazards such as microbes or pathogens for which I may have no resistance. So I was advised to drink plenty if the goon'do drank first, but not at all if they didn't.

They gave me very broad and simple directions that would cover the first three hours or so of the trek after which they said I should be able to see the volcano and simply continue straight for it whether there was a road or a path or neither. Once atop the volcano, I was to complete two full circles and then a third half-rotation so that I would be traveling down a path on the side opposite from which I had climbed. They would await me at the bottom of the far side on the beach at the southernmost tip of the island.

So that was that. It was time to walk. Qat had been silent throughout. I thanked everyone and said, "I'll see you on the other side," and started walking along the road. One of the goon'do immediately rose to his feet and walked to my side.

This brought a wave of laughter from Maru and Goriko. Was everyone on the island going to laugh at me today?

"What's so funny?" I asked.

Goriko said, "She is known as Bobo. She is always known to accompany the boys who she thinks will need the most help." Goriko smiled and continued. "She will take good care of you, and remember, do not drink unless she drinks."

I turned and started walking, Bobo by my side. I found the gravel and tar more comfortable underfoot and stayed on the edge of the road. Bobo preferred the softness of the sand to the firmness of the road and walked there.

I had walked about fifty yards when Qat pulled up in the jeep next to me. She said, "Hey, did they tell you anything about the wild pigs?"

"No," I answered, "what about them?"

"Stay away from them. They bite. They look all cute and cuddly, and then they bite!" she said, as if she was enjoying this.

"Thanks a lot," I said. "Like I don't have enough to worry about."

From down the road, I could hear Maru yelling but in a friendly way. "Leave him alone! Be gone with you!"

Qat just giggled and smiled. "Don't worry about the pigs, John. Just leave them alone, and they will leave you alone. Good luck. I know you can do it. See you on the other side."

She drove off before I could answer.

As I LEARNED after I had left the ship, Barnwell had arranged what he called a "full mission status report," a secure video conference call with Geur, Cheiro, Bert, and Ernie. There was no question at this point as to who was in charge. This was Barnwell's show, and everyone knew it.

Geur and Cheiro seemed content to let their boss pull the

strings. Their initiative in starting this scheme had been the exception. Their full acquiescence to Barnwell and people like him had always been their norm, so Geur and Cheiro said little as Bert and Ernie shared the good news that the islanders would sign the next day.

Barnwell asked a lot of questions, including whether anyone had any idea if I could successfully complete the ritual. He seemed particularly interested in my physical and mental condition. They told Barnwell that I seemed to be a bit beat-up physically but determined to complete the walk and my mission.

"Okay," said Barnwell. "Well done, gentlemen, and that means all of you. What you are doing here will make you rich, but more than that, it will change the world for the better. You can all feel good about your mission."

He paused for a moment and then continued, this time directing his comments to Geur and Cheiro. "And you two, if we make this happen, I promise that you will not be forgotten. I know I gave you a hard time, but you will get the credit you deserve for having thought this up in the first place. It was nothing short of genius."

Cheiro and Geur seemed sheepish as if they were waiting for the other shoe to drop, but no unwelcome surprises came. Barnwell seemed to be genuinely pleased and grateful.

Geur simply said, "Thank you, sir."

Barnwell continued. "Okay. Assuming Frum gets the job done today, I expect to hear from you guys as soon the papers are signed. I don't care what time it is here. We will have press releases ready to go. Good job, everyone. Thanks again." Then he was gone.

Less than a minute later, Barnwell was on another conference call, this one even more secure. This one was with Smith and Wesson.

"Report," he said simply, foregoing any greeting.

"Did you review all of the photographs and recordings we sent?" asked Smith.

"I have," Barnwell replied.

"Then you know as much as we do," said Smith, never overly talkative. "Do you have any further instructions or questions, sir?"

"Yes, as a matter of fact, I do. You will keep a close eye on this Frum motherfucker, and make sure that he and the two lawyers get there on time tomorrow to sign the fuckin' papers!"

"Yes, sir," Smith replied.

"I don't know shit about this guy, and that means I can't trust him. You tell me. Are we losing him?"

"Losing him how, sir?" asked Wesson.

"Well, let's see," said Barnwell. "He's kissing the prime minister's daughter, wrapping his cock, and walking across the island and up a volcano. That's a pretty full day in my book. Can either of you tell me with any level of certainty that he is fully on our side and will stay that way, or is he getting a little too touchy-feely with the locals?"

Neither man answered immediately.

"I am waiting for an answer, gentleman," said Barnwell.

Wesson said stiffly, "He believes in the mission, sir, and he appears to have every intention of seeing it through to completion."

Barnwell seemed unconvinced. "Good," he said, "for his sake. I am sure I need not remind you of your own mission parameters."

Barnwell waited for a moment for both men to offer a formal "Yes, sir" before continuing. "You will inform me immediately upon his return to the vessel. You will inform me whether he was able to complete the ritual as soon as you know the outcome. Thank you, gentlemen."

He ended the call.

Of course, I knew none of this at the time. All I knew was

that I had a long day ahead of me. It was not overly hot, maybe 85 degrees, but I was already sweating in my full uniform. No doubt it would rain at some point because it rained almost every day sooner or later, but for now, the skies were clear. Once I had walked far enough that I could no longer see the elders, I turned and introduced myself to my companion.

Bobo was a beautiful female goon'do. All of the goon'do I had seen looked more or less the same in build, and the only way to tell them apart was by their color. They were all cute with their short, soft coats and prominent light brown whiskers. Bobo was mostly tan with some black on her legs. If she were my dog, I would have called her Boots.

When I turned to her and kneeled, she sat down in the sand as if to accept my greeting. I stroked her head and scratched her ears. In return, she licked my face. She was clean and had a perfect coat. It then occurred to me that every goon'do I had seen looked perfectly clean and healthy. "Well," I said out loud, "I guess it's just you and me, kid. Thanks for coming along." I rose and continued walking, Bobo by my side.

My instructions were to stay on this road for about an hour. When the road started to veer to the east, I would find a path on the right side of road. I was supposed to stay on that path for about three hours even as it intersected with other roads. Where the path ends, I would be able to see the volcano in the distance. At that point, I was to keep the volcano in sight on a variety of roads and paths until I got to the base. Then there would be only one way up, and there would be no mistaking it. If I were going the right way, I would not encounter any villages or signs of civilization other than roads. If I did get lost and happen to wander into a village, I was permitted to ask directions, but I was not supposed to seek out people or ask for help otherwise.

Well, if anyone could get lost, it would be me. I'm from Queens. We don't have a lot of jungles or volcanoes. Following the road was no problem, and I had no difficulty finding the path when we reached it. By that, I mean Bobo had no problem. She left my side just long enough to walk toward the path, and I followed. I think it had been about an hour. My only way of telling time was by the sun—and did I mention I am from Queens?

The path was a combination of dirt and sand, and in most parts it was no more than a foot or two wide. Bobo took the lead and walked just ahead of me. Although the surroundings weren't dense, we were in a jungle with trees and vegetation of every kind imaginable, both large and small. Light still filtered through, and the path ahead was clearly defined. For the first time, I saw the fruit bats clinging to the side of almost every tree. Like most Americans, I had some unfounded fear and loathing for bats, but these were actually kind of cute with furry little orange faces. For a moment, I felt a bit of remorse about eating the fruit bat soup. However, they were considerably less cute when they would unfurl their wings and fly seven or eight at a time from one tree to another. The first time that happened, I stood straight up, for the sounds of their beating wings startled me more than anything. Bobo was unimpressed.

The footing on the trail was decent but soft in a lot of places. My shoes were already covered in dirt but still dry. My uniform from the knee down was considerably less white than when I had started. I was indeed thirsty, and I could tell Bobo was too, but she seemed unconcerned. We had passed a couple of streams, but she had shown no signs of stopping. Soon we came to a small lake of breathtaking beauty. The whole setting looked as pure and pristine as a beer commercial, but Bobo did not stop to drink, so neither did I. I had begun to talk to her, and she seemed to like the sound of my voice.

"What was wrong with the lake?" I asked. "Aren't you thirsty?" She just kept walking.

We soon found our way into a small clearing, and Bobo

stopped suddenly. Bobo had seen them first, three wild boars less than thirty feet to our left. Two were lying down, and one was standing. They were lazing around a mud puddle while the other looked for insects on a nearby tree.

My first thought was that Qat had quite a sense of humor. These were not even remotely cuddly or cute. They were gray and matted, gnarly-looking, shit-covered boars. And they were huge. The smallest was at least a hundred pounds. Unlike with the fruit bats, I felt not the slightest bit of remorse over the pork meatloaf we ate last night. These were seriously ugly animals with huge heads punctuated by a massive round nose. Disney pigs they were not. I knew they were just pigs, but believe me, they were menacing.

I didn't have to convince Bobo. She wanted nothing to do with them either. She led me to the right, off the path and into some dense foliage. Together we made a large half circle leading away from them and eventually back to the path.

That part was tricky. A machete would certainly have come in handy. More than once, Bobo stood and waited for me to clear a palm frond or vine from her path so we could continue. By the time we made it back to the trail, I was covered in sweat and dirt. My feet were now caked in mud, but I got the feeling that it was much better than the alternative.

Did I mention I am from Queens? Did I mention those pigs were huge and nasty?

I had never fooled myself into thinking this was going to be easy, but I was beginning to have one of those moments when I began to reflect on what wrong turns I might have made in life that led to this particular moment. I was already exhausted. Despite what I had said, both of my ankles were throbbing and aching with every step. My shoes and socks were soaked through. My uniform was filthy with mud and what I can only describe as "jungle goop." My hat felt suddenly heavy. I removed it to find a glob of something stuck to the top—bird shit. My only consolation was that I was wearing the hat as opposed to wearing the shit. I shook the hat and wiped off as much of the goo as I could before returning the hat to my head.

There was only one thing to do. We were back on the path after having circled around for a quarter mile or more. I looked down at Bobo who was waiting patiently and said, "Shall we?" I think I heard her say, "We shall," as we resumed our travels.

I had no idea how much time had passed or how far along we had gone. I guessed that it wouldn't be long until the path ended, and the volcano would be in sight, but that may well have been wishful thinking. We were on a section of the path where the trees and bushes were so dense that I couldn't have seen anything, much less a volcano. We had to be satisfied with staying on the path and hope to encounter some water or maybe a nice snack bar. A diner would be nice too.

I entertained myself with the idea that we would turn the next corner and find a nice café or water fountain. No such luck. However, it wasn't too long until we found some water that was up to Bobo's high standards.

Ahead of us was a small pond, more like a very large puddle atop a small ravine. The water from the pond wound down the crevasse gently and splashed generously off a giant rock, the bottom of which was a bit higher than Bobo's head. I would never have thought of it myself, but Bobo situated herself a foot from the rock, opened her mouth, and lapped up the splashing water.

It didn't take me long to figure out that if I just cupped my hands, I would be rewarded with water. It didn't taste all that different from kava. In other words, it tasted like dirt. It was delicious.

Both of us had been so eager to drink that we had not noticed we had company. In a small tree right behind us was a monkey, a tiny one. I have no idea what kind it was, but it was no more than two feet tall and weighed maybe ten pounds.

Bobo wasn't startled by the monkey, so I assumed there was no threat. Bobo simply glanced at the monkey and went back to drinking. I did the same. The little creature sat patiently on a branch as if it were waiting its turn to drink.

As it turns out, that is exactly what it was doing. As soon as we finished and took a couple of steps away, the monkey jumped onto the rock. He cupped his little paws and shoveled the splashing water toward his mouth.

"Have some water," I told him. "It's Bobo-approved dirt water, only the finest."

He ignored me, and Bobo started down the path with a slightly impatient turn. I started to wonder if this is what being married is like. Maybe Bobo saw me as a foolish child, wasting time looking at the monkey.

I definitely felt better after drinking the water, and I felt like we were making progress. Of course, that was when it started raining. There had been no warning because we were in jungle so dense, we could not see the darkening sky, but I could hear the pounding of the rain against the jungle canopy. I later learned that the Bohlin have at least seventeen different words for rain in their native language. I don't know the right word for what was coming down, so I will just call it "a fuckin' downpour" or "instant mud."

To call it rain would not do it justice because there were no actual raindrops. These were more like six-inch shards of surprisingly cool water slapping downward. It was incredibly noisy but not really frightening to either Bobo or me. There was no lightning and little or no wind, just massive amounts of water.

Puddles formed everywhere as we walked until the path was one long, sloshy puddle stretching out ahead of us, but we kept moving. We made it out of the dense jungle and onto an open road. Now we could see the dark storm clouds above. As dark as they were, they remained almost directly overhead while all around us was late afternoon sunlight with slices of sunlit orange and grey near the storm clouds. I knew it would not rain much longer.

Meanwhile, Bobo had stopped momentarily. Then she started up the road. As the rain began to lighten, I realized that the greyish-brown blur on the horizon was indeed the volcano. All I had to do now was keep it in sight and head for it. I halfway expected Bobo to peel off at this point, but she stayed with me. Just as the goon'do have always been for the Bohlin, Bobo was now for me my guide and protector.

It turns out that keeping a volcano in sight is a little trickier than I had thought. We stayed on the road for a while until it seemed to veer away from the volcano. Bobo then took us on a path through some forest with tall trees covered in a canopy of vines. The rain had stopped, yet it might as well have been night. The cover of trees was so dense that aside from the occasional puddle, the ground was mostly dry. When we finally emerged into a clearing, I could see the volcano again. It was closer now but definitely not where I expected. This happened two or three more times. I would lose sight of the volcano and then find it again. Each time, the volcano loomed closer and larger.

We were now on a clearly defined, open path with the volcano straight ahead. I had never seen one before except in photographs or movies, and it was not what I expected. Mount Garak was a wide, squat-looking thing with a broad, black, jaggedly circular hill leading to an almost perfectly round cone at the summit.

We were still perhaps three-quarters of a mile away from its base. Vines and flowers of at least a dozen different colors surrounded the path we were on. A botanist would probably say that the beauty and variety of the foliage was the result of the soil absorbing the nutrients of a thousand ancient eruptions. I can only say that it was beauty on a scale I had never before seen.

Only at this moment was I sure I was going to complete this journey. Bobo seemed to sense it too. She was walking in that way only dogs can when they're happy, showing that little bit of proud swagger in her step as if to say, "Can you believe it? I schlepped him all the way here!"

It didn't take us long to reach the base. I could now see that the black of the mountain came from the covering of a powdery, ash-like substance. The path to the top looked unobstructed, but even that was black and ashen.

Bobo had completed her part. I somehow knew she would not go up the mountain with me. The rest would be solely up to me. I knelt next to her, and she nuzzled my face. I gave her a kiss on her cheek. She, in turn, put her entire tongue in my mouth. Not to spoil the moment, but that was a bit much. A respectable fellow should be wined and dined first. I scratched her ear and thanked her for keeping me safe. She turned and walked back the way we had come. I, on the other hand, took my first steps onto the base of the volcano.

Mount Garak had not erupted or spewed lava during the five hundred or so years since the Bohlin have inhabited Volavo, but geologists have determined that the volcano is millions of years old and has had hundreds if not thousands of eruptions throughout its lifetime. In fact, the nearby caves that house the vast deposits of corbomite were formed by the lava flows of ancient eruptions. Even now, as a supposedly dormant volcano, the mountain shakes underfoot with an unsettling rumble every minute or two and sends a trail of grey smoke into the air several times a day. Clearly, people who use "dormant" as a term are not actually standing on the volcano as I now was.

The flank was not too steep and even as tired as I was would not have been a problem— except that it was slippery, really slippery. Each step needed to be thought out, every footfall a heavy one. Though I tried to be careful, I slipped and fell at least five times, each fall raising a cloud of grey and black dust that stung my eyes and clung to the sweat on my skin. I had not felt abandoned by Bobo, but now I fully understood why she had not come along. She could not have kept her footing.

The sun was now lower in the sky, so I made it my business to keep moving as fast as I could even as I slipped and fell. The footing was tricky enough with light, and I certainly didn't want to find out how hard it would be in the dark. It took me about an hour to make it to the summit, a rocky cone around the volcano's opening, about a quarter-mile around.

There was no ash at the top. The ground was more like a dusty, clay surface and the openings in some parts more than twenty feet wide. Even from the top, the crater itself was not visible. I had imagined that I would be able to peer over its edge and see into the crater, but its sides still rose fifteen feet or more above the mostly flat surface I was on. Still, I was not too disappointed. The slight rumble in my ears and shaking beneath my feet were enough to let me know I was now atop a volcano. That was good enough for me.

I had been instructed to make two full circuits of the summit and then half of a third before going down the path on the other side. It occurred to me that no one would know if I didn't go around twice, but I did anyway. If I am going to do this, I might as well do it right. By the time I finished, it was almost completely dark.

I was saved from total blackness by a bright enough half-moon, a moon that had never looked closer. I found my way to the downward path but took only a few steps before I realized I had a problem. The trail had been slippery on the way up, and the descent was not much steeper, but I realized I had no footing. I was slipping with every step. I could actually plummet down the mountain if I wasn't careful.

I took a couple of steps back onto the summit and had an idea. First, I removed my shoes. I thought for a moment about tossing them into the crater and then immediately thought better of it. I'm pretty sure the gods would not have approved. I then removed my shirt and wrapped it around one foot, tying it off at the ankle. It took me a couple of tries, but I secured it well enough to protect my foot and give me some traction. I then used my undershirt to tie around my other foot the same way. The cotton of the undershirt gave a little more padding but a little less traction. Nevertheless, it would have to do. I took my shoes and shoved each of them toe first into my trouser pockets and headed down the mountain. Traction was what I was looking for, and traction was what I found. My idea worked.

The footing was still difficult, but I managed to stay upright. In the moonlight I could see the ocean in the distance, and it wasn't long before I could also see people. Five jeeps with their headlights on were parked on the beach. I wanted to shout and wave, but I didn't want to be a smartass and lose my footing and end this journey by rolling down the rest of the way. It then occurred to me what I must look like at the moment.

I was wearing a hat covered in bird shit. My face was covered in ash. I had on no shirt or shoes. My shoes were sticking out of my front pockets. My formerly white uniform pants were covered in mud, and my feet were wrapped in shirts. And finally, let's not forget the triangle of the namba sticking out of my fly. If I were the image of a god, it wouldn't be one I was familiar with.

All of that was of no matter to the people awaiting me on the beach. As I descended and drew closer to them, I could see only familiar faces in the glare of the headlights and the glow of the moon. All nine elders had come. Kavu was there and, of course, Qat.

Qat sat in the jeep with a goon'do at her side. It was Bobo! As I approached, the elders arranged themselves in a circle in the sand. Kavu walked forward to greet me first. We walked toward each other until I was close enough to see his outstretched hand. As I reached to grasp it, he said with a very serious face, "Are you ready to begin the journey?"

He couldn't maintain the façade for more than a moment before smiling. "You made it!" he said. "I knew you could do it!"

I pulled him into my chest and wrapped my arms around him. He returned the hug and then coughed a couple of times from the dust and ash coming from my clothes and body.

"Come and complete the ritual," Kavu said and led me to the circle.

The men parted as I entered and stood at the center of the ring of elders. They stood silently for a few moments. Finally, Kepal stepped forward. He was senior among the elders and the first elder I had met.

"We tell our boys that when they complete this ritual, they had gone up this mountain as boys and had come down as men. That will not do for you, will it? So I will say that you have gone up the mountain as a stranger, a man who came to us as a god, but you come down the mountain as one of us, a member of our community."

I nodded and said, "Thank you. Thank you all. And as a man of this island—"

Ishka walked over and interrupted since the men had already begun to wander off.

"Yes, that's very nice, but the boy who completes the walk doesn't get to say anything, and neither do you. Besides, we are all late for our kava ritual, so if you want to keep talking, then come join us."

I started walking with him towards the jeep where Qat was sitting. Bobo had jumped out of the jeep and was now running toward me excitedly. Qat tossed me a bottle of water as I approached. I have to admit I was a bit disappointed at Qat's greeting, but I guess it made sense, given the company and the way I must have smelled.

I heard Ishka say to Qat, "I guess I have to hand it to your boy here, Qat. He's got some balls."

Qat answered, "He does at that."

I sat down heavily in the passenger seat of the jeep, just in time to catch the leaping Bobo, who landed in my lap. She licked my face and knocked my hat off into the back seat. I left it there. Smiling at Bobo, I said, "Well, at least someone is happy to see me."

Ishka invited me to the kava ritual in his village, but he did not seem surprised or disappointed when I declined. I was tired. Having finally sat down, I found that I was sore in places that I didn't even know were places.

All but one of the elders and Kavu had already waved goodbye and hurriedly climbed into the jeeps and left, lured by the call of their kava ritual. I guess I should feel honored that they had showed up at all. Ishka said his goodbyes and did the same. He called out to Bobo and asked her if she wanted to come home. She gave me one last lick on the face before jumping out and getting into the jeep with Ishka. I should have known she came from his village.

Just like that, Qat and I were alone on the beach with just the sea and the moonlight and the sound of the waves. At this romantic moment, Qat turned to me. She looked even more beautiful in the moonlight. She said, "My god you stink!"

Those weren't exactly the words I was hoping for, but as usual, she had a plan. She hopped out of the jeep and pulled a thin strap behind her neck and shimmied her dress down and onto the sand, revealing a one-piece, white bathing suit.

She said, "Let's go, boy. Strip! It's time to rinse you off!"

It had never occurred to me that pretending to be a god would involve this much stripping, but I dutifully removed the shirts from my feet and took off my now almost-black uniform pants. I turned my back to her as I carefully removed the namba.

She had thought of everything. In the back seat were four towels and a change of clothes for her. A simple black T-shirt and drawstring shorts were waiting for me.

"I guess we are going swimming," I said.

"Yes, sir," she replied.

"But I thought you hate the beach."

"Desperate times call for desperate measures," she answered, pointing at me and holding her nose, "and these are desperate times."

She grabbed the towels out of the back seat, and we walked toward the shoreline. She laid out a towel for each of us and put a second one, still folded, on top of it. We walked side by side until our feet reached the water. I could see that the ocean ahead was calm with only the gentlest waves rolling to the shore.

I reached out to her as we walked and felt a quiet rush as she held my hand. We walked until the water was up to our waists. It felt warm and soothing on my aching body. We separated a bit, and I tried to rub some of the collected dirt off of my chest and legs.

Qat watched with amusement and said in a serious tone, "Try not to splash around so much. The movement attracts the sharks."

Sharks? I hadn't considered sharks. I dutifully began cupping the water carefully now, all the while looking around for a telltale fin in the moonlight.

With a grin and a playful look, Qat said, "Don't worry, John. I was just kidding. We don't have sharks here. Let me help you."

By now we had moved into water up to our shoulders. She approached and stood in front of me and cleaned my face, gently rubbing away the ash and grime. She stopped for a moment to look at me. I watched her lips curl into a smile when, without warning, she put a hand on each of my shoulders and pushed me under the water.

I emerged from the water just in time to hear her say, "There. Now that's better."

I wrapped my arms around her, resting my hands at the base of her back. I didn't need to pull her in as our lips finally met.

I am not a great actor by any stretch of the imagination, but I was taught by some of the finest, and I can "Hollywood kiss" with the best of them. If they gave out Oscars for kissing . . . well okay, I wouldn't win, but I'd like to think I would have at least been nominated. Those thoughts went out the window as I kissed Qat with a hunger I had never felt before—ever.

My hands explored her back as she reached up and stroked my hair. We separated for just a moment before again coming together as if assuring ourselves that the moment was real. It was.

We stood staring at each other in the moonlight. I knew she would break the silence, and she did. "My goodness, Mr. Frum, you are just full of surprises."

I said with a laugh, "I would be willing to bet a bowl of fruit bat soup that you are not the least bit surprised."

We returned to our towels, and I wrapped hers around her and threw mine around my shoulders. It was a fairly warm night, but we were both a bit chilly. We sat side by side with my arm around her waist.

"Whatever it is we are up to is going to have to wait," she said with complete assurance.

"Agreed," I said, which was a complete lie. I wanted to make love to her right there and then on that beach. I wanted to sleep nestled next to her in my tiny bunk back on the ship. In other words, I was fucked.

We finished drying off and went back to the jeep. Well, she

did, not me. I stood facing the ocean while she changed out of her bathing suit. She did the same while I took off my wet underwear and put on the T-shirt and shorts she had brought me. She held out a plastic bag for my wet clothes.

"I'm keeping this," she said, referring to the uniform I had put in the bag. "It will be a souvenir for future generations. I'm guessing you have plenty more."

We drove back mostly in silence. As we pulled up to the gangway, she said, "I have to ask, and I am only going to ask you once because I trust you. Does the contract offer the best deal for our people?"

I answered as honestly as I could. "I don't know if it's the best deal, but I do believe it's the safest deal."

"That's good enough for me," she said.

This time she kissed me. It felt even better than it had earlier because now I knew she wanted me as I wanted her.

She broke away from me and said, "Be at my father's house at ten tomorrow morning. Bring the lawyers. I'll see you then."

Again, Smith and Wesson secretly got their pictures and were gone by the time I reached the gangway.

13

SHIT, MEET FAN. PART TWO

It was a happy ship the next morning. After all, it was the morning before John Frum Day, and today we would sign the agreement. Tomorrow it would be announced to the world as part of the celebration.

For the first time since we arrived on the island, we were all together in the galley, sharing a meal. Captain made a rare appearance, and even Smith and Wesson joined Bert, Ernie, and me. Everybody could see the light at the end of the tunnel. Of course, you could never tell with Smith and Wesson. They were their regular, polite, helpful, stoic selves.

Ernie had not liked anything about this mission except the money he was going to make at the end of it, but even he seemed in good spirits. I told him that we were going to walk to the minister's house to sign the papers, and he wanted to know why he would have to walk when they had sent a jeep for me.

"I'm a god, and you're a lawyer. Gods ride; lawyers walk," I said.

He actually laughed before saying, "Well at least I get to get off this goddamn boat for the first time in a week."

Bert chimed in, too. "Hey," he said, "with any luck, we could be off this island and on our way home tomorrow night."

That got me thinking about Qat. This was my fifth day on the island, and an awful lot had happened. I hadn't given any thought to what I would do after I completed the mission. One thing had simply led to another, allowing no time for reflection. What I did know for sure was that I had feelings for Qat that I hadn't felt for anyone for a long time, maybe ever. I was hoping I could stay for a while after the papers were signed. That is, if they would have me, or rather if Qat would have me.

"I might not leave with you," I told my crewmates.

My pronouncement might as well have been a fart in church. The room suddenly got quiet. I explained that I didn't expect them to understand that this was a beautiful island with amazing and unique people.

Smith and Wesson, of course, understood. They had pictures, but they would certainly never say anything—at least not to me.

Bert, Ernie, and I left the ship at exactly 9:50 for the short walk to the minister's house. The two of them looked at their surroundings and commented that it was more modern than they thought it would be. I didn't show it, but their comments annoyed me. I had similar thoughts myself just a few days earlier, but it bothered me to think that they would just assume this was a backward culture. I now knew it was anything but.

As we approached, we saw a young man standing in front of the minister's home. It was the same young man from the other day. He welcomed us and asked us to wait while he checked to see if the minister was ready to see us. He returned less than a minute later and ushered us into the living room.

I knew right away that something was wrong. The minister sat in one of the chairs. Kavu and Qat sat next to each other on the sofa. Qat had an odd look on her face, like she wanted to tell me something. If we were here to sign contracts, it would certainly have been better suited to meet in the adjacent office rather than the living room. Kavu and the minister rose from their seats. The minister introduced himself to Bert and Ernie. He gestured to Qat, who remained seated, and introduced her as his daughter and advisor. He was about to introduce Kavu when his son interrupted.

"I must tell you something, Father," said Kavu. "I went to the ship to meet with Bert and Ernie. I sought knowledge to help you with your decision. I did not tell you earlier because I learned nothing you do not already know or understand."

The minister seemed unfazed. "Do not worry, my son," he said. "I do not question your loyalty, only your wisdom. It is something I myself might have done at your age."

With the introductions complete, the minister gestured for us to sit. I sat in a chair next to the minister. Bert and Ernie sat side by side on the other sofa.

"Gentlemen, before we go any further, I must advise you," he said, "the cat is out of the bag."

Kavu used the remote control to turn on the television. "Let's start with this," said Kavu. It was a *BBC World News* broadcast.

"We continue to bring you developments in the story of the tiny South Pacific island of Volavo. You may recall that earlier this morning, we were reporting a peculiar public statement from the prominent American Evangelical leader Jerry Gramm. In his statement, Gramm said that he had learned that Volavo possessed vast deposits of a mineral that could provide energy to the entire world. He further claimed that a false god was trying to steal the island's resource by posing as what he called 'their godless pagan deity John Frum.'

While the news anchor spoke, we saw a photo of Gramm appear in the corner of the screen, his face pudgy and flush in a secret, heavy drinker kind of way. His hair was a painfully obvious toupee.

"The BBC and other news organizations have now been able to confirm some parts of the reverend's statement. We have learned that there are, indeed, vast deposits of the rare mineral corbomite on the island. Further investigation has now revealed that chemical and technology giant Womansanto has developed a process that can safely process the mineral. Scientists have long maintained that corbomite can produce cheap, virtually limitless energy. Womansanto has offered no public comment so far.

"The news has provoked comments and reactions from across the globe. There are reports that the United States Navy Pacific Fleet command in Pearl Harbor, Hawaii, has already dispatched several vessels to the region. Russian and Chinese vessels are reportedly en route as well. Ships from several other nations are also expected. There has been a flurry of diplomatic activity and hurried phone calls among world leaders.

"It seems for the moment at least, the tiny island of Volavo has become the center of the universe..."

Kavu flipped through the channels. Every network from every nation was covering the story to the exclusion of everything else. Volavo was indeed the center of the universe.

14

THE (FORMER) GOOD REVEREND GRAMM

I already knew who Jerry Gramm was. He had been the president and son of the founder of Rapture University, which was the evangelical college I had attended in the United States. I even met him once briefly at my graduation. At the time, he was still Reverend Gramm. The allegations that would turn him into the *former* Reverend Gramm had just begun to surface in the press in the United States.

Gramm had been not just a religious leader in the U.S. but a potent political force as well. Millions listened to him on the radio and watched him on his television show, *Wonder Words*. The show had been on the air for more than thirty years and had also been started by his father, the Reverend Bobby Gramm, who had passed away some years earlier. The younger Gramm commanded a vast charitable trust with millions of regular donors and a retail empire with sales of more than a hundred million dollars annually. Even I owned a set of "Jesus Jammies," which are still a popular item to this day.

The army of voters they influenced was a reliable friend to every right-wing candidate and cause in the United States, but not a hint of that was ever evident to me on the college campus.

Everyone from the janitors up to President Reverend Gramm himself were always kind, welcoming, and inclusive.

Gramm and his friend, the now *former* Reverend Billy Fowlball Junior had run into a little trouble. Fowlball himself was a second generation TV evangelical and lord over his own political and broadcast empire. The two were good friends and frequent collaborators. There was shock and disbelief when the first rumors of gay foursomes and drug abuse became supermarket tabloid fodder. There was consternation mixed with dismay when they were indeed photographed leaving a disreputable bathhouse in San Francisco. It turns out the bathhouse and other gay bathhouses were owned by . . . you guessed it—a shell corporation traced to Wonder Words Ministry Incorporated. There were also massive allegations and eventually convictions against Billy Fowlball Junior but never against Gramm. Fowlball did time for fraud and embezzlement. His wife left him and formed her own ministry. His three kids each wrote a tell-all book in which they all came out as gay.

Gramm's punishment was less severe. He was defrocked, but his wife stood by him and joined him in his tearful apology and prayer from the steps of Rapture University, my alma mater. He was forced to resign all of his official positions in the ministry of Wonder Words Incorporated. Officially, he handed over the reins of his still vast and powerful organization to his eldest son, The Reverend Billy Joe Ray Gramm. Jerry accepted his reduced role in the company and his much reduced public profile.

Then as fate would have it, some missionaries on the tiny island of Volavo reached out to him. In the old days, some nobody missionaries sponsored by *Wonder Words* from some shitty island might have had to wait weeks to talk to a man of Gramm's stature if they could reach him at all, but these days he was answering his own calls, and now he was glad of it.

It turns out there were some strange things happening on

Volavo. The missionary told him that there was a man pretending to be the cargo-cult god John Frum. Gramm had to do a little research before he had any idea of what she was talking about, but it didn't take him long to figure out what was going on. The ship, the mineral, the uniform, the religious fervor—if there was one thing he knew, he knew a big story when he saw one.

Gramm knew what to do. He was going to go public with the story and be the hero. He would dare the mainstream, lamestream media to fact-check the story, and when it all shook out, he, the former Reverend Jerry Gramm, would make everyone forget his past indiscretions. He would regain all of his past prominence and power, as was his God-given right, just as the good Lord had promised.

Everything was going as planned. The media was hesitant at first, as Gramm knew they would be, but soon they would discover what was going on, and they would be his pawns in revealing the evil plan, whatever the evil plan was. He didn't exactly know, but the Lord had told him it was evil. It had to be. There were false gods, heathens, pagans, and savage island people, a Satan's brew at best.

Gramm's phone rang once again. On the other end was Grant Barnwell, CEO of Womansanto. "Good morning, Mr. Gramm. This is Grant Barnwell of Womansanto. Do you remember me?" Barnwell took great pleasure in saying "Mr. Gramm" to the defrocked reverend.

This was a demeaning question, and it was meant to be. Of course Gramm would remember him. They had met dozens of times. They had been to each other's homes and attended numerous prayer breakfasts together. Barnwell had even been asked but had refused to join the board of directors of Wonder Words Inc.

Gramm said, "Of course, Grant. What can I do for you?" Gramm had purposely called Barnwell by his first name in an effort to regain some power and control over the conversation, but that ended abruptly.

Barnwell said, "Well, for starters you can shut the fuck up about Volavo, and mind your own fuckin' business . . . whatever is left of it."

Gramm was blindsided but recovered quickly. "Why should I?" he asked. "There's something evil going on there, and the world should know about it."

Barnwell was unrelenting. "Do us both a favor and save your holier than thou shit for the rubes, and stay out of this. It is my operation."

Gramm felt empowered by the revelation and pushed back. "Really, and what kind of operation is it that you need false gods and—"

Barnwell cut him off. "Before you ask me any more questions, I want to ask you one. Do you think anyone knows how much meth you were moving out of those bathhouses you ran? Do you think they know that the trail leads straight to your offshore accounts? Sorry, that was more than one question. Last one, I promise. How long do you think you can stay out of prison when people do find out?"

There was silence from Gramm for close to thirty seconds. Finally he said, "Thank you for reaching out to me, Mr. Barnwell. It was truly a pleasure to hear from you. The Lord and I wish nothing but the best for you and your family. We also wish you the best in your blessed endeavors on Volavo. Is that what it's called? You know I know so little of international affairs. Thanks again for calling."

Barnwell did not speak again. He simply hung up the phone. He had made sure Gramm now knew John Frum would not be his personal savior, and he, the former Reverend Jerry Gramm, would not be anyone's hero at all.

15

SHIT GOT REAL

For almost an hour, we watched news reports from all over the world. One thing was clear. Virtually overnight, Volavo had become the most strategically important place in the world. A few of the broadcasts had reports from scientists. They explained that corbomite in abundance was the holy grail of energy. It would change the world with cheap, abundant power. The question that remained would be who would control it.

My father motioned to Kavu to turn off the TV. No one spoke for a time as each of us absorbed what we had seen. On some level, I think all of us had already understood the significance. We understood the vast consequences for the island and the world, but seeing and hearing about the issue through the eyes of the world somehow made it real for the first time.

Today was February 14th. John Frum Day was the next day. It was already far and away the most important day of the year on Volavo. Christmas was celebrated on the island, and it was a big deal. Many of us exchanged gifts and put up decorations. We even celebrated July 4th as a sort of mini John Frum Day, but nothing compared to February 15th, the day John Frum had promised to return with the motherlode of cargo. Tomorrow would be the biggest holiday of them all. John Frum had returned.

Of course we knew that John was not a god, but this John Frum had proven himself to be worthy of the Bohlin people, and make no mistake. Tales of his exploits had already spread among the people. A new legend was being born. This morning a woman had stopped me in the street to ask if it was true that the mountain had trembled beneath John's feet as he walked the summit of the volcano. She had heard that the crater had spit fire and smoke as he walked its peak. He may not be *the* god, John Frum, but he may very well turn out to be *a* god, John Frum.

This would be the biggest John Frum Day of them all. The day would start with a ceremony at Port John at noon. Normal attendance for the celebration was about 2,500 in an amphitheater that seats about 500, so it is already standing room only with the crowd spilling out onto the docks and into the adjacent street. Tomorrow, we expected more than 5,000 to be in attendance.

WE HAD DECIDED that my father would make his ceremonial speech. He usually asks for the return of the great god, John Frum. This year would be different. He would turn to the sea and call out to John Frum, and John would answer and then join him on stage. John would then announce that wealth and happiness had come to us in the form of the island's bounty of corbomite. It was also then that he would announce the agreement with Womansanto.

My father spoke first. He directed his comments to Bert, Ernie, and John.

"Gentlemen, I think we can all agree that this changes things in a way that perhaps we should have foreseen. Nevertheless, I cannot sign your agreement until we have had some time to consider and discuss what has transpired."

Bert had a response, and it was a good one.

"It's more crucial than ever that you sign the agreement immediately. It will act as a shield to protect the Bohlin people from the onslaught of the outside world. It's the only was to save your island from the firestorm that's brewing. Don't you understand? There are foreign navy vessels on their way to your waters!" he said.

I have to admit he made a convincing argument, and it made perfect sense. However, I also knew my father. He was not a man who would be rushed by anyone. We listened as he spoke.

"Even if everything you say is true, it will be no less true an hour from now or tonight or tomorrow."

He turned to John. "I mean no disrespect when I say that your shipmates are lawyers by trade."

He turned to Bert and Ernie. "And I mean no disrespect to you when I say that you now act as salesmen. It is what you are being paid to do. I understand, but a salesman will show you only what will sell. A salesman will tell you only of the sweet taste of the treat, not the rotten teeth that will come much later. I must consider both."

Ernie tried to interrupt, but my father spoke louder.

"And that is what worries me. It is what has stolen my sleep since your arrival. Grant Barnwell may very well be an honorable man."

Bert and Ernie looked at each other, surprised that the minister knew of the Womansanto Chairman.

"He may have every intention of honoring this agreement forever, but his duty is not to me or this island or my people. His sworn duty is to his company and its shareholders. What will happen when the shareholders demand that he squeeze the lifeblood from this island in the name of their bottom line?

It will happen. It may not be Barnwell or me but our successors who preside over the death of this island and its people as a unique culture, but it will happen. Can any of you promise that it won't? Can any of you promise me that the sweetness of today will not become the rot of tomorrow?"

Bert and Ernie looked at John and then at each other. It was Ernie who spoke.

"Minister, you are indeed as wise as I have been told. What you have said contains a great deal of truth, but even as a salesman, as you say, I can tell you that this agreement is still better than the alternative, which I believe to be chaos, danger, and possible occupation by a foreign military power."

Truth is truth no matter where it comes from. I could see in my father's eyes that he believed Ernie.

He said with a smile, "What are your names, gentlemen? Not your names from *Sesame Street*, your real names."

They told him without hesitation that Bert was, in fact, Donald, and Ernie was Howard. "Well, Donald and Howard, you have both done a magnificent job and have earned the bounty you will no doubt collect when I sign these papers, but it will not be today. For the moment, we have a more immediate problem. As we speak, there must be an army of journalists trying to figure out how to get here, so first things first. What do we do about that?"

John had been listening intently but had remained silent throughout. When he finally spoke, he said, "Minister, I have been giving this some thought, and I have an idea. I think we should shut down the island. No one goes in or out until at least the day after tomorrow."

The minister instantly agreed. In fact, everyone seemed to agree. This would help to keep things manageable, at least for a while.

My father turned his attention back to Bert and Ernie. He thanked them again and then asked that they return to the ship. Before they left, he reassured them that he still had every intention of signing the agreement and would send for them when he was ready.

Bert and Ernie seemed to understand and made no further attempt to change his mind. They both paused for a moment when they realized that John had not been included in the request to return to the ship. They knew he intended to remain with us.

John saw their hesitation and reassured them. "I will be right there, guys. I just want to help make sure that the media wolves don't eat all the sheep," he said, forcing a small smile.

Both Bert and Ernie looked like they wanted to say something but thought better of it, so we said our goodbyes. The minister's guard who was stationed in front of the residence would walk them back to the ship.

As soon as they were gone, John told us that he had another idea, obviously an idea that he would rather not share with his shipmates, but my father interrupted him. He spoke to John in a way that I had heard him use to speak to Kavu and me so many times over the years. He had noticed the reaction of Bert and Ernie when John had chosen to stay behind.

"You must be careful that your associates do not come to believe that you have switched sides and now work on behalf of the Bohlin people rather than in the interests of your employer, Womansanto."

My father instinctively knew that with stakes this high, John could be in grave danger. John listened but seemed honestly shocked that his shipmates might ever question his intentions or pose any sort of threat to him.

John said, "Even if they did want to hurt me, how could they do it? Would they land some mercenary force on the island? That seems pretty farfetched to me."

My father patiently asked John about the role served by the three other men observed on the ship since its arrival. John said that one was the captain and the other two were Smith and Wesson. Their job was to provide security, but they functioned as a sort of jack-of-all-trades. They were cooks; they made coffee; they did laundry and anything else the captain asked of them. They had even helped him put on his namba.

As he spoke, it finally dawned on him that Smith and Wesson *were* the mercenary force. Their real purpose was to do any dirty work that might be required. At that moment, John understood that his helpful angels might very well be anything but. The realization seemed to leave him a bit shaken. Womansanto didn't need to send a mercenary force to the island. They already had one.

16

MOTHERS AND SOLDIERS

As usual, the minister seemed to have a knack for putting things into perspective. Doesn't he ever get tired of being right? The idea that Smith and Wesson could be dangerous had not occurred to me, but it made perfect sense. It also had not occurred to me that anyone could possibly consider me disloyal. All the same, from the viewpoint of my shipmates, anything that didn't serve the goal of getting the minister's signature on those contracts could be considered disloyal. Armed with this new vantage point, I was now even more certain about what to do next.

Mary Disir is the only agent I ever had in show business. When I first started out, she was working for a massive talent syndicate, but after some time off, she had formed her own agency and PR firm, and I had moved over with her.

Her industry is dominated by sharks, and truth be told, Mary is a shark, but she had always done right by me, and by that, I mean that she had always told me the truth even if it was a truth I wouldn't like. She had never told me that I was going to be the next big thing, but she said I did have a certain appeal that would keep me working unless, of course, I called someone "Toots." But Mary had always taken time for me even as her business had grown, and her firm was taking on bigger and bigger clients. I had taken to calling her Mother Mary despite the fact that she was only a couple of years older than me. She had started calling me Joey Toots, mostly to bust my balls.

I told the minister that my idea was to contact Mary and have her act as the island's press agent. The first order of business would be to quickly get the word out that the island was shut down to anyone trying to enter. She would be able to issue press releases to all of the world's media organizations simultaneously. That would buy us some time.

The minister agreed without hesitation. We all went into his office where he had a satellite telephone. He put it on speaker as I called Mary.

"Mother Mary!" I said when she picked up the phone. "It's your favorite unemployed actor calling."

"Joey Toots!" she responded. "How the hell are you?"

"I'm doing fine, thanks. We'll catch up later. Right now, I called to see if you've heard any of the news about Volavo."

She was quiet for a few moments. "Quit dicking around, Joe. Of course I've heard about Volavo. That's all anyone is talking about. Are you on the moon or what?"

"No, not the moon, but I am on Volavo," I said.

I think all of us in the office jumped a little when we heard Mary yelling on the other end.

"Oh my fuckin' god! It's you, isn't it? You're the false god that idiot Gramm was talking about. You're John Frum!"

I think that was the first time I had ever seen the minister laugh. It was the softest of chuckles at Mary's reaction.

At some point during her tirade, I told her that yes, it was me.

"Holy shit, Joe! I hope you know what you're doing. You know there are at least ten countries sending military personnel to that island, including a frigging Chinese aircraft carrier. You're at ground fuckin' zero over there!"

Finally I interrupted. "Yeah, that's kind of what I wanted to talk to you about. By the way, you are on speaker with the leaders of Volavo. I would like to introduce you to Prime Minister Karbina. You may call him Minister. I've got his son and daughter here, Qat and Kavu. They're also his trusted advisors."

"Nice to meet you all. Sorry about the salty language. Hey, Joe, you could have told me I was on speaker. Never mind. You never did have any manners. Anyway, how can I help?"

The minister took over and explained that he would like for her to be the official press agent for the island of Volavo. The first order of business would be to issue a press release informing the world that the island would be off limits until further notice.

The minister is a cautious man, so he did not delve into the details of the situation or the decision he faced. When he finished, Mary agreed that the lockdown was a good idea, but she also had an idea of her own. She proposed that they allow in a single reporter with an additional crew of three. Her argument was that there should be a reporter that can immediately transmit events from the island directly to the world, unfiltered.

"May I be blunt?" she said and continued without waiting for an answer. "Right now, all the world knows is that an island full of false-god-loving savages holds the key to the entire future of the world's energy. That's what they've heard from that dickwad Gramm. He doesn't exactly have any credibility, and he has already faded out of the news cycle, but it is still what the world heard first, so some of what he said will stick unless you tell the story from your side. Don't get me wrong. The reporter I can send you is still a reporter. She won't work just for you, but she is fair, and she will get the real story out to the world if you give her a chance."

The minister pondered Mary's proposal for just a moment and then agreed. It was a good thing that the reporter was one of the army of journalists that were already on their way here. She and her crew would be the only ones who weren't disappointed. She was already in Auckland and could be on the island by tonight. Her name was Hannah Cronkite, no relation to Walter Cronkite, but the name had still helped her through college and in her long career as a journalist. Mary would reach out to her, and Kavu would tend to all of the logistical details for her arrival.

The minister told Mary that the announcement to the world would be part of the John Frum Day celebration. The actual announcement would be made at exactly noon tomorrow, island time. Hannah would be free to link up to the satellite and broadcast it live to the rest of the world.

Mary was always the professional. She didn't try to change the minister's mind, but she did caution him that whatever the announcement was, it should be carefully crafted and considered.

"You get only one shot at a live announcement," she said. "Be sure you don't miss. And Joe, it's way too late for me to yell at you for getting involved in this shitshow—Oops! Sorry!—without telling me, but be careful. Playing God can be all fun and games until somebody ends up on a cross, you know what I mean?"

"Yes, Mother," I said sarcastically. "I'm starting to figure that out."

"Good. I'm going to get to work on a press release immediately. When I release it, it should be only minutes before you see it on news outlets around the world.

"If you need me, I'll be available to you any time. I'm going to cancel everything on my schedule for the next twenty-four hours."

The minister was grateful for Mary and her advice, and he told her so.

"Don't thank me until you get my bill. You might change your mind," she said with a laugh.

Mary insisted on going over the plan one last time.

"I am issuing a press release on your behalf. It will inform the world that no one may arrive on the island of Volavo until further notice. Moreover, at noon tomorrow island time, the leaders of the island will broadcast an announcement to the world that details if and how the mineral corbomite will be distributed.

"By the way, has anyone given any thought as to who will actually make the speech? If I get a vote, it should be you, Joe. You're comfortable in front of a camera, and I bet you look good in a uniform."

We all looked at each other for a few seconds before the minister spoke. "I will introduce him, and it will be John Frum who will make the announcement."

Mary said, "Okay, it's settled, then. I'm going to get to work. Call me right away with any changes or updates."

Qat looked at me with a playful grin. "Well, hello, Joe. How nice it is to finally meet you."

I RETURNED TO THE SHIP. The happiness and optimism of just a few hours ago was long gone. To Bert and Ernie, it had been washed away in a downpour of doubt. They were the only ones who awaited me in the galley. We had a lot to talk about, but first they wanted to show me some things on their tablet. It too was linked up to the satellite.

Mary had done her job brilliantly—as always. News shows from around the world breathlessly told of the lockdown on the island and of the big announcement to come tomorrow. Even late-night television host Steven Myers did his monologue about Volavo.

"So in case you live under a rock, the whole world is talking about the tiny Pacific island of Volavo. And speaking of rocks, they happen to have the only rocks that can power the whole world, and wait a minute. If that's not enough, the people there pray to a god they call John Frum who's supposed to come on February 15th and bring them a bunch of cargo. No, no, really. Calm down, everybody. The Reverend Gramm is very upset about this. Rumor is he was planning to open a bathhouse on the island. But seriously, this John Frum thing is not that crazy. One delusional guy is called a lunatic. A hundred delusional people are a cult, and a million delusional people . . . Well, in L.A. we just call them Raider fans. We'll be right back . . ."

"Barnwell hasn't called yet," said Bert, "but it's a pretty safe bet that he's seen all of this and more."

Ernie was beside himself. They both agreed that the agent and the lockdown were good ideas to keep control of the situation, but they seemed disappointed that I had not spoken to them first.

On some level, they were right. After all, we were a team, and this is exactly the kind of thing that they were sent on this mission for, but in the big picture, it was the best thing to do, and the minister may not have agreed to it if Bert and Ernie had pitched it instead of me.

"So where does that leave us?" asked Bert.

I explained that I still thought the minister would go for the deal, and that was the truth. He had been buying time since we got here, and this really wasn't that different or out of character for him. I didn't want Bert and Ernie to be blindsided, so I told them about Hannah Cronkite and her crew being given exclusive access. They would know soon enough anyway.

That information seemed to put them at ease a little, but it felt like the relationship had changed between the two lawyers and me. Maybe it was just in my head. Maybe it was everything the minister had told me, but one thing was for sure. They would be watching. So would Smith and Wesson. And of course, watching all of us was Barnwell.

Barnwell at that moment was talking to Smith and Wesson, who were in their cabin. Not surprisingly, they had sound-proofed the cabin for just such an occasion as this. Bert and Ernie had dutifully told Smith and Wesson of the events at the minister's house. They, of course, passed it along to Barnwell, who already knew everything else. Barnwell, through his contacts in the media, even knew that Hannah Cronkite was being permitted to visit the otherwise locked down island.

"Okay, gentlemen, it is just about showtime. This is where we all justify our big fat paychecks. Consider this as a mission summary, reset, and action plan." This was language Smith and Wesson understood.

"Let's start with this. There will be a public announcement tomorrow at noon. A single reporter who is being permitted on the island will carry it live. Everything I know about this minister guy tells me that he won't sign until after they have made the announcement tomorrow. He is no dummy, especially now that the word is out. He's going to try to buy as much time as he can. I wouldn't be surprised if he tried to weasel a few extra percentage points out of us, but that is the least of our worries. Our biggest problem is Frum."

"Frum, sir?" asked Wesson.

"Yes," said Barnwell. "We know a lot about him—dead parents, no close family, no serious relationships past or present. He has no bad habits, no drugs, and no unsavory sexual appetites. He's so clean that it almost makes him even more of a weirdo. Everybody I've ever seen has something to work worth but not him, not a single skeleton in his closet. Even worse, he has plenty of money, and I can't even find where he spends any of it."

Smith responded. "Frum has performed in the exact manner outlined in the original mission plan."

Wesson continued. "We have observed and noted minimal areas of concern in regards to his relations with the locals, but all of his actions are justifiable within the parameters of mission objectives."

Their point was that I was supposed to get close to the locals and make them like me. Once it was clear that they were not accepting me as God, at least they would see me as their friend, but Barnwell wasn't buying it.

"Yeah, does that include playing kissy-face with the minister's daughter? How am I supposed to know where his acting stops and his hard-on begins? I do not have that luxury, gentleman. I cannot afford to stake the future of this company on the whims of an out-of-work sitcom actor.

"He will almost certainly be making the announcement tomorrow, and here is the bottom line. If he says anything other than we have a deal with Womansanto, you two are going to blow his head off."

Smith responded. "Well first of all, sir, considering our firing position aboard the vessel, it would be inadvisable to attempt to target a head shot. It would be a much lower percentage kill from that angle."

Barnwell interrupted. "Cut the crap. Head, chest, I don't give a shit. Just kill him."

Smith and Wesson remained silent. Barnwell correctly assumed that their silence meant respectful disagreement.

"C'mon, fellas. I've seen your dossiers. You can't possibly have a problem with this. That's the reason we hired you."

"It's not that we have a problem with it, sir," said Wesson. "We just don't see how it would further the objectives of this mission."

Barnwell was quick with an answer. "First of all, that's none of your fuckin' business. That is also why we hired you, because you know the difference between what is and what is not your business, but since you asked, and it shows you have an interest in the success of this mission, I will explain it to you.

"If the minister has any ideas of fucking us over, I promise you he will change his mind when he looks down at the corpse of the great John Frum. I also promise you he will be begging to sign before he even washes Frum's blood off his face and hands. Does that sufficiently serve the mission objective, gentlemen?"

The soldiers, Smith and Wesson, did not answer. There was no need.

17

EITHER/OR

John, or maybe I should start calling him Joe, had returned to the ship. My father was no longer in the mood to talk and retreated upstairs to his bedroom. He stopped along the way up the staircase to look at each photo of my mother that lined the stairway. He had a lot to think about.

John—I have decided to keep calling him John—returned in the afternoon. He came in and joined Kavu and me in the living room. We continued watching news broadcasts from around the world. The stage was certainly set, both literally and figuratively. News of the lockdown and tomorrow's announcement had indeed spread around the world in minutes.

On the island, preparations for John Frum Day had kicked into high gear. Every villager was busily readying costumes. Workmen were setting up for the ceremony in the port. There would be a stage adjacent to John's ship for the announcement.

AFTER A WHILE, all the news reports blurred together. Finally, Kavu suggested that we go have a meal. We had agreed that we would go together to meet Hannah Cronkite and her crew at the airstrip, but we still had a couple of hours to kill before she was scheduled to arrive.

We walked over to Siskos and got an out-of-the-way table where we could talk without fear of being overheard. Along the way, at least a dozen islanders approached us. They all said the same thing to John— "Thank you."

When we were finally seated, John asked us why the people were thanking him since he hadn't actually done anything, unless you count walking, jumping, and kava-drinking. Kavu and I didn't know either, but I told him that they were probably thanking him for what he would do, rather than what he had already done. After all, the islanders had televisions too. Many had computers as well. They knew what was going on and what was going to happen tomorrow.

The conversation soon turned to my father and what his decision might be.

I said, "The problem is that the choice was framed as an either-or situation. Either we agree to the terms laid out by Womansanto, or we risk chaos or worse."

John agreed. "What your father said about Womansanto in the future was also true, and it's a valid concern. Womansanto would take ninety percent of the proceeds from the sale of corbomite, and they alone would set the price. The problem isn't that ten percent is not enough for Volavo. That ten percent would probably be enough to buy every Bohlin a new mansion every year. It would be more than enough.

"The real problem is that over time, Womansanto would accrue unheard of wealth and power, and like any corporation, they would have no choice but to use it. Whether it's Barnwell or some future CEO, if they can make even more by gouging the world, they will. They must. They owe it their sharehold-ers. If they can make even more by crushing the Bohlin people and culture, they will. They must. They owe it to their shareholders. And if Barnwell refuses, not that he would, he would be gone, fired. If the next CEO refuses, he would be gone, fired.

"A corporation cannot act morally. By definition, it is always a hungry animal and will always behave as such, and it will, sooner or later, devour us. So it becomes a choice between the beast that will eat us tomorrow or the one that will eat us eventually."

Kavu had sat quietly and listened as John and I spoke. Finally he said, "I have a question. Why exactly do we think that an agreement with Womansanto will protect us? How does it stop any country out there from sending an occupying force to the island? In other words, why can't they just attack us anyway, and take what they want, agreement or not?"

John thought for a moment before he answered. "It doesn't really completely protect us. A rogue country could still act against us, but what the agreement does do is to make an attack instantly illegal according to international law, which means almost every country on earth could and would act against the invader. The agreement protects us only psychologically but powerfully. It forces any country that might harm us to be afraid that every other country would harm them."

Kavu had listened intently and seemed to be deep in thought before he spoke, but it was almost as if he were talking to himself. "Okay, so the agreement protects us by making them afraid of each other. Looking at it another way, it's in everyone's best interest to protect Volavo's best interest."

Kavu's voice was barely audible, like he was trying to work something out in his head.

"I have another question," he said louder and with confidence. "Is there any other way to make every country *want* to protect us?"

I started to see where he was going with this. If the agreement with Womansanto protects Volavo because it is in every country's own best interest, is there any other way to achieve the same result?

Seconds passed as we all sat, each of us thinking about what we had just heard. Finally, John and I both mumbled something at virtually the same time.

"Give it away."

Kavu 's face lit up. "That's it! We can give it away!"

John said, "Hold on! Hold on! Let's think about this for a second. What exactly would happen if we just gave corbomite away? There's plenty for everyone, right?"

I said, "Yes, enough for hundreds of years."

Kavu said, "Okay then. No one would dare touch us if we were giving it away. It's even better than the agreement!"

John said, "True . . . but wait a second. We can't give it away."

The mood at the table had become nothing short of jubilant until John said that. Then we all looked like a seven-year-old who had just dropped his ice cream cone.

"Why the hell not?" I asked.

"Like it or not," John said, "Womansanto did invent the process to harness the power of corbomite and absolutely deserves to profit from it even though the process is not patentable. What's more, we would be failing to serve the Bohlin people if we earned nothing for them from this bounty."

We spent the next hour working out the details and overcoming each other's objections. But that's not too bad, right? An hour to change the world? I'm pretty sure it took more than an hour to invent the wheel.

We came up with the plan to present to my father. John would announce to the world that we would be giving corbomite away to the whoever wanted it in whatever amounts as long as it was for their own use, but it wasn't completely free. Each country would be expected but not required to pay tribute to Volavo each year on or before John Frum Day, February 15th.

Each country could decide how much to pay each year. It was completely voluntary, and the amount was at their discretion, and since we are the Bohlin, we would accept the payment either in currency or as cargo delivered directly to the Bohlin people on John Frum Day.

We did not forget Womansanto. Each nation would be expected to pay directly to Womansanto ten percent of the value of what they gave Volavo. Why would Womansanto accept this? Womansanto would have to accept it because the entire world would instantly agree to these terms. Womansanto would have no allies anywhere in a legal fight for more, and as John said, "Ten percent of something is a whole lot more than a hundred percent of nothing."

It is hard to describe the excitement we felt. It was as if we had all drunk ten shells of kava. Together we had found another way. We all thought the plan was airtight and perfect, but it would mean nothing unless my father agreed.

We couldn't wait to bring him the plan, but we would have to wait. It was almost time to meet Hannah Cronkite at the airstrip.

We walked back to the house where there were three jeeps waiting for us to drive out to the airfield. If we each drove one, we would have enough room for Hannah, her crew, and their equipment. Kavu took the lead jeep, and I jumped into the second one. John would follow in the third.

I had made sure that he got the one with *The King and I* in the eight-track player. It was just getting dark as we made our way out to the airstrip. As we approached, we saw the plane fly into sight. It was tiny and hardly seemed large enough for the passengers and the equipment. We pulled up as it was landing.

Hannah popped out of the front passenger seat. She looked like an American TV news reporter straight out of central casting. She was thin, blonde, and high cheek-boned. She was very fit, in her late thirties, and dressed in jeans and a massive camouflage jacket atop a black T-shirt. She walked directly over to us as her crew got out and started unloading their equipment.

"Hi, I'm Hannah Cronkite. You must be this god Frum guy that has Jerry Gramm all worked up."

"That's me," said John. "Let me introduce you to Qat and Kavu. They are the children of and advisors to the prime minister of this island."

We all shook hands with Hannah. Like the good reporter she was, the first thing she asked was to interview John. He politely declined.

We laid out the ground rules for her: She may speak to anyone who will speak to her. She may record any video she likes, but nothing may be broadcast until after the announcement tomorrow. She accepted the terms as reasonable and thanked us for the opportunity.

I made clear that the reason for her exclusive access was that she alone cover the announcement. I would meet up with her in the morning to make sure she had everything she needed for the satellite link. I would also make sure she had a secure position in front of the stage for the announcement.

Hannah said, "I don't suppose anybody wants to tell me who's making the announcement and what the revelation is going to be. Every talking head on the planet is speculating, but as usual, they don't know shit."

The three of us just shook our heads and smiled. We were all still giddy about our plan, which we had yet to present to the minister.

"I will make the announcement tomorrow at the request of the minister," said John, "but only the minister knows what the announcement will be. We will all find out together tomorrow."

"Okay," said Hannah, "I guess that's it, then. I hope you all understand that I have to at least ask. That's my job."

We all assured her that we understood.

By this time, her crew had taken all their gear from the plane and loaded it into the three jeeps. The pilot had sealed the doors, turned the plane around, and took off for his return to Auckland. Hannah introduced her crew.

They were a grizzled, middle-aged group of men consisting of a sound guy, a cameraman, and a spotter. The four of them together were the classic foreign correspondent team and had worked together for more than a decade. They had covered events large and small the world over, and even they seemed to share our sense of excitement at what was going to happen on Volavo.

I was a little surprised when Hannah jumped into the jeep next to me, leaving her crew to split up with John and Kavu for the drive to the hotel. She seemed to notice my reaction and confessed that she thought she could learn more about John Frum from me than she could from John himself.

"He looks familiar," Hannah said. "I feel like I know him from somewhere."

It turns out that Mary hadn't told Hannah anything other than she would get exclusive access to Volavo, but I didn't think any harm could come from telling her that he was Joe Fray from *Friends Without Benefits*. She reacted with an "Aha" look on her face and said, "I knew it!"

She told me that the world didn't know who he was yet and that there had been millions of searches on the internet for "John Frum," "cargo cult," and "Volavo." They were far and away the most popular searches over the last twenty-four hours. It seemed the whole world was learning about our little island.

Hannah seemed perplexed. "Wait a second," she said. "If you know that he is not the cargo-cult god, John Frum, then why is he making the announcement? Why is he still walking around in that uniform?"

Before I answered her, I reminded her that whatever she might learn between now and tomorrow was off the record until after the announcement. She again quickly agreed, so I told her a little about the last five days and that we had figured out early on who he actually was. I told her that my father had also used this time to gather information he would need to make this most important decision, and that in the process, John had proven himself as a friend to the island and the Bohlin people, regardless of the circumstances of his arrival. I also explained to her that when it came to religion, the Bohlin people held beliefs that were much wider than they were deep. The belief in the god, John Frum, was more like a pastime and a fun one at that. Besides, if one is inclined to take religion seriously, who's to say that Joe Fray was not sent here by the hand of God during a time of great peril and promise?

By now we had pulled up in front of the hotel. The men had unloaded the gear and left us alone as we spoke.

"Wow," said Hannah, "it makes me wish I had been here for the last five days. I'll bet it would make for a great book."

I laughed and said, "Yeah, I guess it would. I just hope it has a happy ending." John was approaching, so I quickly added, almost whispering, "Oh, and he is wearing the uniform because he didn't bring any other clothes."

Hannah and I shared a laugh as John got to the jeep and looked at us quizzically before speaking. "You are all checked in, and your equipment is safely stored, courtesy of Minister Karbina. I hope you enjoyed your ride across the island," John said with an exaggerated formality that betrayed his suspicions about what was discussed on the ride over.

Hannah responded with a wry smile. "Oh yes, very much, thank you."

Kavu had now joined us too. We said goodnight to Hannah and her crew and told them we'd see them in the morning. We were still eager to talk to my father.

The hotel was across the street and a couple of buildings

down from our home, so we simply left the jeeps where they were parked and walked together back to the house. John, Kavu, and I entered to find my father seated in the living room, flipping through the channels on the satellite. He looked weary and bone-tired. He was being truthful when he had said the weight of his decision had robbed him of sleep.

The only time I could ever remember seeing him this way was when I had first returned from America after the death of my mother. In those early, dark days, I would find him awake in the middle of the night. I would be awakened from the creaking of the steps as he walked from one photograph to another on the stairway. Often Kavu would wake as well, and the three of us would sit together and watch American television until the sun rose.

FATHER GREETED us as we entered and gestured for us to sit. He pointed to the TV and said, "Look, children, everything is going to plan. Now if we only actually had a plan . . ."

All three of us started speaking at once, and the words came out as if our grand plan was the hastily babbled excuse of children explaining a broken window to their mother. My father raised his hands and said, "Okay, okay. Calm down. When all speak, no one listens."

He pointed at me. "You! Tell me what's going on." He looked at Kavu and John. "You two, shush!" he said, bringing his index finger to his lips.

I quickly composed myself and said, "Father, we have an idea, one that we think will enrich both Volavo and the world while also keeping us safe. What if we announced that we are giving the mineral away?"

My father first frowned, and then his lips curled into a soft smile. Again, we all began to talk at once, and again, my father raised his hands to quiet us. Kavu spoke, laying out our reasoning in a very calm and lucid manner.

"If the deal with Womansanto would protect the island, at least for a time, then our plan would protect us even more and quite possibly forever." He provided my father with the details we had already discussed. "All of the world's powers, great and small, would have the same vested interest in our safety and protection."

When Kavu was finished, my father sat lost in thought for more than a minute. Finally, he had a question. "What of Womansanto? Why would they accept this arrangement?"

John answered, eager to allay my father's doubts. "Womansanto will agree for much the same reason as the rest of the world, pressure from everyone else. It will be in everyone's best interest, and they will have no choice but to go along. They won't be completely left out. I have no doubt that the people of the world will be generous with Volavo far beyond our needs. What they choose to pay Womansanto each year will still be a very large amount, and that money will eventually come to be seen by Womansanto's shareholders as a yearly bounty that costs them nothing to earn. They would not dare challenge it."

When talking about Volavo, John's reference to "our needs" was not lost on any of us, and my father was not afraid to address it.

"You speak as one of us, and I am proud that you do. I cannot yet find any flaws in your reasoning, but that does not guarantee that I will not discover any as I deliberate further. If I have served this island well, it is because I am slow to judgment. I think we can all agree that this decision deserves at least that much, but know this right now. My heart swells with pride for all three of you, no matter what is decided, no matter what the outcome."

I don't know why, but I had begun to cry quietly as my

father spoke. Smiling tenderly, he got up and hugged me. "You . . . you are the strongest of us all."

He looked at the boys and said, "None of us can know what tomorrow will bring. We may never be all together again. Please remember this moment and your part in God's grand plan, whatever it may be. As for our plan, I will make my decision in the morning."

He turned to John. "Come to me in the morning, early, just after the sun rises. We will talk then, but for now, I must be alone."

As usual, my father was right. We would not be together again, at least not before the announcement. I would be coordinating with Hannah. Kavu would be overseeing the final preparations of the stage in the port. John and the minister would meet in the morning to coordinate their speeches. A part of me did not want this moment to end. We sat perched above a moment in history. If only we could freeze a moment in time . . .

18

LOVE?

I didn't want that moment to end either, but end it did. Both the minister and Kavu had gone upstairs to their rooms for the evening, leaving Qat and me alone in the living room. We did not speak for quite some time. The silence was broken only by the sound of the TV.

There was a feed from Chinese state television, in Chinese of course, with dubious English subtitles. The first thing I noticed was the breathtaking and casual racism, at least by Western standards. The Chinese government had, in fact, sent an aircraft carrier. Actually, they had sent an aircraft carrier, two destroyers, and half a dozen gunships, all of which were now fifty miles off the coast of Volavo. This, they claimed, was to make sure that the "Brownies" (presumably the Bohlin) did not cheat the Chinese people out their rightful share of the bounty of energy that was present on the island. Of course, they weren't the only ones to send ships. The United States, Russia, France, Great Britain, and at least half a dozen other nations already had ships offshore. It had to be getting pretty crowded out there, and there were more on the way.

Qat had been sitting in one of the chairs, only somewhat

watching the news reports but mostly just lost in thought. Finally she got up and sat next to me on the couch. She curled up next to me and rested her head on my shoulder. I put an arm around her, still without a word spoken. It wasn't long before it seemed as if she were asleep.

I flipped through the channels on the satellite. It was still all Volavo, all the time. After a while, my own eyes started to feel heavy, so I gave her a gentle nudge and said, "Hey, Qat. Wanna see my gunship?"

Still half asleep, she smiled and said, "I thought you'd never ask".

We walked hand in hand back to the ship and up the gangway. I was past the point of caring whether my shipmates saw Qat or what they might think. As it turns out, Smith and Wesson were no longer watching. There was nothing more for them to learn.

I didn't offer her a tour of the ship, and she didn't ask for one. We passed through the empty galley, which was barely illuminated by a single bulb over a small table and chairs. Outside my cabin were two clean, pressed, and neatly folded uniforms. No doubt the work of my helpful angels Smith and Wesson.

My cabin had been constructed specifically for this mission. It was small but neat and functional. I myself have never been particularly tidy, but I hadn't spent more than a few minutes at a time in my cabin unless I had been sleeping. I had no opportunity to cause clutter or make a mess. It had no toilet, but it had a fairly large shower enclosure, a closet, and a bed that was custom-built with a mattress just a little bit bigger than a twin.

"Not too shabby for a seventy-five-year-old," I said, referring to the ship.

"No, not too bad at all. You don't look a day over sixty," she said with a wry smile.

"That's about how old I feel," I said as I closed the cabin door.

I turned and looked at her in her pale blue, cotton dress, standing in front of me, her eyes bright in the dim light of the cabin. For the first time, she seemed small, yet she had been my fierce protector since the moment I had arrived. Now I realized that I wanted nothing more than to protect her. I wanted her to feel my body around hers, and I wanted to feel her body on mine. I wrapped my arms around her. I didn't kiss her. Instead, I put my lips to her ear.

It was Qat who turned her head and placed her lips on mine. She held me with a strength I had never known. I held her as tight as I dared, feeling the warmth of her body against mine.

Soon she moved her lips to my ear. "Do you want to have sex?" she whispered, but I could feel her smile against my skin. It wasn't a teasing voice, but she knew as I did that it was still not yet our time.

She plopped down on the bed, kicked off her shoes, and lay down, pulling the blanket over her. I quickly shed my uniform and wedged myself behind her in the small bed, sharing the pillow. Again, our bodies were pressed together with my hand on her hip. There wasn't a sound in the cabin, and I thought for a moment that she might have already fallen asleep. Then she turned her head slightly and said, "I can never tell you I love you."

I was about to ask her what she meant when she continued. "Everyone in America hunts love as if it were a beast with magical powers. They see movies, and then the moment their loins stir, they think they are in love. They harm each other in the name of love in ways they would never, ever think of harming a stranger."

I was quiet for a moment. "I thought you were asleep, not

deliberating the nature of love, but I think I know what you mean. Love is sometimes just a word."

She didn't reply, so I continued. "Please forgive me, but it is a word I have to say because I can't be sure I will ever have another chance. I do love you. I love you."

She lay quietly in my arms, and it wasn't long before her even breathing told me she was asleep. It was not long before I, too, was asleep.

I awoke, alone, to the first rays of the morning sun shining through my cabin window. I knew I was expected at the minister's home, but I halfway sleepwalked through a shower and getting dressed in my uniform. In spite of everything that would happen today, my thoughts were of the words Qat had said the night before.

I think I understood what we she was trying to say. I knew how she felt about me, and I definitely knew that I wanted her, even loved her. In spite of my feelings, the word "love" felt shallow and hollow. Real love is sharing a life. Real love is knowing and caring for another person as you would yourself. Real love is walking the stairs of your home in the middle of the night just to look at pictures of the love you lost too soon.

No, love is not a word. It is a life, or it is nothing. I finished getting dressed and forced myself to put those thoughts aside.

There was a knock on my cabin door. It was Wesson. He and his partner had never looked particularly happy, but at this moment, he looked especially dour. He said simply, "John, please come with me."

I could tell from his face that this was not a simple request. Looking back at this moment, I probably should have been scared, but I wasn't. I figured they probably knew that Qat had stayed on the ship and might have something to say about it, but it didn't occur to me, at least not yet, that they could hurt me.

Wesson led me to the cabin he shared with Smith and

opened the door. Smith was inside, and I heard him say, "Here he is, sir."

I saw a large monitor set up on a table with a webcam. Smith ushered me over to a chair in front of the screen. As I sat down, Smith and Wesson left the cabin and closed the door behind them.

On the screen in front of me was Grant Barnwell, sitting behind an impressive desk. He loomed large on the screen, so large that almost no background was visible. Seconds passed as I waited for him to speak.

"Good morning, Mr. Frum. It is indeed my great pleasure to finally meet you. Please forgive me for not introducing myself. I am Grant Barnwell. Do you know who I am?"

I said nothing but nodded instead.

He saw my acknowledgement, smiled, and continued. "I can see why you were cast for this role. You really do look the part . . . amazing. Anyway, I am sure you wouldn't be surprised to learn that I have been following your exploits with some interest, and quite frankly, I could not be more impressed. What a performance! Too bad there is no Oscar for best actor in the role of a false god. I always thought you were pretty good on *Friends Without Benefits,* but wow! You really pulled this off."

I interrupted him. "I haven't pulled anything off. The islanders don't believe that I am John Frum, the god."

He brushed it aside. "Nonsense," he said. "That hardly matters. The legend of John Frum is alive and well. Have you been watching television, John? The cargo-cult god, John Frum, is now known throughout the world, and that's all thanks to you! When this is all over, you can probably restart your acting career, and I can help you with that. I know people in Hollywood and all over the world. I sit on the board of directors for three streaming services. I can open doors for you that you didn't even know were doors. The sky is the limit!

"So speaking of when this is over, John, tell me. Where are we at? When will the minister sign?"

I am definitely not the best actor in the world, but one thing I do know is when the bright lights come on, and they were certainly on now. This was showtime.

"I don't know," I said. "The minister has not shared with me what his decision will be."

Barnwell was silent for a few moments as if he were pondering tactics or what to say next. "C'mon, John, you've spent five days on that island. I sent you there specifically to influence the minister's decision. You can't honestly tell me you don't know what he will do."

I interrupted him again. "You didn't send me here," I said. "I was hired by Geur and Cheiro."

His response betrayed the first signs of anger. "They work for me!" Barnwell said tersely.

"Well then, maybe you should ask them!" I replied.

Again there was silence. He glared at me on the screen as if his gaze could bend me to his will across the thousands of miles between us.

"Now you listen to me, you sack of shit stuffed into a fake uniform! You will get those papers signed, and you will do it before this big fuckin' announcement to the world—"

I interrupted him once more. "That is not within my power. The elected minister of this island, not me, will make the decision. I came here and completed my mission. What happens now is up to him, not me."

Barnwell just glared, and then, ignoring my last response said, "You will get the agreement signed, and I will tell you why. I know you, Joe Fray, and I know you will never work again unless I say so. I know you don't give two shits about money, but I bet you give a shit about your family in Queens and your family in Switzerland or Sweden or wherever the fuck they are. I also know about this little island whore you've been dicking around with since you got there. So you will do exactly as I fuckin' tell you to! Understood?"

I'm not going to lie. I was a bit intimidated. After all, here was one of the world's most powerful men threatening me. But I had met men like him before. I had met studio executives who could offer a carrot and stick with the best of them. It was true that none of them had quite the power of Barnwell, but I had seen the tactic before . . . if it was, in fact, a tactic.

Part of Barnwell's strategy was intended to intimidate, but it was also meant to enrage me in a way that would leave me feeling powerless and paralyzed. Sorry, no dice. To be honest, if he had spoken about Qat that way in my presence, I would have happily pounded his face in for him.

I let him wait for a response. I sat looking at him, and I tried putting on my best demoralized face. I wanted him to believe, if only for a moment, that he had pounded me into submission. "So tell me something, Grant. This whole charming psychopath act . . . That normally works for you, does it?"

He was a formidable man, and if he was surprised by my reply, he would not permit his face to reveal it. "It is not an act, and you would be wise to remember that before you open your mouth again," he said ominously.

"Okay, okay. I got it," I said. "Then how about this, then? How about . . . if you . . . go fuck yourself!" I gave him no chance to respond. I quickly stood up and walked out of his sight and out of the cabin.

I found Smith and Wesson sitting in the galley with Bert and Ernie. I gave them a small smile as I walked past. I looked at Wesson and said, "That went well" and nodded my head vigorously. I didn't give anyone time respond and quickly went above deck and down the gangway. I was running late to meet the minister.

The normally quiet port was a flurry of activity. There was not yet any sign of Qat, Kavu, or Hannah and her crew. A low, wooden platform was set up as a stage with the back of it running almost parallel to our ship. Actually, it wasn't set up as much as it had been rolled into position. It looked old and creaky, and it already had a microphone and lectern in place. Behind the microphone were nine chairs set up in a semicircle. No doubt it was the seating for the nine elders and their goon'do. Hundreds of folding chairs were being placed in front of the stage, and U.S. and Volavo flags were everywhere.

The port was already full of islanders. Some were working on the setup, and others seemed to be getting an early start on today's celebration. Many wore native costumes, but more were dressed in makeshift American military uniforms of every variety. It seemed that everyone noticed me as I walked through the port on my way to the minister's home, but no one bothered me. One after another, they would simply walk over to me and say, "Thank you, John Frum." I wanted to ask them what they were thanking me for, but there was no time.

No guard was stationed in front of the minister's house, so I just walked to the front door and knocked. There was no answer, so I knocked again and then a third time. Still there was no answer, so finally I slowly opened the door. I leaned in and called, "Hello?"

I could hear the television. I looked over and saw the minister sitting in his chair, alone, his eyes glued to the television. He finally noticed me and wordlessly waved me over to the couch to join him.

"The U.S. is going to invade us," he said and pointed to the TV. I had seen a similar report the night before. Apparently, the American president had asked his military advisers to draw up plans for a bloodless invasion of the island, as if such a thing were possible.

"They say it would be to protect us," said the minister, "but many of our neighbors will tell you that their protection comes at a steep price, and is impossible to refuse."

He was referring to centuries of colonialism that many of the neighboring islands had been subjected to, colonialism that Volavo had so far avoided.

I spoke to encourage him. "That is why we are here, Minister, to find a better way."

He turned his attention to me and saw my concern. "Of course, John. Do not worry. I have not given up hope. I am simply learning as much as I can for as long as I can about the challenges we face, but we are almost out of time."

"Have you made a decision?"

He thought for a moment before answering.

"I must answer your question with a question. How much danger are you in if we deny Womansanto their bounty?"

I chuckled to myself. As always, this man was way ahead of me. Obviously, he had no way of knowing of my confrontation with Barnwell. He was simply a master of acquiring and assimilating every morsel of information at his disposal, truly a born leader. He did not know Barnwell, but he knew that Womansanto was a dangerous animal, and right now it was a danger to me.

I looked at him reverentially, the same way I can still remember looking at my father years ago. "I am not tired of living," I said, "nor am I eager to give up my life, but if I had to choose a cause worthy of that sacrifice, this would be it."

"Then we will find a way to give this gift to the world and also to keep you from the grave," said the minister. "As we both know, you have much to live for. My daughter is the most beautiful of souls, and she has chosen you. She is in love with you— or whatever you people call it."

I smiled, and of course he noticed.

"Good. You will not bother to deny it, nor should you deny your love for her. It is more obvious than the sun in the sky. My daughter gave up her dreams of America out of a daughter's love for her selfish father. It is only right that her love for you should rekindle that dream.

"Did you think I did not know how of her desire to stay in America? She came home to protect a broken man who could not serve his people without the help of both his son and his daughter."

The minister was a brave and noble man, and it occurred to me that it was indeed part of his strength that he knew when he was weak, when he needed help. That same strength enabled him to accept my help, and it made me able to have the utmost trust in his judgment.

Together we crafted the speech I would deliver. We agreed that he would introduce me, and then I would walk down the gangway of the ship and join him and the elders on the stage. The details of the speech would be almost word for word what Qat, Kavu, and I had cooked up the night before. We had decided that corbomite would indeed be given as a gift to the world from the Bohlin people. Each nation of the world could have as much as they need as long as it was for their own use. Corbomite could not be sold or traded. The Bohlin people would accept tribute from any and all of the grateful nations of the world, and tribute could take the form of cash or merchandise, which we of course refer to as cargo. Tribute payments were to be made each year either on or before February 15th. The Bohlin people would be grateful if the nations of the world came together to designate February 15th as John Frum Day to commemorate the day on which the world gained energy independence. I would say that Womansanto Corporation had graciously offered to share their method for processing corbomite with the nations of the world, and they had also offered to mine the corbomite from our volcanic caves on Volavo. The Bohlin people would ask that the nations of the world offer voluntary cash tribute to the Womansanto Corporation each year to offset their costs and demonstrate appreciation for their efforts and scientific prowess. We would ask that the tribute equal at least ten percent of what would be offered to the Bohlin people each year.

I am an actor not a writer, but I wrote most of the speech. The minister was only concerned that we get to the point quickly in case anything went wrong. We both also understood just how short the world's attention span was. It was actually his idea that the speech go out as a press release to the world as it was being delivered. That way, no matter what may happen on the island, the word would get out to the world. There would be no turning back.

For the press release, we would need Mary, and God bless her, she was true to her word and answered on the first ring.

"Talk to me, Joe," she said when she answered the phone.

There was no playfulness in her tone, no kidding around, and no calling me Joey Toots. Just as we had, Mary had watched the explosion of news reports around the world. She knew that close to a hundred ships of war sat in every direction just off our shores. She knew that what happened here in the next couple of hours would alter the course of history—for better or worse. Mary was all business, and I felt incredibly lucky and grateful to have her on our side.

"Okay, Joe, lay it on me. What are you going to do, and how can I help?" she asked. She didn't wait for me to answer. Instead, she said, "Oh, before I forget, I think you should know Hannah is broadcasting from the island."

The minister and I looked at each other with surprise. We had not seen anything on the satellite, but it made sense. It was probably only on *Triple N*.

"Any decent journalist would do the same thing," said Mary.

The minister replied, "I'm not shocked or worried by what you say. I understand that this is a story too big and too tempting for any reporter to resist."

Mary and I both agreed. No journalist worth a shit could be expected to sit on a story like this, and there really wasn't anything Hannah could reveal that could harm anything. In fact, it was probably a good thing. Even Mary said that it was almost certainly a positive. Hannah was doing interviews with islanders and showing off the beauty of the island. The more the world got to know Volavo and its people, the better off we were. When it comes to PR, it's always better to define yourself before someone else does it for you. Now the world would know us for the people we are and not the backward savages the blithering former Reverend Jerry Gramm imagined us to be.

Since we hadn't seen the coverage, Mary recounted for us what she had seen. So far, Hannah's newscasts had indeed been flattering. The island looked like a travel brochure, pristine, beautiful, and unspoiled, except for the volcano, which had none of the majesty she imagined. It resembled, in her words, "a giant black pimple."

The islanders interviewed by Hannah spoke nearly perfect English and were eloquent with a wicked sense of humor. The minister told Mary that it sounded like a fair representation of the island and the Bohlin.

"What I don't understand," said Mary, "is how virtually no one ever heard of the place before this. How are you not overrun with tourists?"

The minister answered. "We welcome tourists, but we don't exactly encourage tourism. Ours is a small island, and we already have everything we need. We don't mind sharing our island with some tourists, but we don't need tourism."

"That makes sense," Mary said. "You get the benefits without losing your identity.

"Oh, and Joe, one question. Did you by some chance make the volcano erupt?"

The minister and I looked at each other, puzzled. "Um, no," I said, "but I did walk up to the top of it."

"Well, the islanders think you did. Apparently, you made the mountain shake, among other magical deeds. They also said that you were the one who put the corbomite in the caves, cured people of the clap, and the dog gods talked to you."

"Well, I did talk to the dogs, but as far as I know, they didn't talk back. Seriously, Mary, I don't think the islanders actually believe this stuff. I think they are just having fun."

"Maybe so, Joe," said Mary, now completely serious. "But this is how legends . . . and religions are made, and it usually doesn't end well for the prophet. Anyway, tell me, gentlemen, what exactly do you have in mind here?"

I started out by first explaining to her what Womansanto had been so eager to offer. Basically they would pay all the costs of the mining, and they would oversee all the sales. Most importantly, they would set the price and receive ninety percent of the proceeds.

Mary listened and then paused for a few moments before speaking. "That's not terrible. Don't get me wrong. It's bad, but it's not awful. It is a whole lot better than having the Russians or Chinese come and shoot the place up, but that's not actually what we are doing, is it? I have a feeling you guys have cooked up your own plan. Okay, out with it!"

I spent the next ten minutes or so going over our announcement, word for word. We could hear her on the other end, typing furiously as she listened, taking notes so she could prepare the press release.

She started laughing when we got to the part about designating February 15th a worldwide holiday. She interrupted me to say, "You know? The funny part is that if this fakakta thing works, the world will probably do it. Maybe we should call it Joe Fray Day or Joey Toots Day, or is your ego not that big?"

"Are you done?" I said with exaggerated impatience. "You know, we don't have a hell of a lot of time here."

"Sorry, sorry. Go ahead," she said, still laughing quietly.

When I had finished going over the plan, there was a long pause. We could still hear Mary typing over the speakerphone. Finally, the typing on the other end stopped.

"Okay," she said. "Let me see if I understand this. Corbomite is free to any country that wants it . . . and believe me, everybody will want it. They can choose to pay whatever they want every year on or around Joe Fray Day—sorry, couldn't help myself—John Frum Day. Countries will give ten percent of that directly to Womansanto because they will do the actual mining, and they were the ones who came up with the method of turning these rocks into juice. Does that about sum it up?"

"Yes, that's about it" I said.

"I like it," said Mary. "Womansanto is not going to like it, at least not at first. However, once you announce it, I don't see how they'll have any choice but to go along. They aren't stupid. Ten percent will still be massive, even for them.

"On the news today, they were saying that the projections are that within five years, corbomite energy could replace two trillion dollars worth of fossil fuel costs worldwide every year.

"Hold on a second. Let me do some quick math. Yeah, that's what I thought. Even if the world is stingy with you guys, you're still probably looking at a couple of billion a year for Volavo and at least a couple of hundred million for Womansanto. That's not chump change even for them, but honestly, Joe, the brilliant part of this is that every country will see how it is in their best interest to protect Volavo and just leave you alone.

"It's like you've invited the whole world to a dinner party, and all they have to do is bring a chocolate babka. Whoever came up with this should probably get a medal or something."

The minister interrupted. "My children thought of it," he said proudly, "all three of them."

"Okay, guys," said Mary, "you know me, so you know I am going to go over this one more time. It's too important to risk screwing anything up. Besides, I have to justify the massive bill I am going to be sending you when this is all over."

The minister laughed and said, "If this works, I am pretty sure we can afford you . . . and Mary, please accept my thanks. I cannot help but feel as if you and John were sent to us by the hand of God."

"Thank you, Minister," said Mary. "I am not a religious person, but I will take all the grace I can get."

Before we hung up with Mary, we agreed that she would craft the final wording of the press release and have it ready in about half an hour. She would call the minister back for its final approval. Then she would watch our speech and release the announcement to the world at the precise moment I began speaking.

I said goodbye to the minister and made my way back to the ship. The next time I saw the minister, he would be introducing me on stage. All that was left to do was to find my "helpful angels," Smith and Wesson.

19

GETTING TO KNOW YOU, PART TWO

Hannah had indeed been broadcasting all day. I had suspected it from the moment she first started taping, but I would wait to call her out on it. She had an uplink to the satellite available to her, and with the flip of a switch could broadcast directly to the control room at *Network News Now* in their main offices in Chicago. *Triple N*, as it was commonly known, was Hannah's current employer. They would receive the raw footage, and from there, they could broadcast live or record and edit the footage for later use. As it turned out, *Triple N* had chosen to air huge chunks of Hannah's reporting live and unedited so a curious world got to see a whole lot about our tiny island in the hours leading up to the announcement in Port John.

I had awakened well before the crack of dawn. John and I had somehow slept soundly in a bed that was barely big enough for one. I awoke facing John with our foreheads almost touching, his hand resting on the swell of my hip.

I covered him with the blanket and softly touched my lips to his. He was still asleep, but he smiled and rolled over, clutching the blanket to his chin. I left him sleeping with no worry that he'd oversleep. I knew one of his shipmates would certainly wake him before too long.

I didn't encounter any of those shipmates as I left the still barely lit ship. I practically ran home to get showered and dressed for the day ahead. The television was still on when I went into the house, but it was otherwise quiet, and there was no sign of Kavu or my father. I got ready quickly, and it was still mostly dark as I walked over to the hotel to meet Hannah and her crew.

I was not surprised to find them already waiting for me next to the jeeps in front of the hotel. Although the morning light was faint, that didn't stop Hannah from seeing me as I approached.

"Good morning," she said and reached out to shake my hand. "I hope you don't mind. I took the liberty of asking the boys to load up the jeeps. We were hoping to get started as soon as possible."

"What exactly did you want to get started with?" I asked.

"Not much," she said with a wide smile, "just everything. I'd like to see as much of the island and meet as many islanders as possible and be back at the port by ten to give us time to set up for the speech and the announcement at noon."

We took two jeeps. Hannah and I were in the first jeep leading the way, our back seat full of equipment. The three members of her crew followed in the other jeep. We set out toward Mount Garak, the volcano. I figured it would give us a little time to talk, get to know each other. Not surprisingly, most of her questions were about John.

The first thing she wanted to know was who sent John to the island. She had assumed, correctly of course, that someone had sent him for reasons of their own.

I try never to lie, but let's just say that I left some things out. I told her that someone had sent him, but we didn't know who or why, and I certainly said nothing about Womansanto for one simple reason. If our plan was going to work, the last thing we would want was to expose Womansanto or call them out publicly for their greed. If we wanted them to accept what we were offering, publicly shaming them would just make that harder.

Hannah was friendly, personable, and even a little bit charming. Most of all, she was a smart and professional journalist and immediately steered her questions back to ones I could easily answer for her. She had done some background research on Volavo, the John Frum religion, and cargo-cult religions in general.

"Are you a believer?" she asked me.

Instead of answering, I asked her a few questions of my own.

"Do you believe in a bearded, white man in the sky who judges your intentions as well as your actions? Do you believe in Zeus or Odin? Neptune or Jesus? Have you ever seen any of these gods? Do you know anyone who has?" As I drove, I turned to see her smiling broadly at my questions.

"No," she said. "I have never seen any of them, but you . . . you have seen John Frum. Your parents and grandparents have seen him too."

I interrupted. "And whether or not he is the real John Frum hardly matters in the end, does it?"

We had reached a spot where we could view the volcano, parking on the beach where John and I had gone swimming after he had completed the ritual walk. Hannah's cameraman had already set up a handheld camera and was taking video of the ocean, volcano, and other surroundings in the now full morning light.

"The Walk," I told Hannah, "is something our elders asked of John. It's usually a rite of passage to welcome the boys of the island into manhood. It ended right here, on the ocean side of the volcano, but it started on the other side of the island. John climbed the volcano from that side and descended pretty much right where we were standing."

"Why do you think he did it? Why did you even want him to?" she asked.

"I think my father wanted him to prove himself to us, and I think John did it for the same reason."

"Well," she asked, "how did he do?"

"It took him almost all day, but he made it, and that's no small accomplishment! He had to wear a ceremonial namba while doing it too. That's sort of a cloth sheath for his, um, you know . . ."

"Penis?" Hannah asked helpfully.

She laughed, and I could see the wheels spinning in her mind. I'm sure she was imagining John in a full dress uniform with a triangular dick tent sticking out of the fly.

As we spoke, a group of six island men approached. Three goon'do accompanied them. The crew turned their cameras to the men and recorded their approach.

"May I speak with them?" Hannah asked.

I nodded my approval.

"Good morning," Hannah said to the men. "My name is Hannah Cronkite, and I am with *Triple N* news. May I talk to you for a minute?"

The men gathered around. They were clearly happy to talk with her. They were dressed in shorts and T-shirts and carried with them gear for early morning fishing. They put the gear aside, and each man introduced himself. Then they introduced each of the goon'do by name.

The cameras started rolling, and Hannah spoke to the camera and the world. "Good morning from the island of Volavo. As most of you know, later this morning we will be covering the announcement from the capital of this island. I report to you now from the oceanfront base of Mount Garak, a volcano on this beautiful island. I have with me some local men of the island and their dogs—"

One of the men gently interrupted her. "Excuse me, miss, but the goon'do," he said, gesturing toward one of the dogs, "are not *our* dogs. They are our partners, and they belong to the island and the gods. They do as they wish."

"I see that," said Hannah, who had leaned over to pet one of the goon'do and had received an enthusiastic greeting in return.

"I have learned that the man claiming to be the god John Frum completed the ritual known to the Bohlin people as The Walk and climbed this volcano. Gentleman, do you know of this?"

The men laughed. One of the men leaned into the microphone and said, "He did more than just climb Mount Garak. It trembled beneath his feet. It threw smoke and fire into the air in his honor."

"You saw that happen?"

"Of course!" said another man "We all saw it, and we all know, but that's not all. He speaks to the goon'do, and the goon'do speak to him!"

Hannah looked at me, and I shook my head as if to say I could not confirm these tall tales.

Hannah turned to face the camera and said, "Of course, the goon'do are our cute, furry friends here, but so far, they have not talked to us."

"Of course not!" the man said with a laugh. "We are not gods!"

Hannah laughed along with the men but then turned to more serious matters.

"The Christian Reverend Jerry Gramm has said that the Bohlin people are savages who intend to keep corbomite for themselves. What would you say to him?"

The men grew silent for a moment as if pondering the

question. Finally, one of the men said, "There have been Christians on this island for more than sixty years. They are kind and gentle. Their Christian God is wise and kind. I do not think that the Reverend Jerry is a Christian."

The other men listened and nodded in agreement. "Like you, I wait for the announcement. Our Minister Karbina will find justice as he always has."

Hannah had been listening intently. When the man finished speaking, she thanked the men for their time and turned to face the camera.

"This has been Hannah Cronkite reporting for *Triple N* from the Island of Volavo."

The men picked up their gear and continued to the shore. Hannah looked at me and said with a smile, "Is everybody like this?"

"More or less."

I had a feeling that they were already broadcasting live, or they were at least live-feeding to the studio rather than just recording, and I was right. "Listen, Hannah," I said. "It wouldn't be the end of the world if you are broadcasting live, but just check with me first along the way, okay?"

She smiled at me, and rather than apologize just said, "You got it. Thank you."

We didn't have a lot of time, so I took her on a quick tour of the island. I drove a route that approximated the path John had walked. Hannah was suitably impressed.

She said, "He walked all that way through the jungle and up a volcano in full uniform and—what did you call it, a dick tent? —and those patent leather shoes, no less."

Her crew was filming everything as we drove. With my permission, Hannah was recording the audio of our conversations as we went. She made a point of turning off the recorder before she asked me what I personally felt about John. I don't think she could have sensed my feelings for him, but who knows?

"John is a man who came to us pretending to be a god, yet he had a quality about him that somehow made him the most real man I have ever met."

Hannah looked at me. "That's exactly what actors are paid to do."

I laughed. "I do not believe that John is a very good actor, but I do believe he is a very good man."

There was nobody around, but I stopped by the lakeside location where John had jumped from the platform with vines around his ankles, and the crew started filming the site. Hannah had never heard of land diving, our other rite of passage.

I gave her a very quick lesson about the origins of the legend and the history of the ritual. I finished by saying that this is where the boys practice by jumping over the water. From where we were, she could see the scaffolds with the two platforms and vines. Some of the vines had been neatly coiled and stacked by the platform. Others were still dangling over the edge.

"He really did this," she asked, "from the top one?"

I answered, "Twice!"

"Wow!" Hannah said. "He must have been trying to really impress somebody." She stared at me.

"Don't look at me," I said. "I was trying to talk him out of it. I was pretty pissed at him that he did it at all, let alone twice. I just thought he was being a macho idiot."

I could see that Hannah was genuinely shocked by my words. She kept looking at the vines and the top platform and how far it was to the water below.

"Those vines are like ropes," she said. "They're not like bungees. There is no give to them. I don't care who you are, that has to hurt! Did he get hurt?"

"He wouldn't admit it, but he definitely looked sore when he was done. Did I mention he made these jumps the day before he did The Walk?"

She shook her head. "Incredible," she said. "I don't know whether he is very brave or completely nuts. Probably both."

I found it funny to see a reaction like that from an outsider, but I guess it makes sense. At the time, John's actions all seemed so normal to me, even logical given the circumstances, but I guess I had to agree that a grown Westerner jumping off a platform sixty feet high, vines attached to ankles, probably seems just a little bit crazy.

Hannah asked if it was okay to report what I had been telling her. She thanked me when I agreed that she could. There could be no harm at this point.

I tried to show her as much of the island as I could in the short time we had. Our last stop was at Banyu Cepete or "The Rush" as we call it on the island. John and I had walked this beach on our first day together. No one swims here, but there were people on the beach. A small crowd of about a dozen islanders with a half dozen children saw the men with the cameras and came over to see what we were up to. Of course, I knew all of them, and they knew me.

Most of the women and children were dressed in ceremonial garb while the men wore the island version of a U.S. Navy uniform, which in this case was pressed white shorts with a black belt, black shoes, and a green camouflage T-shirt. Three of the men had chosen to wear a namba, which was prominently protruding from the fly. They were on their way to the port for the party and the announcement. I could see Hannah working especially hard to keep her eyes from drifting downward to the nambas. Her efforts were mostly successful.

All of them quickly gathered around Hannah and her microphone in front of the cameras. Her cameraman counted down, "Three . . . two . . . one."

"This is Hannah Cronkite once again reporting from the island of Volavo. We are here on the beach at Banyu Cepete, or as the islanders call it, "The Rush." I have with me a group of people on their way to the John Frum Day celebrations in Port John, not too far from here."

She turned to the gathering. "So you are on your way to the party. Have any of you seen John Frum on the island this week?"

A boy of about thirteen politely raised his hand and looked eagerly at Hannah. She leaned over just a little with the microphone.

"I have seen him," said the boy. "I watched him jump twice from the high platform," he said with excitement. "Once, he went into the water, but the water itself feared him, so he did not get wet."

The other islanders all nodded in agreement, and Hannah quickly explained on camera the ritual of land diving and spoke of the practice location by the lake she had just visited. A woman seemed eager to speak, so Hannah first thanked the boy before turning to the woman and reaching out with the microphone.

"The great John Frum cured my husband of the gout," she said and gestured to the man next to her. He at first looked surprised but then quickly smiled and nodded in agreement.

There was a young girl dressed in a simple, white cotton dress with her hair carefully pulled back and decorated with a white bow. Hannah asked her who gave her the pretty dress, and the girl pointed off camera at me and said, "I am dressed like our princess Qat! And God John brought me the best toys in the world!"

Hannah turned and smiled at me. It seemed to Hannah, and it came across on camera, as if the islanders were playing a fun game. The game was to see who could come up with the tallest tales of the exploits of the great god John Frum.

After the group had moved on, I explained to Hannah that this was pretty typical of our people. "In the West, you have storytellers of all kinds: writers, filmmakers, priests, and poets. Here, we all take turns creating and shaping our legends. Do we believe them? I don't know. We can if we want to or if we need to. The legend of Banyu Cepete tells the story of the ship and the storm that first brought the Bohlin people to Volavo. That is a true legend, one which we all believe."

It was time to head back to the port. I knew that if we waited any longer, it could be a difficult drive. Volavo was an island virtually without traffic jams, but on John Frum Day, the roads would be full of vehicles and pedestrians making their way to Port John. The drive back was slow but steady with Hannah's crew filming continuously along the way.

We drove directly into the port. A narrow path had been cordoned off, and we were able to drive the jeeps past the stage and park them dockside, next to the stage and in front of the ship. Hannah's crew unloaded their equipment, and I found a couple of workers to drive the jeeps back from the port. This gave Hannah and her crew a working area just to the left of the platform with a clear filming sightline to the stage. During the speech, I would allow the cameraman to stand on the stage itself. From the view of the audience, he would be to the left of John and my father as each spoke.

20

SHOWTIME!

There was less than an hour until the announcement. Port John was now packed with revelers. Hannah used the time to interview as many people as she could, sometimes with hilarious results. My fellow islanders seemed to be competing to see who could come up with the tallest tales of John Frum. One man told her that John Frum himself had put the corbomite in the caves, and it had not been there before his arrival. Another man said that the warships at sea had already sailed away, fearful of the wrath of John.

Hannah would ask people what they thought the upcoming announcement would be. One after another, the islanders expressed the greatest faith in their minister and John Frum, but they also enjoyed their flights of fancy.

"Volavo will become America's fifty-first state," said one man with absolute certainty. "Minister Karbina will be governor, and they will make John Frum president of America!"

Hannah took me aside and asked, "Is it my imagination, or does everybody love your father?"

I smiled. "Naturally, I'm biased, but my father is the wisest and most honest man I have ever known."

Hannah was still a journalist and couldn't help but ask the occasional provocative question. She had asked several of the islanders what they thought of Jerry Gramm, the man who had been so thirsty for attention he had publicly called the Bohlin people savages. He had gone as far as saying that Volavo had a history of cannibalism, which even his own missionaries on the island had told him was nonsense.

Hannah interviewed an older man and asked him if he had ever heard of cannibalism on Volavo. There was a long and uncomfortable silence as the man just stared at her. Soon his gaze came to rest on her arm and the hand that gripped the microphone.

Finally Hannah said to the man, "I am sorry, sir, if I have offended you."

Still he stared at her hand and arm. Finally the man broke his stare and asked, "Dear lady, are you right-handed or left?"

Hannah was a veteran journalist, but the man's behavior had rattled her.

"Um, I am right-handed, sir, but why do you ask?"

The man smiled broadly and replied, "I am a chef in my spare time, and I have found that the meat from the dominant arm is often tough and stringy. I prefer the tender meat of the lesser-used arm. It is a true delicacy. So you are right handed, you say?"

The man had sprung his trap, but Hannah was now in on the joke and laughed along. The man said, "You will never find a more gentle people than the Bohlin. Like our minister, we have always found strength in kindness."

Hannah thanked him, but before he turned away, he said, "You know, on the other hand, reporters do make for a tasty treat." Hannah smiled at him but pulled the microphone away.

I knew that every bit of Hannah's observations and interviews was being broadcast via satellite, and I wondered what type of picture we were painting for the world. One thing was for sure. It was a true picture, an accurate picture. My people were smart, funny, painfully honest, and they definitely enjoyed a good story, especially the story of John Frum. The bigger the tale, the better.

The port had become even more crowded with revelers. Music and anticipation filled the air. Kavu arrived and went up on stage to make a final check of the lectern and microphone. This had been his job every year for nearly a decade, so the crowd reacted, knowing that the final soundcheck meant that it was almost time.

Kavu came to talk to me. He quietly told me that we would be announcing the plan we had created, and Mary would be releasing it to the public simultaneously with the announcement. I had pretty much assumed that would be what would happen, but this was the first time I had gotten confirmation.

The island's elders began making their way onto the stage one by one. By tradition, each elder was accompanied by one of the village goon'do. Ishka was accompanied by Bobo. Hannah was of course continuously broadcasting live, and Ishka stopped along the way to introduce himself to Hannah, telling her and also the world that this goon'do was Bobo. This was the dog that had helped John to complete his walk across the island. Soon all the elders were seated behind the lectern, each of them with a goon'do at his feet.

Kavu made his way back to the lectern. Hannah and her crew now had a second camera in position. The crowd had begun to cheer when they had caught sight of the minister, who now walked along the front of the stage where there was a line that had been roped off between the stage and the crowd. I knew my father had never been comfortable with crowds and even less so with public appearances and speeches, but you wouldn't have been able to tell as he smiled and waved, making his way onto the stage and approaching the lectern.

Each of the elders in turn rose and briefly embraced the

minister before returning to his seat. His greetings completed, the minister approached the microphone. Kavu stood several feet behind him and to the right. The crowd grew quiet in anticipation. It was showtime.

"Good afternoon and greetings to all of you here with us today and to all of you watching around the world. I am Karbina, the prime minister of Volavo. Those of you in attendance know that I am not one for long and boring speeches, and today will be no different, but what is different today is the company we keep and the announcement we will make. We welcome the world to our John Frum Day Celebration, but more than that, we welcome the man who would be John Frum himself, in the flesh . . ."

This drew a loud roar from the crowd. The minister paused briefly before continuing.

"Some of you may be surprised to learn that the man you are about to meet is, in fact, a man and not the god John Frum. Some of you may be disappointed that he is merely a man, but I can tell you that he is a man I have come to know, and I can also tell you that while he is no god, I have come to believe that he is the hand of God, God's grace."

He paused for a few moments and looked out over the audience. "Suffice it to say that I believe in the decision I have made as we deliver it to the world today, and I believe as well in the man who will deliver it. I present to you, John Frum!"

The crowd was now in a near frenzy. Some of the people had seen him at some point during his stay. Certainly everyone knew he was here and what today's event was about, but anticipation had given way to excitement as John walked down the gangway and onto the stage.

Again in turn, each of the elders stood. They offered a handshake as he passed by. Up until now, the goon'do with each elder had remained serene and almost motionless, but when Ishka rose to shake John's hand, Bobo could not contain herself and jumped up on his leg, demanding his attention. Even as the world waited for an announcement of historic significance, John stopped to greet her.

Everyone in the crowd had heard the tales of John and Bobo on The Walk. They roared with laughter as John got down on one knee and embraced Bobo. Her tail and backside shook, and she put her face to his, licking his cheek. Finally, Ishka sat down and Bobo reluctantly broke the embrace and returned to sit quietly beside him.

John shook hands with the remaining elders and then hugged Kavu and my father. Finally, he approached the microphone. The crowd once again grew quiet.

"Greetings to the blessed people of Volavo and everyone watching around the world. I have come to know the Bohlin people, and they have come to know me. The Bohlin are wise and kind, and it is without a doubt the greatest honor of my life that they have chosen to accept me as one of their own and chosen me to make this announcement on our behalf. Today I speak to you as John Frum, a deity to the Bohlin who promises to deliver unto the people great prosperity and happiness."

John paused while applause came from the audience along with an occasional shout of "Yes!"

"I am here to tell you that I am not John Frum the God."

From the crowd came cries of "No!" and "Yes, you are!"

"But I do come with a message that will bring prosperity and happiness not just to the Bohlin people but to the entire world!"

The gathering cheered again.

"As you all know by now, our island alone possesses a resource that can offer the world virtually unlimited energy, but corbomite alone is not enough. Scientists from the great company Womansanto have developed a method to safely unlock the vast power of corbomite. With this mineral and their process, we can bring cheap, safe, and almost limitless energy to every corner of the globe."

Now the crowd grew quiet.

"And best of all, it will be for everyone, everywhere. The events of the last twenty-four hours have reminded us all that with great power comes great danger—and even greater responsibility. Even now, mighty military forces from around the world encircle and threaten our island and each other."

John's voice grew louder and more powerful.

"We will protect this island from the world! We will protect this world from itself! There is enough corbomite on this island to power this planet for centuries.

"On behalf of Minister Karbina and the Bohlin people, we hereby offer corbomite as our free gift to the world!"

Pop! Pop!

The blasts did not sound like gunshots at all. They sounded simply like *pop, pop*. The crowd was cheering, so I'm not sure if most of them had even heard the sound of the shots. John had started to raise his arms but abruptly lowered them and seemed to fold himself over the lectern. When he did, I could see a splash of red across his upper back and left shoulder. There was another splash of red on the left side of his ribcage. John had only a look of confusion on his face. There were two more quick *pops*. They sounded louder this time as the crowd had quickly grown silent. John's body turned as he almost lurched over the lectern. Two more splotches of red appeared at his lower back.

John sprawled backward and away from the lectern. All the elders had jumped from their seats. It was Ishka who reached John first. He wrapped his arms around John in a now futile attempt to protect him. The two men fell backward, Ishka cradling and protecting John's body with his own as they fell. They landed together in an almost seated position with Ishkas arms wrapped around John's midsection as if he could hold his body together out of sheer will. Bobo was now by their side, whining and trying to get to the two men now lying on the stage floor.

The crowd, who had been at a crescendo of excitement just moments before, was deathly quiet. I ran onto the stage. John now lay prone, his eyes closed, his breath still. I could not cry. I saw his once bright white uniform now covered in red. I kissed his forehead as my father and the elders looked on. Kavu had run to alert an ambulance parked just outside the port gates. Hannah had remained at a respectful distance, but one of her cameramen had come on stage. All the world was witness to every moment.

The Bohlin people are indeed a special breed. No one moved when the shots had been heard. There was no panic. There was no stampede. There was just calm, sad pain for the loss they had just witnessed. Guns are almost unheard of on the island of Volavo. Maybe they were just slow to realize what they had just seen and heard, or maybe we are just a brave people with no history or knowledge of what it means to fear.

The ambulance came slowly into the port with Kavu leading the way through the narrow passage between the stage and the audience. My father asked that I stay with him rather than ride in the ambulance with John. I am not sure if he meant to protect me from pain or if he simply needed me by his side, but I obeyed and watched as they put John's still body into the ambulance. Ishka helped to lift him into the back and then climbed in. He was joined by Bobo, who insisted on not being left behind.

I can't tell you how long all of this took because for me, time had stopped. The ambulance soon made its way out of the port. I don't think anyone who wasn't in that ambulance had left the area.

In the quiet moments that followed, the elders once again took their seats. My father returned to the microphone. This time I was standing at his side. The joy and excitement from earlier had now been replaced with somber resolve.

"Again I speak to my friends here on the island and around the world. We have all just witnessed what evil is capable of, but we will not bow to violent cowards and hatred. We are undeterred! We will give corbomite as our gift to the world! We will see a world transformed and freed!"

He then spelled out everything that John was going to say. It was identical to the press release, which by now had gone out and was already becoming known to the world. He recited the details almost word for word from memory, without a written speech or notes.

I had told John that I could never say "I love you," and that is true, but he is the only man I have ever known that I could see spending my days with, all of my days. And now he is gone, taken from me. The ship that had brought him was gone as well. After the shots had been fired, the ship had slipped out of the port and disappeared among the hundreds of vessels off the coast.

EPILOGUE
FEBRUARY 15TH – JOHN FRUM DAY

One Year Later

It hadn't been that hard to talk Smith and Wesson out of actually killing me as Barnwell had ordered. It was slightly harder to convince them to pretend that they *had* killed me. After all, they were intelligent men with a profound sense of honor and duty. They certainly knew a turning point in history when they saw one. The technical details had been easily worked out. As it turned out, they had access to a cargo hold full of weapons of war and deception at their disposal.

After meeting with the minister in the early morning, I had returned to the ship, looking for Smith and Wesson. I found them in their cabin, and they did not look surprised to see me. Barnwell had made clear to them that their assignment was to assassinate me if I said the wrong thing at the ceremony. I think they had sensed that I already knew I might be in danger. Even if I didn't know that, they would be the ones to kill me.

Smith put a finger to his lips to quiet me as soon as he opened the door. It was only then that I realized that everything aboard the ship was being recorded. He gestured for Wesson and me to follow him. We walked silently until we were on the ship's deck, almost to the bow before he spoke.

"This is the only place on the ship that I am sure we are not being listened to," he said. "And I have a feeling this is not going to be a conversation that any of us want recorded."

"What can we do for you, John?" asked Wesson flatly.

It is not often that a man comes face to face with his would-be assassins, but here I was. The only thing I could do is make my case and hope for the best. For all I knew at the time, they could simply kill me right then and there. These were men who had made a career out of honoring the chain of command and following orders. However, they just listened intently as I laid out the plan for the distribution of corbomite to the world and my "assassination" at their hands.

As I spoke, I searched their faces for signs of sympathy or agreement, but they had remained predictably stoic, revealing no hints of their thoughts as they listened. I was offering them the opportunity to change the course of world events for the better, and by the time I finished speaking, I think they knew it —if they hadn't known already.

They stood silently facing each other for what seemed like an eternity but in reality was less than a minute. There was no conversation between them. It seemed to me that they must have already thought of and considered every conceivable possibility and outcome, including this one, and were deciding together whether to come along, to go all in.

Finally it was Smith who spoke. "Okay," he said, looking back at Wesson, "I can only imagine the look on Barnwell's face when he sees this."

I felt myself exhale deeply with relief. "By the way, guys," I said, "would Barnwell...Would you have really killed me?"

The angels Smith and Wesson only smiled.

They had actually released the dock lines as they took the "shots." While I lay "bleeding" on the stage, the ship was on its way out of the harbor. Later, it was scuttled somewhere out in the middle of the Pacific. Bert, Ernie, and Captain made their way to safety. I am told that Womansanto made good on its promises to them.

Smith and Wesson were men who were perfectly capable of disappearing, and that's exactly what they did. They disappeared.

There's been a great deal of speculation about who these men were. Who did they work for? What did they want? Did they act alone?

A bestselling book was released a few months ago that claimed, correctly, to know exactly who the two men were. *In Search of Smith and Wesson* details how the two started out as roommates at the Naval Academy in Annapolis. After graduation, they again roomed together while attending the Navy and Marine Corp Intelligence Center training in Dam Neck, Virginia. Both had distinguished decades-long careers in military intelligence.

The two men agreed together to leave public service when they realized they could never reveal what they had always been—a couple. They had been life partners almost since the day they had met and as men of honor could no longer bear to live in the shadows. They retired from military service and moved into the world of corporate security and espionage. In that world, no one cared who you loved. The only thing that mattered was whether the job got done. That's how Smith and Wesson came to be my helpful angels. And they had certainly gotten the job done.

After I was "shot," I waited until the ambulance was safely away from the port before opening my eyes and sitting up. I tried not to laugh at Ishka's reaction. He had been sitting at my side, his eyes filled with tears and his hands clasped together in front of him. He screamed so loud when I rose that I thought he would be heard back at the port. The poor man was in shock, but Bobo wasn't. I think she had felt my heart beating all along. I explained the ruse to him and asked that he take me to his village where I could hide out until we figured out what to do next.

Qat was very, very angry with just about everybody involved when she was first brought to Ishka's village and discovered I was still alive. That, of course, was after she had run to me, kissed me, and squeezed me so hard, I thought I might actually die. Only then did we face her wrath for making her endure the experience of my death.

I manned up and took all the blame. I had told only the minister of the scheme, and I had only told him so he could approve it. I knew, and he agreed, that the secrecy was warranted, and genuine reactions were needed. As it turns out, I am a better actor than Qat thought.

I have spent most of the last year in either Ishka's village or the minister's home. Eventually, Qat brought me some regular clothes, thank goodness, and I am happy to say that I have not at any time over the last year worn a namba.

The media blackout on the island has been faithfully maintained over the last year. Hannah and her team were asked to leave shortly after I was "killed." It was not meant as a punishment. We all felt she did an amazing job of getting the word out to the world. Because of her, the world got to see the Bohlin for the people they really are. No tourism has been permitted for the last year either, but the minister tells me that they will soon allow it again but in very limited numbers.

The minister made no announcement about my condition or whereabouts, but the whole world had watched me "die" on that stage. Rumors that I was still alive began to circulate around the world soon after the events of last year. The rumors could not be confirmed with certainty and only served to enhance the legend of my sacrificial "death."

Not unexpectedly, the legend of John Frum had grown during the year since that notable day. "John 2.15" has become shorthand for events on the island and had suddenly begun appearing everywhere. The Navy style officer's hat I wore on the island had become the symbol of sacrifice for a greater good. I wouldn't quite call it a religion, but people have started holding up signs at sporting events around the world that read "John 2.15." It could be seen on T-shirts and jewelry, graffiti and billboards, bumper stickers and tattoos— just about everywhere.

If you're wondering about Hannah, she has been busy as well. She has spent the last year investigating the Bohlin legend of the islanders' origins on Volavo. It came as no surprise to us that she did a good job at that too. Her research led to the discovery of a shipwreck just a half-mile off the shore of Banyu Cepete. The ship is about six hundred years old and sits on the ocean floor, split almost perfectly into two sections. It is precisely as described in the Bohlin legend, and scientists have postulated that ocean currents in that area could easily have swept survivors to the shores of Volavo. Hannah's documentary premieres tonight on *Triple N* and ends with her saying, "Not only can our legends give us comfort and tell us who we are. Sometimes they are even true."

Barnwell and Womansanto were quick to act. Barnwell immediately made appearances on the news and talk shows. He told the world that he was "disgusted by the cowardly act" he had seen on TV along with the rest of the world. He offered his deepest condolences to the minister, the elders, and all the Bohlin people, and of course he and Womansanto would be proud to accept the very fair arrangement that had been proposed by the wise and generous people of Volavo. A formal long-term agreement was signed soon after with Mary and her legal team making sure it was airtight.

He was almost as magnanimous with Geur and Cheiro. They did not receive the untold millions that they had dreamed of, but they did receive modest promotions and a generous bonus presumably in exchange for their continued silence on the matter.

I'm not sure if Barnwell would have sought revenge against Smith and Wesson had he been able find them. Barnwell strikes me as the kind of fake tough guy that might very well be afraid of the genuine tough guys that are Smith and Wesson.

No, Barnwell's revenge was reserved for the man whom he blamed for ruining the plan, the man who had outed it to the world, the good, former Reverend Jerry Gramm. Federal prosecutors found themselves suddenly and mysteriously in possession of indisputable evidence of meth labs and a distribution network operating out of the bathhouses under Gramm's management. The charges against Gramm came in just under the wire of the statute of limitations. It seems Gramm would be a *former* reverend for the foreseeable future. The only title he would now carry is "inmate."

Before I forget, if I could speak directly to Grant Barnwell, here is what I'd tell him: "Mr. Barnwell, I don't like you. That is a bit surprising because I can find something to like about almost anyone, but not you. You're a bully, a coward, and a shithead. Once again, go fuck yourself!"

Like Womansanto, the nations of the earth were eager to express support for the plan we had announced. They were so eager that they immediately wanted to show their appreciation by offering gifts to Volavo. The United States, Russia, China, and other countries instructed their ships to prepare some form of tribute from whatever they had on hand. The minister allowed these ships to visit one at a time in the days following. Some of the vessels sent tenders. The smaller vessels docked in Port John in the same space my ship had been just days before.

The cargo they brought ranged from the thoughtful to the practical. There were recipes and prepared foods from the ship's galley. There were rations, cookies, cakes, wine, and more than a few bottles of vodka. The always generous people of Volavo responded in kind. Many of the gift-givers returned to their ships with packaged bundles of kava root along with instructions for its preparation.

Many of these tributes came with notes of thanks or condolences from their leaders, and there were even a few personal thank-you notes from their crew members and officers. I laughed when Kavu and the minister told me that three different countries had sent them live chickens. Cheiro would be happy to know that he wasn't the only one who thought the islanders might want them.

A special session of the United Nations was convened. One after another, world leaders stood at the lectern and pledged their support for Volavo along with their eager acceptance of the terms. All of them promised they would be happy to pay tribute each year in the form of cash or cargo, and they would also be happy to compensate Womansanto fairly for their nation's use of corbomite. A UN resolution was passed in record time.

Today is February 15th, exactly one year later. It is once again John Frum Day on Volavo. It is also John Frum Day in eighteen other countries as declared by the leader of each of those nations. By next year, it may very well be a worldwide holiday as declared by the United Nations. It is safe to say that the world has been grateful . . . and generous. Over the last year, Volavo has received just over four billion dollars in cash and cargo from a grateful world. So far no live chickens have been reported.

Womansanto was paid more than four hundred million.

Their mining operation has been in full production for more than six months, and Volavo has hardly noticed them. The workers are housed on offshore ships and tender to the island. Womansanto has kept their end of the bargain and has been rewarded.

The very first corbomite-fueled power plant will begin operation today. In my honor, a location in Long Island, New York, less than five miles from where I was born, was chosen. Hours from now, it will open with great fanfare. It will provide energy to all of Long Island from a single power plant no bigger than a McDonald's. By next year at this time, there will be hundreds of these plants scattered throughout the world. Within two years, there will be thousands. Today, the era of cheap, clean energy begins.

And then there is Qat. The best part about all of this is that I have gotten to spend the last year here on Volavo with her. Yes, she was furious with me about the whole not-telling-her-I-wasn't-really-dead thing, but it didn't last long. Although many people in this world spend their days looking for things to be mad about, Qat is definitely not one of them. In the days that followed, it became obvious that our little plan had worked. For a while, I stayed hidden away in Ishka's village, but as time passed, I spent more and more of my days outside and more of my nights with Qat. To the people of this island, I am not a god. I am something even better. I am one of them.

Later today, I will appear again at the John Frum Day celebration. Once more it will be broadcast to the world. Afterwards, Qat and I will fly to New York. We will stay in America for as long as she likes.

I know I won't be able to stay under wraps much longer, and I know we will have to deal with the media, but like everything else, it will pass. Besides, I still have Mary to help me. Today the minister will once again introduce me, and I will once again appear before the world in my uniform. In the crowd will be hundreds of people wearing T-shirts with "John 2.15" or "He died for you."

I have one last surprise for Qat. As I stand before the world with Qat at my side, I will turn to her and get down on one knee to ask her to marry me. I just hope she's not angry.

END

ALSO BY DAVID L. LITVIN

The Monochrome Solution

All In: The Poker Musical

Silencer's End

Why the Fuck Not?

ABOUT THE AUTHOR

David Litvin has spent most of his adult life in two worlds. The first was in the Basque sport of Jai Alai. He was the U.S National Amateur Jai-Alai champion in 1990. He played jai alai in the Campeonato De Mundial (World Championship) in Havana, Cuba, as part of the Pan American Games. As a representative of the United States, a fourth-place finish earned the U.S. a berth in the 1992 Olympic Games in Barcelona, Spain. Later, his attention turned to the world of poker where he was a profitable, professional player and later a poker dealer, poker tournament director, and poker room director.

His previous work is a musical stage play about the world of high stakes poker, *All In: The Poker Musical,* which featured original songs by Grammy award winner Vini Poncia.

He tries to keep his needs simple and his masters few.

Reach Me:

dlkosmo@gmail.com

DavidLitvin.com